CARMELO'S *Malice*

For all content inquiries, please check out my website:

Dedication

True strength isn't just in broad shoulders or battle scars. It's in the spine that won't bend, the heart that won't break, and the fierce fire you carry within.

PROLOGUE

Carmelo

How did I end up here?

My arms are trussed up above my head and my body is swinging over a darkened cement floor, which is darkened with what can only be bodily fluids. I can smell the ammonia and iron plainly from here.

Voices sound from my left, but it's hard to see that side with my eye swollen shut, and my body hurts too much to force it to turn. They warned me this could happen, that fucking with these people would have me killed.

But she was worth it.

Being a Torres by blood hasn't been easy considering where it's gotten me, but I can't help that. I'm not too worried because my name also means people are coming to help me. I can rest assured I'll either be rescued or avenged. The DeRucci Family has no idea what they're in for.

My Aunt Ember needs little convincing to fight or shed blood, and I can only hope I'm alive when she rips this place apart for me. That's a sight I want to see.

Suddenly, the voices have hushed, and I don't know how long it's been this quiet. Then I hear a creepy whistle sounding from down the corridor. I try to swing my body to see better out of my one eye, but it's fucking useless. The sound grows louder as they grow closer, anxiety tightening my chest.

Are they whistling "Kissin' Cousins" by Elvis Presley? Then it dawns on me. I know exactly who the fuck that is, and I don't know whether to be elated or petrified. I keep trying to turn, but the pain becomes too much on my shoulder blades, so instead, I wait for them to find me.

Once the whistling is directly to my left, I swing slightly and come face-to-face with the source. Their face is covered in blood, both drying and fresh, and a sinister smile lines their lips.

"Just hanging out, I see."

Chapter One

"Fucking concentrate!" Uncle Emmett slaps me on the side of my head and I throw it back with a groan.

"I'm tired!"

"Yeah?" he growls. "I'm fucking tired of you being tired."

He's been relentless in my training, and it's doing little to improve my knife-throwing skills. I can work a gun and my aim is good, but when I throw a knife, it flies in a different direction.

"I hate flinging these little shits around," I whine. Yes, I fucking whine as I twirl a little black knife around my forefinger.

"Start acting like the man we named you after!" Uncle Emmett yells, and my vision bleeds red.

"Yeah?" I scream back, getting in his face. "How the

fuck can I do that when he was killed before I was even born?"

The room falls silent as Uncle Emmett's face crumbles, guilt seeping into his features. "Fuck," he mutters and turns around.

"That was pretty harsh." Her voice floats into the room.

I turn to find Trent's daughter, Catalina, leaning against the wall, one of those little knives rotating around her finger in perfect arcs. She flicks her wrist forward and the knife sails past my head before lodging into the dummy I've been trying to hit all day. The knife sits firmly between its eyes, and I slap down the piece of metal I was holding onto the table in front of me.

"Fuck this," I snap and storm from the room.

"Carmelo!" Uncle Emmett calls to my back, but I'm already gone.

I slam my fist into the wall of the corridor at the sound of my name. Carmelo. They named me after a man I never met and it's a constant reminder. Where I came from is a mystery, and I can't figure out who I am because that vital part of me is missing. I am nothing like my mother. I don't even look like her, and I struggle every day with the realization that I may never know who the hell I am.

"Daddy issues can be a bitch."

"Go away, Cat," I hiss at her, not bothering to turn and face her.

"You sound like a little bitch too." Fuck, I want to punch this chick in the face. Catalina loves to push every one of my buttons, and I have never wanted to hit a woman as much as I do her.

I've known her for four years now, and with each year

that passes, she becomes more fucking annoying. I used to try to get into her pants every weekend in the beginning. We were in high school and sticking my dick into a pussy was my favorite pastime. I tried with Catalina, but she never even let me get close. Then that attraction turned into annoyance and now I can barely stand the sight of her. Doesn't help she's a good little soldier for her daddy, a well-trained soldier, and fucking deadly with almost every weapon. I say almost every weapon because the one she has between her legs is the one she doesn't know how to use.

I storm away from her and lock myself in my room. This compound is my home for three weeks out of the month, and the fourth I spend in Whitsborough with my family. Mom gave me an ultimatum: If I want to be a fighter, then I have to let Uncle Emmett and Aunt Ember train me, but I can't do what they expect of me. I used to love fighting, though now it feels like a fucking chore.

I fall across the bed and pick up my phone. I wonder what my cousins are up to back in Whitsborough. Cameron is now in his final year of university and living the fucking dream, and Ivy is practically married. Soon, it'll just be me and my need to make someone bloody while they become domesticated bitches.

Me: Tell me your dick is deep in a tight pussy.

Cam: I wish, bro. How are the knives?

Me: I can't do it.

Cam: Yeah, you can. You said the same thing about guns and then the same thing about proper fighting techniques. Keep at it.

He's right, but fuck, I'm so frustrated.

Me: I have a fight next weekend.

Cam: I'll be there.

He's always there for a fight, no matter where or when; he makes the time. He's my number one supporter. Cameron Williams is the son of my stepdad's sister and my mother's half brother. Our family is so intertwined that it makes dating in Whitsborough dangerous. I never know who I may be related to or if someone is a distant cousin.

Catalina pops into my mind and I snort to myself. That girl is like a fucking glacier and I will never chase that tail again. It took me three years to realize it, and each time I tried to get her to go out with me, her rejections became meaner. She and I were made to hate each other, it seems.

Speaking of hating each other, I wonder how my cousin, Ivy, and her fiancé, Neil, are doing. She graduated from university after studying social services and now works for Uncle Travis at the Whitsborough Center for abused women and children. She says it's her calling and loves what she does.

Me: Any chance you can come to New York next weekend?

Ivy: Fight night?

Me: Yeah, you don't have to watch, but I want to see you.

Ivy hates watching my fights, and no matter how much I tell her I've gotten better, she still shies away from it. Neil likes to watch a good fight though, and if she doesn't agree to come, I'm hitting him up next.

Ivy: Sounds good. I want to see you too.

My heart warms and I grin. Now I have something to look forward to.

There's a sharp knock on my door and then it creaks

open, stealing the grin and warmth out from under me.

"Carmelo?" Uncle Emmett says into the room.

"Yeah." I blow out my breath.

He lets himself in and shuts the door behind him, his face pinched in concentration. "I am so sorry." Solid start. "I shouldn't have said what I said, but I meant it." I know he did, and I think that's what hurts the most. "But you were right. How can you emulate the man if you never had the chance to know him?" Bingo.

As I watch him stand there in shame, I don't say anything. I love him, but he gets terrible cases of verbal diarrhea and it's time he faces the consequences of the shit that literally rushes out of his mouth.

"I need to head home now, but I'll be back next weekend. I want to help you learn more about Carmelo Senior."

I sit up on my bed and cock my head. "What?"

"Yeah, there's so much you don't know about the man who fathered you, good and bad. I think you need to know everything. You down for that?"

"Yeah." I nod and swallow. "Yeah, I am."

My mother knows next to nothing about the man and calls my existence a quick whirlwind affair. So I'm a product of lust, and before it could've developed further, he was murdered.

"Okay, cool." Uncle Emmett scratches his chin. "Ember will be here next weekend too. She'll help."

"Okay." I exhale the tension still swimming inside my chest.

"I love you." His eyes lock on mine. "You mean a lot to me, you know that, right?"

I do know that. "I love you too." It's rare Uncle Emmett admits when he's wrong, and in this case, I refuse to hold it against him.

"Okay, I'll see you next weekend." He leaves the room and I fall back against my pillows.

Uncle Emmett was the closest to my father, and he's always telling me I look exactly like him. I remind him of the older brother who was taken away too soon. In the beginning, that made me feel special, loved, and needed. Now, it does nothing but rub salt in a deep, festering wound because I don't know the fucking man. Except, now that may be changing.

Learning more about the man who sired me can only help me know more about myself, right?

CHAPTER TWO

Cameron

I drop my phone back down to the bed and continue to plow into the girl under me.

"Who was that?" she rasps, her voice breathless.

"None of your business." I roughly grab her hips and slam into her.

I need to stop sleeping with the same girl more than twice. They grow attachments and then that festers into… feelings. I shudder as I empty myself into the condom and shudder again when I think about attachments. Did she come? I look down into her face and find her looking up at me with annoyance and, yeah, frustration. Whatever.

"That was pretty anticlimactic," a monotone voice hits the back of my head. "Did she even finish?"

Saxon Greene, a motherfucking thorn in my side and one of my favorite people all rolled into one. I pull out of the girl and roll onto my back.

"Sax…"

"I'm guessing the answer is no if that's what you're

working with." He points at my dick and I flick him the finger.

"Fuck off, I'm a grower." The girl beside me snorts and sits up before grabbing her clothes.

"He is a grower," she confirms while she slips on her bra. "And no, this time I didn't finish."

"Pity." He shrugs, sounding insincere, and I cackle. "Probably time to move on."

"You're probably right," she answers and looks at me over her shoulder. "I'll call you."

I don't answer her as I sit up and remove the condom from my deflated dick. Even soft, it's still impressive. I don't care what the asshole says. The door clicks and I look over to find her gone and Saxon still leaning against the wall.

"That was fucking creepy," I point out.

"Yeah, it was. Your ass needs waxing."

"Can you fuck off?" I snap and laugh. "What do you want?"

I pull on my track pants and open the bar fridge by the bed, then pull out two cans of beer, throwing one to Sax before popping mine open. Living in a dorm in Toronto has been lonely as fuck. I don't have Carmelo here anymore, my cousin Ivy has a life in Whitsborough, and her brother, Saxon, is in his final year of high school. Although, the shithead really likes to surprise me by showing up some weekends.

"I had to bring the Ducati in for an oil change. Thought I'd wait it out here with you." He takes a drink from the can. "I regret that now."

"You didn't have to watch!" I exclaim. This is a first, having someone who is practically family watching me have sex.

"What else was I supposed to do?"

I chuckle and shake my head. Saxon's got to be the most levelheaded person I know. Nothing fazes him and he can endure just about anything. He's quiet mostly, and many people mistake that for shyness, but it's not. He just can't be bothered interacting with people unless he needs to. Even with me or his family, he will talk and listen, but it feels perfunctory. Despite that, he's always there if one of us needs him.

"Carmelo has a fight this weekend," I tell him as I take a swig of my beer.

"Are we betting on the hits he'll take again?" He grins. "If he takes another one to the head, I'm requesting he sign his brain over to me when he dies. I want to cut it open and see the damage."

"Fuck, you're weird." I laugh and shake my head. "Nah, I wanted to see if you were down to come with?"

"Sure, I guess." He scratches at the little growth on his chin. "I'll let you know."

"I think your sister is going," I reveal, hoping it sweetens the deal.

Saxon and Ivy are brother and sister, but they don't really hang out unless it's necessary. They are completely different. Where Ivy is emotional and expressive, Saxon is not. Dahlia, their baby sister, seems to be the only one who draws any emotion from him, and she knows the power she has over her big brother.

"So she can cry every time Carmelo takes a hit?" He shakes his head and swallows a mouthful of beer.

"He needs support, and Ivy is supportive." I shrug.

"She is," he agrees.

"What's happening at Precious Blood Academy? How're the twins?"

Samuel and Sonja are Emmett's, Travis', and Adrianna's kids. Yeah, it's complicated. They're a few years younger than Sax and they all attend my old high school in Whitsborough, a small town outside of Ontario, Canada.

"Boring." He rolls his eyes. "They bring some amusement to the school day. Although their bickering makes me feel murderous."

"You find a girlfriend yet?"

"Nope." He shakes his head. "Girls my age are so… immature." His mouth turns down at the ends. "I want someone I don't need to spend so much time on."

"That's a relationship, dude." I chuckle. "You need to take care of each other."

"Why?" he questions. "How about we take care of ourselves and then do things we mutually find fun from time to time?"

See what I mean? He's logical to a fault and so analytical that anyone who gets close to him eventually despises it. Except for me. I like that about him, and I like that he's brutally honest. I never have to guess where I stand with Saxon.

His phone pings and he pulls it from his pocket, swiping it open and reading a text.

"Bike's finished." He sets his can down. "Let me know what time we're leaving for New York."

"Yes!" I grin at him, happy he's coming with me. "I'm gonna get you laid."

"I do well getting myself laid, you idiot." He smirks,

giving me a pointed look. "I'm just picky about the pussy I like."

"Are you calling me a whore?" I raise my eyebrows.

"Nah, you're a slut." He opens the dorm door. "Whores at least get paid to fuck around." Then he pulls it shut behind him.

Brutally fucking honest.

I crush the empty beer can and head to my bathroom. I got lucky this year and moved into one of the few units with its own bathroom. The last three years, I spent bathing in the communal showers, and it wasn't comfortable in the least. The steam rises above the glass stall when I turn on the shower and let the hot water run.

My reflection is worrisome. The bags under my blue eyes are becoming darker and my blond hair is getting way too long. No one prepared me for how hard it would be to do this school thing without my family. Ivy used to make sure I was studying and helped me with things like food and sleep, Carmelo provided distractions, and I wasn't sticking my dick in girls to pass the time, not that it's a dangerous pastime. I'm just over it and I miss my family.

I should go back home more often, but I don't really mesh with my parents. They're good people, but they like things a certain way and expect me to be one of those things. Mom works constantly at the bank and Dad works as a mechanic for the Greene family. My father, Tommy, was a gangbanger in his youth and one of his jobs was to steal cars and tear them apart to sell for parts. He's transparent about his past, but he's also tough on me because of it. He likes to lecture and is pushing me to finish this business degree. I fucking hate this business degree.

I continue with it though because I don't have a fucking clue what I want to do or what I'm good at. Besides fucking, that is.

My stomach growls and I press my hand to the lean muscle. When was the last time I ate? I think back to last night and groan when I remember beer funnels and not much else. I stare at my chest and grin when my eyes settle on the tattoo etched into my skin. Blood Deep. Carmelo and I got these done during his last year of high school, and it means our blood runs deeper than anything else. We will always have each other's backs.

I drop my pants as the smell of sex wafts up to my nose, and I crinkle it in disgust. I need to stop this sleeping around bullshit and figure my life out. My parents are going to continue to expect great things from me after I finish college. I don't know if I have the greatness everyone else seems to have though.

My family is filled with overachievers and they've all become these great societal figures. Mom is the manager at the only bank in Whitsborough and she's a big fucking deal. I'm an only child, which means I need to do even better than they did. There are some huge fucking shoes to fill, but I don't think I'll ever come close to doing it.

I step into the shower and let the hot water run off my head and down my back, trying to ease the doubts in my mind.

There has to be a place for me somewhere.

Chapter Three

"Get your arm up underneath mine here." Aunt Ember demonstrates. "And then flip me on my back."

I do as she says and grin when her back meets the mat. "Yes!"

She grins back up at me, but I don't miss the wince when she goes to stand. I know she's getting older, and it saddens me that soon, she won't be able to train me anymore. Aunt Ember is the best fighter I know.

"Hey!" Aunt Ember's youngest daughter, Dahlia, calls out. "Don't hurt my mom."

Aunt Ember and Dahlia came a day earlier so we could do some training before the fight. Just a few short years ago, it took me taking a beating before my adrenaline would kick in, and then I would fight in a blind rage. Now, I am trained and capable of fighting before my face turns to minced meat.

"Is this a qualifying match?" Aunt Ember asks.

I have been trying to become a UFC fighter for three years now but it's hard to get their fucking attention. There are so many who want to fight, and I am literally a needle in a haystack.

"Not this time." I shake my head.

"Going pro is boring." Aunt Ember's eyes shine with mischief. "Who wants to always fight by a set of rules?"

Exactly. I smile back at her because she just fucking gets it. I just like the notoriety that comes with being a UFC fighter, but she assures me I can still get there without it.

"Your Uncle Emmett told me the guy you're fighting is smaller than you," she states, and I snort.

"Yeah, it should be a breeze."

"A breeze? Is that what it's like when I have you screaming on the ground in two seconds flat?" Shit. "I bet that's what you mean, right? The breeze you feel as you fall?"

"Right." I hate when she's right. No matter the size of my opponent, I need to be prepared all the same.

"Never underestimate someone because of their size. That's a good way to lose. Always be prepared for the unexpected," she lectures as I nod.

Aunt Ember is full of wisdom. Uncle Emmett told me about a fight she was in a long time ago, where her opponent pulled a knife. He slashed her stomach, and let's just say he didn't walk out of that ring after that. Aunt Ember has a fierceness inside of her, something that's cold and calculated, and if you're not a part of her family, she doesn't give a second chance. Uncle Emmett says she's a lot like their father.

Before I came to live here, I admittedly knew little about my father's side of the family, save for what Aunt Ember and Uncle Emmett told me. In the last year, I have heard some rumors, and I am biding my time for when I can ask for explanations. I heard my grandfather on the Torres side was a tyrant who ran the Eastside Rampage with an iron fist and torture was his favorite pastime. He liked to play with his food before he fucking ate it. The stories I've heard tell of a psychotic man who killed others because of his paranoia.

I've also heard that Aunt Ember is the same.

Which is hard to believe. I see the patient, loving person she is with her family, and the respect she shows the people here. I can't for the life of me imagine her as a killer, but I can't ignore the whispers either. She killed her father, but only after torturing him first, and she kills those who threaten the well-being of our family. She's a deadly weapon in the way she fights, but I've never seen her handle a gun or knife, so I don't know if the rumors are just that... rumors.

"You're deep in thought." She chuckles as she throws a towel at my sweaty face.

Might as well get it over with now. "I've heard things," I reveal, dropping my voice so Dahlia can't hear.

Her eyes quickly flick to her daughter as she sits on a bench, her phone in her hands as most preteens do. Then they come back to settle on my face as she gives a brief nod.

"I figured you would eventually." She sighs and dries her face. "I'll come by and talk to you before the others get here."

I nod and head out of the gym. "Hey, Dahlia!" I stop and call out to my little cousin. "Want to play some Mario Kart?"

"Yes!" she squeals and jumps to her feet. "Prepare for defeat, Carmelo," she states as she runs past me.

"She's intense," Aunt Ember warns with a laugh.

"I can't see where she could've gotten that from." I roll

my eyes and start after Dahlia.

"Her father!" my aunt calls out, and I laugh.

Uncle Vin is the chillest man I know. Everything rolls off his back like water, and I rarely see him worked up.

Nice try, Aunt Ember.

There's a quick rap on my door later that night, and I drop my phone to plod over to the door, opening it to Aunt Ember.

"Hey," she greets and looks over her shoulder. This is the closest to nervous I have ever seen her, and the sight of it has me feeling anxious.

"Hey." I close the door behind her and see she's holding a six-pack of beer. "Uncle Emmett will kill me if he knows I drank before a fight."

"Don't tell him." She shrugs and sits in my chair.

The rooms in this compound are dark and without windows, given we are underground. The top half of this place looks like an abandoned warehouse while underneath is a labyrinth of interconnected tunnels and rooms, designed over fifty years ago. Again, by my paranoid grandfather, whose murderer may very well be sitting down and drinking beer with me.

"What's up?" I ask as I open a beer and take a swig.

"Why don't you tell me?" Her brow raises as she effectively counters my question.

"Did you kill your own father?" Might as well bite the bullet and avoid dancing around the subject.

"Yes." She doesn't break a beat as she sips her beer.

My heart picks up speed and I can feel my mouth dry. "Did you torture him?" My voice cracks.

"Yes." She nods, her eyes boring into mine. My limbs go numb and my chest tightens as apprehension travels through me. "Don't you want to know why?" Her face is still, not revealing anything, her emotions locked up tight. Just like Saxon.

I nod and take another swig of the beer, anything to help me calm down right now.

"It's a long story." She exhales loudly before setting her beer down. "But you should know all of it. With that being said, my children do not know this. So, if you can't keep this information to yourself—"

"What?" I cut her off, my mouth working faster than my brain. "You'll kill me too?"

Her brows jump to her hairline and she drops her head back, letting out a loud cackle. Then her hand grips her stomach as she continues to bellow out a laugh, and I stare at her, dumbfounded. She's clearly psychotic too.

"Kill you?" She snorts once she has finally calmed down. "No, I was just gonna say I won't tell you and would deny everything you think you know."

"Oh…"

"Look." She leans forward, looking deep into my eyes. "Before I start, everything I do is for my family. I protect them at all costs, and that includes you. I would let no one hurt you, understand?"

The tension slowly bleeds from my body as I feel my chest loosen. "Yeah." I should've known all of this already, and Aunt Ember would never hurt her family. Well, not the ones who don't force her to do things against her will, apparently.

"As you know, much like yourself, I grew up never knowing my father. I didn't even know if he was dead or alive. The night my mother died in that fire, they released Raphael Torres from prison, and he saw me in a fight here in this compound. He knew I was his daughter and made a plan to bring me back when I was shipped off to Whitsborough."

Her hand rakes through her hair as she takes a deep breath. "He and your father showed up in Whitsborough a few months later and grabbed me, bringing me here to the compound."

"Grabbed you?" I ask her.

"Yeah, kidnapped, you know?"

"My father did that?" I look at the floor.

"He did." Her hand touches my knee and I look back up into her face. "But under the orders of our very deranged father, who was holding Emmett's well-being over his head. I haven't held onto any ill feelings for Carm. Quite the opposite."

"Go on," I encourage her.

"I arrived at this place, and I knew it well enough, guessing they would use me for fighting. What I didn't realize was what type of fighting I would be doing." Her face pinches as she continues. "They put me in that ring every night and told me to kill or be killed."

"What?" I breathe out. Shock rips through me as her words settle in my mind.

"At first, I didn't think I could do it, taking someone's

life from them, but it was Carm who told me what kind of scum they were ahead of time. So I did as I was told and I began killing them. Until one night, it was Tommy."

"Uncle Tommy? Cam's dad?" I place my beer on the floor between us and run my fingers through my hair.

"Yes." She nods. "I refused to fight him, and Carm pulled out his gun and shot him in the head."

My breath is lodged in my throat and I can feel my blood pounding throughout my body.

"Obviously he didn't die because Carm missed, but he made it look believable. I almost killed him when I got out of that cage." Her eyes lose focus as she's transported back to that time, then they light up. "Anyway, I had also learned that my father started the fire that killed my mother, so I went berserk. Yes, I hunted him down. Yes, I tortured him." Her mouth pulls up slowly. "And then I fucking shot him in the head."

When she puts it that way, I can understand why she did it, and if it were my family being fucked with, I would probably do the same. Well, no. I don't think I have the stomach for torture, but if I had to, I could kill someone.

She sees my pensive face and smiles at me. "Carmelo, you are not like me. I can tell you a bit about your father, but I don't know as much as Emmett."

"Please." I nod, eager for any crumbs of information.

"Carm had this tough exterior and could command a room of seasoned criminals easily. He killed when he had to and he tortured when the time called for it, but he was also loyal. He took a bullet for me," she whispers that last line.

"Why?"

"Whitsborough wasn't always the town it is today.

It used to be filled with cockroaches who bred faster than I could crush them, but bit by bit, I was cleaning it out. I wanted somewhere safe to raise the family I so desperately wanted with Vin. Eventually, I hit the root of evil in Whitsborough and it came to a head, ending in a battle. He bought me time to get out, even though he knew it was a death sentence. Carm wasn't just the sum of all his good deeds, he was also the sum of his bad ones because he always made it right in the end. He wasn't perfect, but he loved hard." She grabs my hand. "That's where I see him in you."

When the first tear drops on our clasped hands, I gasp in shock and touch my cheek. Am I really fucking crying right now? Aunt Ember grabs my beer and places it back in my hand.

"What else do you need to know?" She grins as I chuckle.

I think I know enough to last me a lifetime, at least.

CAMERON

New York is like a little pocket of anxious energy. Everyone moves like they are short on time, and there are so many of them that the streets are always packed with pedestrians, traffic is bumper-to-bumper, and unless you're in Central Park, trees are nonexistent.

"New York always smells like cheese," Saxon mutters as he looks out of the passenger window of my car.

"What?" I snort.

"Or like sour milk. Maybe it's all the fucking people squeezed together and their body odors amalgamating."

"Gross, Sax." I shudder.

He shrugs and continues gazing out of the window while I try to navigate, making our way to Hunts Point. The compound belonging to the Eastside Rampage is huge, and Trent has been holding it down since Carmelo's father was killed long ago. Trent is a hardened man and he doesn't tolerate much bullshit, unless it's coming from the Torres twins, Aunt Ember and Uncle Emmett. And they cause him a lot of bullshit.

Trent likes me though. He thinks I am a pretty boy and he likes my manners. Little does he know, it's the fear he puts in me that brings out those manners. His daughter, Catalina, is hot but intense, and when she talks to you, it's like she's trying to dissect your every word. She makes me so fucking uncomfortable.

For a while there, Carmelo had a crush on her, and even though I told him that pussy was impenetrable, he still gave it a shot. He lost miserably and continued to lose until he fucking buried it once and for all. Some women are just untouchable, and it takes a certain man to make them bloom. I get it. She's still fucking hot though, in like a female Terminator way.

"Why do you have a stupid grin on your face?" Saxon breaks through my thoughts.

"We're going to see Carmelo." I play it off, but the fucker sees right through me.

"That's your 'I'm looking for pussy' grin."

"Huh?" I chance a glance at him as I pretend not to hear him.

"Yeah." He nods and raises his brow. "It's your skeevy look."

"Fuck you." I chuckle and shove his shoulder. "I'm not skeevy."

"You just look like it." Little asshole never cuts me any slack.

"When are Neil and Ivy getting here?" I ask him.

"They left about two hours after us." He glances down at his phone. "Neil says Ivy made him pull over for tacos."

"So they won't be here for another few hours at least," I huff.

I miss my family, and now that I'm closer to seeing them all in one place, it feels like time is slowing down. Carmelo visits frequently enough, but Ivy rarely leaves Whitsborough, and I know it's because she's really busy. So seeing her will be a treat. I miss having the three of us together and fucking shit up. Since she's settled down with Neil, she's been… tamer. I get it, and I don't fault her for that. I just miss her. I miss all of us.

"Now you look like someone pooped in your Cheerios." Saxon's voice breaks up my sad inner monologue and I choke on a laugh.

"Can you stop watching me?"

"There's nothing else as interesting as your face when you attempt to think about stuff," he replies. Fucking asshole.

We finally get to Hunts Point, and because this part of the city is run-down, everything here feels malignant and evil. Thank God our family owns most of it, otherwise I would trade my left nut to never come here.

"I like how still everything here is," Saxon states, and I look at him in shock.

"Because it's abandoned and riddled with homeless junkies."

"It's quiet and you can hear yourself think. Not like the rest of New York." He rolls his eyes at me and turns back to the window.

I get what he means, but this is not a place you want to be caught in walking on your own because the type of people who lurk around here are looking for their next target.

"I can see why he chose this place," he murmurs, and I look over at him.

"Who?"

"My grandfather, I can see what he saw in this place. This is where I would want to be too." He nods.

I stare at him long and hard before I turn my gaze back to the road. The abandoned-looking Rampage headquarters comes into view, and I release my breath. Driving through New York is fucking stressful, but add a budding psychopath into the mix and it's fucking terrifying. I love Saxon, but sometimes I can't help but wonder what he'll become when he's older.

I pull into the lot and park beside Aunt Ember's car. I'm glad she comes here for Carmelo and that he's getting proper training from her over the years. He needs it.

"I'm texting Uncle Trent to open the door," Saxon mumbles as his thumbs fly over the screen of his phone.

We get out of the car and walk toward the large garage-style door. Soon after, we hear the creak and then the motorized door opening. What I'm not prepared for is to see Catalina.

She stands there with her arms crossed over her chest and her hair a mass of curls around her shoulders. Her skin is a deep golden hue and it fucking glows. Her full mouth is turned down slightly in the corners and her near black eyes stare at us like we're rodents.

"I texted Uncle Trent," Saxon sneers at her, and her eyes move from mine to his.

"And he sent me, brat." She doesn't skip a beat.

"Daddy's gopher." Saxon grins at her widely as he walks by.

"Mommy's sicko," she snaps back, and I cringe when Saxon halts his steps.

Then he turns to look at her, and from where I'm standing, his face is obscured, but I see Catalina's eyes widen as she draws in a quick breath.

"Good one." He chuckles before continuing to the elevator.

Catalina closes the door behind me and I wait with her until it's completely closed just to get a good look at her ass.

"There's something not right about him," she whispers, low enough for my ears only.

I don't answer her and choose to shrug instead. Not everyone is going to understand Saxon, that's just facts.

Saxon is holding the elevator doors open for us and we both step in with him. The confined space ramps up the tension and I can see Catalina shooting him quick glances. Sax is unperturbed though as he drums his fingers against his thigh while the elevator slowly drops.

When it finally stops and the doors open, he's the first one out, making a right without a look back.

"That one isn't normal." Catalina watches after him as her brows crush together.

"What's normal?" I ask, really fucking curious.

"What?" She looks at me like I'm speaking another language.

"Seriously, what's normal?"

"People who laugh and joke and feel things," she answers and pulls ahead of me down the hall.

"Well, he's normal." I shrug and then call after her, "But are you?"

Her middle finger flies up above her head, but I'm too busy watching her firm ass sway as she strides down the hall. Fuck, she really is fucking fine.

"Stop looking at my ass, needle dick!" she calls back, and I fucking gasp like an offended girl.

"Listen, whatever Saxon may have told you is wrong!" I scream at her retreating back. "I'm a grower!"

Then I shake my head and head down the corridor that leads to the large dining area. Here in the compound, there are a few cooks who lay out buffet-type spreads for three meals a day. It's not a terrible setup, but it can feel impersonal and lonely at times.

Carmelo has been struggling with connections and family structure all his life, even though his family is great. His parents really try hard to create a loving home for him and his sister, Sabrina, but Carmelo has always struggled with not having his biological father around. I can only imagine the loneliness of meals here and what they're doing to his psyche.

I throw open the double doors and walk into the dining hall. My father practically grew up in this compound. His single mother was a junkie, so he ended up being an orphan at a young age. He jumped from foster home to foster home, but it was this place that finally felt like home to him.

Carmelo is sitting at a table with our little cousin, Dahlia, and she is telling him a dramatic story if her hand movements mean anything. Saxon is walking toward them with a tray of food, which he places in front of his sister, and she tips her head back to smile at him. She adores him and her big brother has a soft spot for her too.

I head to their table, and as soon as Carmelo sees me, he's out of his seat and dragging me in for a hug. He and I have an unbreakable bond. It's hard to explain, but since we were kids, life has always been easier with the other close by, and we feed off each other's energy to push through certain situations. He and I are opposites in looks and personalities, but we click.

"I'm so glad you're here, bro." He claps my back and pulls away. "I need to win this match."

"You will." I raise a brow at him. "Why are you doubting yourself?"

"I don't know." He exhales loudly. "I've been trapped in my head and these thoughts are fucking eating me alive."

"Okay." I nod and look around the busy dining hall. "Let's get out of here and talk it out."

He leads me out of the hall and down a corridor I know all too well. His room here is in the same area as mine and Catalina's. She spends less time here than Carmelo though, because she floats back and forth between here and California. She's one of the DeRucci Family's highest-ranking captains, or capo, and the youngest ever named. Not to mention the first woman, but she's well-trained, and they knew having her would be an asset. An asset for her daddy to spy on the organization and try to slowly bring them down, but that's neither here nor there.

We get inside Carmelo's room and he shuts the door as I open the small bar fridge. I bring out a beer and sit on the chair, waiting for him to unload. I can see the distress on his face, his features tense with it, and his body is coiled and ready to spring. He's right to worry about his fight.

"Aunt Ember told me some shit last night," he begins.

"About what?"

"My father and what he did to her." He paces. "He was a good person, but he wasn't at the same time. He ran the Rampage and he did questionable shit, but I always thought he was good."

"Why don't you think he's good anymore?"

"Because I found out the people I thought were good actually aren't." His voice shakes.

"Bro." I stand and grab his arm. "What the fuck are you saying?"

"Aunt Ember," he whispers, and goose bumps break out on my skin at the fear coating the words. "She admitted to something I've been hearing around here."

"What?" Now I'm whispering with him.

"She killed her own father, tortured him, and when she spoke about it, it was like she enjoyed it." I fall back down into the chair and feel the shock spreading across my face, the muscles freezing tight. "He did some bad things to her though, but that's not what scares me," he continues.

I don't know what to say because all I can hear is the pounding of my heart.

"I am freaked out because after everything she told me, I knew I would do the same thing she did if I was in the same situation," he finishes and sits on the bed.

"He did bad things? Her dad?" I ask, finally finding my voice.

"He murdered her mom and forced her to fight here when she was just a kid… to the fucking death."

Shock hits me immobile again, and I swallow thickly to clear my passageways so I can breathe.

"That was my grandfather," he murmurs. "Am I psychotic too?"

I don't know what to say to him to make it better, and I can't find the words to convince him otherwise. Maybe this whole family is a little psychotic.

Chapter Four

It's clear this whole family has the psychotic gene. Now that I know our history a little better, I can see it when I watch each of them. Aunt Ember always has this gleeful look on her face when she's pounding someone's flesh or a punching bag, and Uncle Vin looks at her like she's the very air he breathes. Uncle Emmett likes knives and guns while Uncle Travis and Aunt Adri love him… together. Ivy may seem put together and completely sane on the outside, but that girl has some dark shit simmering just beneath the surface. And Saxon? I have no need to even expand on that. Dahlia is still young, but she doesn't stand a fucking chance, and neither do my other cousins. We're all fucking doomed. The need to slam my fists into people and watch them bounce off a mat or pavement, or any type of flooring really, is fucked-up enough. That's all that's been running through my mind. We're fucked-up, and the people we associate with are fucked-up.

Great example? I am currently watching as Catalina tangles herself up in ropes hanging from the ceiling before slowly lowering herself upside down toward the ground. Her father pushes her, making her body swing wide from side to side as she lines up her two pistols and aims at the dummies in the room, hitting every fucking one.

I used to idolize the girl, followed her everywhere, and hoped she would notice me. I wanted her skills and I wanted her to be mine. Watching her now, those feelings are gone and all I see is the haughty, arrogant bitch she is. She knows she's good, and no one can deny that fact, but it's the arrogance saturating her expression when she thinks no one is looking. She thinks she's better than everyone else.

My fight is in an hour, so I should stretch and warm up, but instead, I'm watching through a bulletproof glass as this girl swings from a fucking rope. And… I'm fucking hard while I watch her. I scrub a hand down my face and startle when I hear a whistle behind me.

"She's good," Cam says as he stands beside me.

"She knows it," I retort.

"I bet she does." He shakes his head. "The DeRucci capo needs to be in top shape at all times. When does she go back to California?"

"Who the fuck cares?" I snap and turn away from her lithe, swaying body. "I don't know her schedule."

"All right." Cam chuckles.

I bend over, trying and failing to touch my fingers to my toes, and Cam snorts again. I huff and stand back up to glare at him over my shoulder. "I need to stretch, asshole," I snarl.

"You weren't stretching when I came in here, asshole," he shoots back, and I groan.

"My head is fucked-up and I can't concentrate."

"Maybe you should reschedule this fight," Cam

suggests with a worried look.

"No, I just need to find my balls and then my fucking rage," I grit through my teeth.

"Oh, I can help." Cam gets a mischievous look in his eyes as my brows come together in question.

Before I can ask what the hell he means, his fist slams into my cheek and I stagger backward. "Are you fucking insane?" I stare at him wide-eyed as I rub my cheek.

He stalks forward and hits me again in the stomach, making me double over. He's not finished because he knees me in the forehead, making my back hit the mat. That's when I feel it, the sudden rush of scorching, furious fire spreading from my chest outward, and my breathing speeds up. Spit flies from my mouth as I exhale and roll over to my knees.

"I think I'm done here," he mutters and opens the door. "Let me know if you need more." Then there's a click as the door shuts behind him.

My body is vibrating with energy, and I know it won't release me until I have someone bloodied and battered. That's just my fucking psychotic gene. I turn around and flex my fists inside the fighter's tape. Time to pound some shit.

CAMERON

My fist hurts.

When Carmelo gets stuck inside his head, there's no way to drag him out unless he's fighting. I had no choice but to knock the fucking sense out of him and coax his rage out to play, otherwise he would lose this fight. He's stressing about our family right now, but I don't think that's all. I saw the want in his eyes when he was watching Cat, and I know he's been watching that tail for a while.

Speaking of, that same tail sits herself in the chair beside mine, then turns her body to face me and watches me closely. Finally, I look away from the first fight of the night and look at her with my brow raised.

"I saw you hit him," she says with a smirk.

"And?"

"I know why he needs that." She continues to grin.

"Are you going somewhere with this?"

"You were worried he wouldn't be able to win because he's been distracted," she determines, clearly not needing confirmation from me.

I shrug and turn back to the fight before Carmelo's.

"You're a good friend, Cameron." She pats my fucking knee like a child, and I can't decide if I like her touch or if I'm annoyed because I'm being patronized.

I brush her hand off my knee and slightly shift away from her. "He's my family, Catalina."

She nods and folds her hands into her lap, focusing back on the fight as well. I keep my eyes trained on the cage ahead, except for the quick glances I give her from my peripheral. She has a firm jaw for a woman, angular and sharp. Her nose doesn't protrude too far from her face and her cheekbones are prominent. Her lips are the color of lily petals, rosy and satiny. She bites down on the fleshy bottom one when someone takes a hard hit in the cage, and it's not from the brutality. No, she looks like she's turned on by it.

The cleft in her chin deepens with the movement, and when I see a smirk grace those plushy lips, a small dimple winks at me in her cheek. She has a rich, olive skin tone, and it radiates like bronze without a single blemish. I wonder if she looks like her mother because she looks nothing like Trent.

"You could just take a picture," she mutters, and I quickly turn away.

Fuck, how long had I been staring at her? Shit, she has such a fucking big mouth, and I'm worried she'll say something to Carmelo. He would fucking knock me on my ass for it.

"Nah, I'm good." Fuck my stupidity.

The fight is over when a guy is punched so hard, his face smashes into the cage and blood spurts from a gash in his cheek. He slides down to the mat with a thud and doesn't move. KO'd. A few Rampage guys open the cage and rush inside to lift the knocked-out fighter. I look around for Ivy and Neil because she promised Carmelo she'd watch, even though she wasn't watching the other fights.

They showed up late and ended up sleeping before anybody saw them, and this morning, they dragged themselves to breakfast an hour after it was served. I'm glad they're here though, because Carmelo needs us three.

Finally, I see her messy waves bobbing down the aisle and Neil coming behind her. The tension automatically leaves my body, and I stand to greet my cousin and her fiancé. As soon as she sees me, she skips forward with a huge smile on her face.

"Cam!" she yells and launches herself into my arms.

I breathe in her scent and chuckle at her enthusiasm. It took a lot to get Ivy to this point in her life where she's content and extremely happy. I hold out my hand behind her to the man who helped her achieve it. Neil grasps it in his and claps his other hand to my shoulder.

"What's up, bro?" He grins, his bright smile wide as he takes in his surroundings. "Is that blood on the mat?"

"Seriously?" Ivy looks toward the cage and rolls her eyes. "I'd hate to have that cleanup job."

"For real." I chuckle.

Ivy steps around me and waves at Catalina. "Hey, Cat."

"Hi, Ivy." She nods back with a smile. "How's life in Whitsborough?"

"Boring."

They take up small talk as Ivy sits in my vacated seat beside Cat, then Neil sits beside her, leaving me to sit at the end.

"How's he feeling?" Neil asks me.

"I had to pop him a few shots so he could rage out," I mutter, and Neil looks at me with a shocked expression.

"That takes him back a few years," he mumbles. "What's going on?"

"I think he's struggling with how fucked-up our family is," I confess, deciding to go with the truth.

"He really doesn't know the half of it." Neil laughs heartily, and Ivy stalls her conversation with Cat to look over at us.

"If that isn't the truth," I agree just as the lights dim.

"Now it's time!" the emcee booms over the mic. "The main event you all came to see."

The crowd roars and the energy cracks with excitement. I can see how someone would get addicted to this. It's like snorting a mountain of coke and feeling yourself fly. Only I know Carmelo has a completely different reason he's addicted to fighting, and it's about inflicting damage.

"Tonight, we have Malice in the house!" The speakers shake with the force of his voice. "He's angry tonight, folks!"

"Because his boy popped him in the mouth." Neil laughs beside me.

His opponent is introduced and brought into the cage. He's smaller than Carmelo, but he looks fucking fierce and a little unhinged. He climbs up the cage and screams through the holes at the people in the first row, spit flying as he leans back and laughs.

"Charming." Ivy chuckles and Cat joins in beside her.

Carmelo's music plays and the crowd goes insane. In the few short years he's been here, he's really gathered himself a following, and he insisted on doing it without being associated with Aunt Ember—or Blur, as she's known here. He's coming down the aisle with Uncle Emmett by his side and Trent on the other. People reach out their hands as he passes, the top part of his face obscured by a hoodie, but his jaw is exposed and it's clenched tight.

"He looks fucking pissed." Ivy leans around Neil to

look at me. "What happened?"

"I'll tell you later."

"Your cousin got his ass handed to him by Cam so he could concentrate on the fight tonight," Cat fills her in. The bitch.

"Why couldn't he concentrate?" Ivy turns back to me. I know I can't make her wait because she will cause a fucking scene otherwise.

"He had a chat with your mom." I watch as they escort Carmelo into the cage and he rips the sweater over his head, baring his chest and stomach.

Ivy grabs my arm and squeezes, fear potent in her eyes. "About what?"

"I think you know what." I point at her eyes. "We'll all chat later."

She visibly swallows and looks back at the cage, her skin a shade paler. Yeah, she definitely knows what I'm talking about. Funny that. I fucking thought we told each other everything.

The bell rings and Carmelo charges the other guy, a roar escaping his mouth. He's fucking livid, completely raged out, and I cringe when his fist flies. He fakes his opponent to cover his face and then slams it into his stomach instead. This is going to be quick, and I'm hoping Carmelo comes to his senses before he kills him.

The guy takes the hit like a fucking champ and clocks Carmelo with a sharp left jab. Carmelo's head snaps to the side and he jumps back, spitting blood onto the mat. I know what blood does to him and he's already fucking brimming with violence. I feel bad for his opponent.

Carmelo's body is practically vibrating. I can see it in the shake of his jaw and how he can't keep his feet still. He once told me when his adrenaline hits its peak, his body moves of its own accord.

His opponent growls and runs at him, his body bent forward. Carmelo dips his knees, and as soon as the guy reaches for him, Carmelo has him up and flying over his head. The guy hits the mat face-first with a loud resounding thud and his body bounces, only to hit hard a second time.

"He's fucking pissed," Ivy breathes out.

"I love when he's brutal," Catalina purrs, and I bend over to look beyond Ivy at her.

She sounds like she's turned on by Carmelo, but literally has treated him like the shit on the bottom of her shoe for years. Huh.

Carmelo slams his elbow down between the guy's shoulder blades and then drags him back up to standing by the hair on his head. He punches him twice in the face, the second blow spraying blood, and then finishes him with an uppercut to the chin. His opponent flies back and his back hits the mat, unmoving.

The crowd explodes around us, screaming for Malice, but he's already at the cage door, breathing rapidly.

"That wasn't enough for him," Neil murmurs.

No shit.

Chapter Five

Carmelo

My back is to the wall as I wait patiently for him to get in here. After every fight, he comes into this room to congratulate me, but this time, my body is thrumming with the anticipation of releasing this anger on him.

I hear this voice coming down the hall, and even though I know our family may be with him, I don't care if they see us go at it. The door opens, and as soon as his foot appears inside, I grab him and throw him to the floor, my body coming down on top of him. My fist connects with his chin, and he grunts, taking the hit he knows was meant for him from the moment he decided to hit me earlier.

Cameron bucks underneath me and sends me to the floor. Granted, the fight had left me as soon as my fist hit his flesh. That's all I needed to do.

"Guys!" Catalina storms into the room and grabs the front of my hoodie, pulling me to my feet. Then she shoves me against the lockers and holds her hand out as Cam gets to his feet, swiping the blood from his lip with his thumb.

Catalina stands between us, her hand on my chest and

her eyes on Cam. She's breathing heavily, and my eyes are drawn to her low-cut V-neck shirt, her tits pushed together delectably. My cock swells in my pants and I fucking curse as it grows. I let Cat go a long time ago, knowing she was always going to be beyond my reach and I would never be good enough.

Her eyes turn to me and she gives me a once-over, her mouth set in a determined line. "You are family," she grits through her teeth. "Family doesn't fight."

I shrug and fall back against the locker, watching her with hooded lids. Her brows rise as she takes me in, and I grin when Cameron crowds in behind her, walking her body toward mine.

"We are family," he reiterates, his voice low and rough. He's doing this for me, but he may just want her as well.

She looks over her shoulder at him as his hand lands on her waist, her body remaining relaxed at the touch. It doesn't bother me because I trust Cam completely and he would do nothing against me. He takes two steps into her, forcing her body to come flush against mine, those beautiful tits pressing into my chest. I don't touch her, keeping my hands at my sides, but that hand of hers runs from my chest down to my stomach as she peers at me through her lashes.

"What's going on right now?" Her voice is husky.

I smirk as her fingers wrap around the waistband of my track pants and Cam's lips land on her neck. Her eyes slowly close and her full lips open on a gasp as she tips her head to the side, giving him more access. I continue to watch as she enjoys another man's mouth on her. I should feel some sort of jealousy, right? I shouldn't be so turned on that I want to rip her fucking pants down and fuck her raw.

My hands grip her torso and I push her back, her eyes

snapping open.

"As fun as this is, I got shit to do," I say in a bored tone, the sound at war with my tumultuous insides.

"What?" She blinks and slowly brings herself around, realizing just what is happening.

I step away from them as Cam chuckles, fighting my need to smirk.

"You guys have fun. I need a shower and some hot pussy." I know the jab stings as she narrows her eyes. "Good night," I call over my shoulder as I leave the room.

I don't make it ten steps before her shriek is at my back and she shoves me against the wall. "Fuck you, Torres!" Her palm lands on my cheek, making my head snap to the side.

Then she storms back toward the ring and I turn toward Cam's laughing voice.

"That was just getting interesting." He shakes his head.

"You can enjoy that," I dismiss him and start off down the hall. "I don't want to get involved with Catalina."

"Wait," he calls at my back as he jogs to catch up. "It's not like that, you know I wouldn't—"

I cut him off with a raise of my hand. "I'm just making it clear I wouldn't care if you did."

We say nothing else as I lead the way back to my room, bypassing the dining hall and the noises coming from within. They'll be drinking and celebrating my win tonight, and I'm expected to join them. I will, but I just need a moment to chill.

Cameron goes into his room, just down the hall from mine, and I get to my door, looking over my shoulder at Cat's room. Is she in there or in the hall? I shake my head, annoyance hitting me hard, and open my door. Why the fuck does she always work her way back into my head?

I slam the door shut behind me and press my forehead to the wood, the cool surface soothing the ache I feel forming.

"Turn around and face me, you asshole." Cat's voice in my room shocks me, and I spin.

She pushes off my bed and comes to stand in front of me, her chest moving rapidly in anger. Her high cheekbones flush with pink and her face hardens with determination as her palm connects once again with my cheek.

"You made me feel cheap in there." Her growl sounds angry, but there's a touch of pain in it. "How dare you?"

Her hand flies up again, but my fingers seal around her wrist to stop it as my other hand wraps around her throat.

"Do not push me, Cat," I warn, low and dark.

I flip her around and throw her against my door, the thud loud in my small room. Her eyes widen as I take the few steps toward her and crowd her against the wood, framing her in with my arms. Her bottom lip is sucked back into her mouth and her eyes become heavy with lust.

Not tonight.

I yank on her arm and open the door, shoving her outside roughly. "Stay the fuck out of my room."

"You're crazy," she breathes out, and I toss my head back with a laugh.

"You would be smart to fucking remember it too." I point my finger at her face. "If I find you back in here again, you won't be leaving the same way you came. I don't give a fuck whose capo you are." I mock her ties to the crime family.

Cat opens her mouth to say something, but I slam my door in her face, ignoring her protests from the other side. She had a chance with me a few years ago. Fuck, I would've still been willing a few months ago, but that's all changed. She would never get sweet Carmelo now because he's gone, and after learning about my family, she's the least of my concerns.

I whip off my hoodie and drop my pants on the way to the bathroom. I need a fucking shower before I chill with anyone. The first cold spray shocks my skin as I step in. I glance down at my raging hard-on that has not deflated since things went down inside the locker room. The cold water is doing fuck all and my cock is jutting straight out, the water forced to stream around it.

I grasp it in my hand and groan at the skin on skin contact. I haven't done this in a very long time. It's been months since I've given myself relief because I like to use that energy in the cage, but right now, as I glide my fist up and down my length, I know it's been too long. I squeeze hard at the tip and fall back against the tiled wall, too absorbed in the sensations to care about the cold seeping into my back.

I'm two pumps in and can already feel my balls tightening, my orgasm rushing up on me. It's not surprising since I've barely touched myself in months, let alone sank into a tight pussy or a hot, wet mouth. I imagine Cat on her knees in front of me, her eyes wide like when I threw her against the door, and that plush mouth open, waiting for the hot splashes of my cum.

When the first drops of cum fly from my cock, my knees get weak and my head hits the tile, her name sounding like a moan coming from my mouth.

Catalina Costa.

CAMERON

I hear screaming from the hallway and recognize Cat's voice. Opening my door, I lean against the jamb, watching her scream at Carmelo's shut door. Not a single word is in English, so I don't understand a thing she's saying, save for the few curse words thrown in.

"Are you trying to figure out the magic word to open the door?" I chuckle. "Sometimes a knock will do it."

"Fuck you, asshole," she snarls and turns on me. "This is your fault."

"Hold on, what?" I raise my brow at her as I stand up straight.

"That shit you pulled in the locker room. What was that?" She's coming right for me, her face a mask of fury.

"A good time?" I play dumb as her eyes begin to twitch with anger.

"I've stayed away from the whole Torres family on purpose. I can't be associated with any of them." She kicks the wall beside my door.

"What? How? You're in their fucking compound." I don't like what she's saying about my family.

"If the DeRucci Family found out my father was really working with the Torres' and running the Rampage, and I was here shacking up with the heir of the whole damn thing, we would all die." She kicks the wall again.

Trepidation and understanding wash over me at her words, but one thing stands out. "Is that why you stayed away from him?"

"And because I don't fucking want him," she grits through her teeth, and I laugh, unable to hold it back.

"Right, you're just outside his door screaming like a cat to be let back in for a bowl of cream."

"Do you think you're funny?" she shrieks, and I cringe at the noise.

"I think you need to calm down." I step up to her and look down into her angry brown eyes. "And if you want nothing to do with him, then I suggest you stay out of his room and the fuck away from the both of us."

It's brief, but I catch it before it disappears, that flash of sadness, and it grabs ahold of my heart. I've always been soft for sad girls. She turns slowly, her gaze landing on his door, and then she's turning toward her room.

"Cat…" I reach out and grab her arm. "Let's talk."

She looks down at my hand on her arm and then back up at my face. "You just said…"

"I know." I exhale heavily, hoping this rash decision doesn't cost me another hit to the face. "But I think you need a friend. Do you even have any?"

There it is, that sadness making her chocolate browns lighten and her mouth to turn down. I step back and open my door farther.

"Come on, Costa." I motion her into my room. "Let's have a drink."

She looks torn for all of two seconds, and then she's brushing past me into the room. She smells of citrus and bad intentions—exactly how my dick likes it apparently. I need to nip this and fast because I won't go against my boy, even if I have his permission. He's family and I won't lose him, but fuck, this girl was made from the very shit I crave.

I suck in a deep breath and back up into the room, closing the door behind me. Then I look over my shoulder and find her perched on the end of my bed, leaning back on her hands. Her tits are pushed forward and practically pulsing with her rapid heartbeat.

Fucking help me, sweet Jesus.

Chapter Six

Carmelo

My fingers twitch and curl into fists when Cat and Cam walk into the dining hall together. My irritation is immediate and without thought as I try to clear my head with a shake. I know Cam wouldn't do anything behind my back, and even if he did, I gave him my blessing, didn't I? It doesn't stop the rage I feel gathering low in my belly though, the same rage I thought I depleted an hour ago in the fucking cage.

I take a swig of my beer and narrow my eyes when Cam heads to my table and Cat goes to find her father. Why would they separate now? Weren't they together this whole time? Did she go straight to his room after I kicked her out of mine?

"Hey." Cam looks at me warily, but there's no guilt in his eyes. I nod and slide the beer I ordered for him across the table. "She needs to talk to you." He rests on his elbows and tries to catch my gaze.

"Don't get involved in the Catalina drama. You'll regret it," I warn him. Sound advice, if you ask me.

"Cam!" Ivy screams as she runs over to us. "Let's do shots of tequila."

"Tequila makes you feisty." Cam grins at her.

"And then you end up starting fights," I continue.

"And we'd have to fucking finish them," Neil finishes from behind her.

We all laugh, and I can feel the tension leaving my body in a rush. I won't let Catalina Costa come between me and my family. Cam is all I have left since Ivy practically got married, and I won't stand for anything to tear us apart. Pussy is everywhere.

"Two shots max." She steeples her hands under her chin and widens her eyes.

"Fine," I groan and stand up. "Two and that's it."

"Yay!" She claps. "Cat!" My body stills as Ivy calls out to the girl I love to hate. "Come, do shots with us."

I don't check if she's coming as I follow behind Neil to the bar, half listening to Cam and Ivy talking behind us. I find Saxon sitting at the bar, talking to the bartender, looking in deep conversation as his hands fly around his head.

"I will bet a hundred bucks the little shit is talking about how to dispose of a body." Neil holds his hand out to me.

"I'm not betting against that." I swat his hand away. "That's for sure what he's doing."

"Damn." Neil snaps his fingers with a chuckle. "That would've been an easy hundred."

"Are you pimping yourself out again?" Saxon raises a brow at Neil.

"Bro." Neil shakes his head. "Stop coming for me. Are you drinking?" He points to the beer in Saxon's hand.

"Yeah." Saxon takes a few swallows. "Did someone say something about shots?"

"Yes!" Cam clasps Saxon's shoulders and grins. They've always been weirdly close. I say weirdly because Saxon doesn't really get close to people.

When Cat's scent of citrus and musk hits my nostrils, I close my eyes and take shallow breaths. Her perfume and her own personal scent will always be my weakness. I've just gotten better at hiding it over the years.

"Line up shots of tequila!" Ivy yells over to the bartender, and he chuckles as he shakes his head. "Don't puke." Then she points at Saxon.

"No promises." Saxon shrugs.

The shots line up, and I down two in a row, chasing away the scent behind me and the want that courses through me at her nearness. Every time she gets near, it's like I have to retrain my brain and my fucking dick to hate her… until the next time she gets too close.

"We have to take two shots of tequila?" Her voice sounds like velvet. "That's a recipe for disaster."

"Oh, live a little, Cat," Ivy chastises and hands her a shot.

Her hand comes around me from the left, her breasts pressing against my back from the motion. I steel my spine and continue to breathe until I smell Jose Cuervo under my nose.

"To family." Cam raises his shot glass up. I grab the other and raise it as well.

"Family," I repeat, and we all tip back the shots.

"Wow." Saxon lets out a heavy exhale. "Jose needs a new day job." His face is screwed up in disgust.

All of us break out into laughter as Cam claps Saxon

on the back. "It'll put some hair on your balls."

"Great." He nods and gives Cam a look. "But will it help your dick grow?"

"Will you shut up about that?" Cam mumbles, but the damage is done.

"Pardon?" Ivy leans on the bar. "How do you know about Cam's teeny weenie?"

"Fuck you!" Cam snarls at Ivy, but it's drowned out by Saxon's voice.

"I walked in on him the other day humping it into some chick." Saxon sips his beer. "She left pretty unsatisfied."

"Ouch." Cat laughs behind me.

"Whatever." Cam shakes his head, but I see the ghost of a smile on his mouth.

"Nah, he's decent," I speak up for him.

"Do I want to know?" Neil looks at me with humor.

"We've tag teamed a few girls in our time."

"Yes!" Cam slaps the bar. "I'm a grower! Let's drink to that!"

"Ugh… gross." Her husky voice hits my ear, and I take the shot offered to me, tipping it back instantly.

I let the warmth of the liquor burn its way down my throat and into the pit of my stomach, focusing on that instead of her proximity. It's always her overwhelming presence that has me reeling, and I just want my reactions to her to stop. I can't concentrate. Everything about her throws me off, and the worst part is I think she knows it too.

I step forward and my stomach hits the bar, but at

least she's no longer touching me, and I ask the bartender for another beer.

"That was a quick fight tonight, Cuz," Ivy says to me, her hand on my arm. "Is everything okay? I heard you spoke to my mother."

I give her a quick nod and then shake my head. "Your mother is so much more than what I thought, and I fucking thought she was so much already."

"I know." She nods while tightening her hand on my arm. "She's a good person."

"I don't know that everyone would agree, but I agree with you. I understand her reasoning."

"Imagine if those types of people stayed alive," she breathes out and then swallows thickly. "She's just trying to make sure her family is safe."

"Types of people? You mean our grandfather, right?" I lower my voice and step in closer to her. "How many more are there?"

"Oh, shit." Her hand flies to her mouth as she stares at me wide-eyed. "Carmelo, you can't say anything."

"How can I? I don't understand what the fuck you're saying."

She continues to shake her head and keeps her eyes on the bar. If this is even close to what Aunt Ember already told me, then this isn't the time or place to speak about it. To be honest, my first-round talk with Aunt Ember fucked me up and now I'm nervous about what else there could be.

"We need to talk about this later," I tell her, and she nods solemnly.

She knows there's no way out of this, and if I have my way, Aunt Ember will be there for this talk as well. What the fuck has my family been up to? And how many secrets do we have buried under our feet?

I slip away from the bar, and Catalina's scent, to make my way to the bathrooms. The sudden clean air is refreshing, and for a short time, I don't have to remind myself that I hate her. I enter the bathroom and hit the urinal. My head is slightly fuzzy from the fucking tequila. I don't know why I always give in and do shots with Ivy. I always end up regretting it.

The door opens behind me and I think nothing of it until I smell citrus. I languidly tuck myself back in my pants and shake my head. She wouldn't follow me in here.

"You're avoiding me." Yes, she fucking would. Shock tears through me when I hear her turn the lock on the door, then I look at her over my shoulder.

"After nearly four years of pretending I don't exist, now suddenly you're stalking me?" I try to keep my voice level, but my emotions are a mess. Anger and lust are all-out battling, and my stomach is heating.

"We either talk like civil human beings or we fight, and when I win, you'll talk to me anyway. You decide."

"Or…" I raise my brow. "You could always just go talk it out with Cameron."

"You're jealous." Her face literally glows as her full lips stretch into a wide smile, like she has it all figured out.

"I'm observant." I shrug and try to pass her on my way to the door.

I grunt as she grabs my arm, twists it up behind my back, and then shoves me face-first into the wall. If I wasn't so drunk, I would've been able to flip the move around and not have my face touching something someone could've pissed on. Fucking Ivy and her fucking tequila.

"As kinky as this is…" I take a deep breath to stop the rage vibrations I feel gathering. "I'm just not that into you."

I could fight her, and getting out of this hold isn't difficult, but I'm worried about her reaction and possibly having a broken arm at the end of it all. As much as Cat pisses me off, I know she's a well-trained fighter, and even though I think most moves out, others are instinctual. Just to prove her point, she steps in closer and tightens her hold. I feel the pull on my shoulder and continue breathing to calm the rage that's threatening to consume me.

"I bet if I slipped my hand down your pants…" Her voice becomes low and husky. "I would find the complete opposite."

She's not wrong, and just to drive the point home, my dick pushes against my jeans.

"Let's talk then," I grit out as my vision reddens around the edges. I need out of this hold, and now.

"I kind of like you like this," she purrs, unaware of the battle I'm fighting to keep myself together. "Think of the things we could do."

Her foot kicks against mine, trying to widen my stance, and I lose the fight at the contact. My teeth crack as I grind them together before snapping my head back, connecting with hers. She grunts as her hands leave my arm, and I turn on her instantly, my hand wrapping around her throat, her back now slamming against the tiled wall.

I can see the red welt forming on her forehead and thank God I didn't get her in the temple. She's taken worse hits and dusted herself off though.

"What. Do. You. Want." My hand tightens with each word as my face moves closer to hers. I give her credit because she doesn't look scared in the slightest and her eyes darken into something my dick is reacting to.

I press my cock against her stomach and keep a firm hold on her neck as I graze my lips along her throat. She feels soft and her skin smells like something uniquely her. Then I run my tongue along the surface just to taste it. She moans as her hands snake up under my sweater to run along my heated flesh.

"Is this what you wanted?" I ask as I pull back and stare down into her eyes. "Did you succeed?"

I release her throat and cage her in with my arms against the wall on either side of her head, my mouth an inch from hers. She licks her lips, looks at my mouth, and then up into my eyes.

"You don't know everything." Her whisper leaves a fiery trail along my cheek. "You don't know how hard it's been."

I press my thumb against her bottom lip, running the pad back and forth, and relishing in how fucking soft it is, how much I want it on me. "Tell me."

"Kiss me," she begs, her hands gripping the material of my sweater. "Please."

I want to, and as my anger seeps away, I'm left with the overwhelming need to make her mine. To give in to four years of denial and claim what my heart believes belongs to me. I sink into her further, our breaths mingling and her lips glistening.

"I don't want to fuck you in this bathroom." My lips brush hers.

"It's just a kiss, asshole." There's no fire behind her words.

"I won't be able to stop there," I admit as I flick my tongue against her bottom lip. "You good with being fucked in here?"

"Should be interesting for my first time."

The shock of her words has me stumbling back just as someone bangs on the door. I stare at the door and then back to her face, her features crestfallen. She turns and opens the door, apologizing to the surprised guy on the other side, then disappears into the dining hall while I just stand here in shock.

CATALINA

Today is a new record for how stupid I am. Not only did I spill all my secrets to a sweet-faced Cameron, but now I just blurted out my biggest secret of all to someone who can barely stand me. What is wrong with me? Why did I break the one important rule I set for myself almost four years ago? Stay away from Carmelo Torres and his overwhelming sexual aura.

That's all it was, just a reaction to the sexual energy he radiates from his pores, and I can deal with it. Nothing will cloud my judgement again; it can't, and I won't let it. Passing by the bar, I hear Cameron's deep laugh as he ruffles Ivy's weird brother's hair. I slip out of the dining hall unnoticed and hurry to my room. I'll just work off this anxious feeling. The gym always helps to clear my head.

I change into my workout gear and hurry to the gym. I know no one will be there tonight because everyone is working on getting drunk in the dining hall.

The corridor is quiet as I scurry along, hoping not to run into anyone and needing to pound my fists into the bag. I round the corner and breathe a sigh of relief when I see the empty gym through the glass. This is exactly what I need.

I pop my earbuds in and head straight for the bags, my chest finally relaxing and my mind becoming clearer. It's so funny how in a single moment, a lifetime of training can be forgotten and all your weaknesses come tumbling out.

My fist hits the leather of the punching bag and my eyes roll back at the sting on my knuckles. This is the pain I'm used to dealing with. I don't know how to handle emotional pain, but I know it feels so much worse than the physical.

I hear a muffled bang through the music in my ears

and switch it off before turning to see a livid Carmelo standing inside the room. Based on the dust floating to the floor, he slammed the door into the drywall.

"Why did you come here?" His voice is deep and raspy.

"What?" I hold my arms out. "Is it so hard to be in here with a fucking virgin?" My voice becomes high-pitched on the last word, and he cringes at the noise.

"No." He shakes his head, his eyes softening. "I don't care that you're a virgin. It just took me by surprise."

My throat swells shut with shame and I can feel the burn of tears behind my eyes. I haven't cried since I found out the crime family I work for killed my mother. I feel embarrassed. All I want to do is make him feel bad, because that's how I felt when I threw myself at him in the bathroom and he proceeded to reject me.

"Well, I had a momentary lapse of judgment. I wouldn't fuck you if my life depended on it."

His eyes darken with the insult before he slowly prowls toward me. "Cat, we both know if I were to completely disrespect you right now…" Another slow step and a sneer. "Rip down your fucking pants…" Another step. "Bend you over that bench…" His chest brushes mine with his rapid inhales. "And slam my cock into that tight virgin pussy, you would scream my name in pain." His hand grabs my hair, his fingers yanking on the strands, bringing my face close to his. "And you would beg me not to stop."

Carmelo's words bring a flood of wetness between my legs, and I steel myself, begging my hormones to fuck off. His nose brushes against mine and I hold my breath to stop myself from gasping.

"Your tight pussy would squeeze me as she creamed

all around my dick and this pretty little mouth would call me your God."

His arrogant words piss me off, and I am at least grateful the haze of lust is wiped away with it. I clench my teeth and slam my forehead forward, connecting with his nose and hearing the sweet crunch of his cartilage. He rears back with a roar, his hand wrapping around his nose as blood runs out between his fingers.

"What the fuck?" he screams, his voice sounding nasally.

The gym door swings open just as Carmelo is stalking back to me, his eyes on fire and the hand not wrapped around his nose clenched in a fist.

"Whoa!" Cameron jumps in front of him and stops him with a hand to the chest. "What the fuck did you do?" he asks me from over his shoulder.

"Your cousin needs a lesson in decency," I snarl and narrow my sights on Carmelo. "I meant what I fucking said. Not if my life depended on it."

"The DeRucci Family has the perfect soldier," Carmelo's nasally sneer deepens. "Two-faced and frigid, completely untouched."

That fucking kills. Those words were meant to flay, and they leave me sliced open, bleeding profusely at his feet. My heart sinks so low into my belly I fear I'm dying. Is this what death feels like? If it is, then I was stupid to never fear it. It's a pain like I've never encountered from a fist or a weapon, and I feel like my knees are about to give out from under me.

"What is wrong with you?" Cameron bellows at Carmelo and gives him a shake. "Stop speaking without thinking. You'll regret it."

Breathing is becoming more and more difficult the longer I'm standing in Carmelo's direct sight. His eyes are like a ligature wrapping around my throat and cutting off my air supply.

"I fucking hate you, Carmelo Torres." I can feel the vitriol roll through my words. "Thank God your father never had to witness his useless sack of shit for a son."

"Hey!" Cameron yells, but I'm already out of the gym.

I need out of this compound and away from the man who makes me want to commit murder. Maybe a trip to California will keep me from landing my ass in jail. I'll tell my father I want to leave tonight. There's no need for me to be here now anyway, and I can't stand to be in Carmelo's presence. I need him out of my system, and distance will do that.

It's time I go back to ignoring his fucking existence.

CAMERON

"Will you tell me what the fuck that was about?" I press Carmelo as blood streams down his chin.

"Why don't you go ask her yourself?" He brushes past me and out into the corridor. "You two are buddies now, right?"

"Oh." I chuckle humorlessly. "You're mad she was in my room? I didn't fuck her," I confess as I follow his actions.

"I know." He laughs, the sound dark and depraved. "She's a fucking virgin and practically begged me to fuck her in the bathroom earlier."

I'm stunned to the spot, my feet no longer able to move as my head tries to wrap itself around the words. A virgin? That can't be true. It doesn't seem to fit the woman who was in my room earlier and lounging across my bed. She exudes confidence… and I'm sounding like an idiot. Just because she is confident in herself and her training, that has nothing to do with her sexual experience, or the lack of it.

"For real?" I ask, and Carmelo turns to look at me.

"Why?" A nasty grin spreads across his face. "Did she put you in an arm hold and threaten to grab your dick?"

"What the fuck?" And… I'm hardening in my jeans.

"Never mind," he huffs and continues toward his room.

"Wait." I jog to catch up. "None of this explains what the fuck I walked in on or why she busted up your face."

"Because I wouldn't fuck her in the bathroom? I don't even really know." He shrugs before his shoulders deflate. "It doesn't matter because I agree with her."

Then he opens his room door and heads inside with me hot on his trail.

"What do you mean, you agree with her? About what?" I throw my hands up in exasperation.

"I'm thankful my father isn't here to see his worthless sack of shit for a son."

With those words, my heart breaks for my family and my best friend. I knew her words would affect him. I just hoped they wouldn't cause him to spiral, and right now, I can see he's on the brink. Carmelo has never felt like he lived up to his father's image and he's always trying to find validation.

"You sound pathetic." It's the only way to crack him open. I need him to get pissed off. "This self-deprecating bullshit is becoming annoying."

His body turns slowly, and with each second, his spine grows rigid, his breathing speeding up. That's it. "Watch it."

"Is there ever going to be a day that goes by when I don't have to hear you whine for your daddy?" I give him a smirk.

He grabs the front of my polo and throws me against the wall, his body vibrating with anger. "I will fucking kill you." His spit lands on my face.

"How about"—I throw his hands off me and step into his face—"you call your fucking mother and your baby sister? Speak to your family who are alive. They miss you."

His face relaxes and he scrubs his hand along the five o'clock shadow on his cheek. "Yeah." He sounds guilty, but it needed to be said. Sometimes he needs reminding that he has a family outside of these walls, and I'm usually the one to do it.

"How long this time?" I ask him.

"I spoke to Mom three weeks ago."

"Call her and talk to them." I shake my head and walk back out into the hallway. "Regardless of what your dead father would think, you still have a family who deserves better."

He nods, and I let out an exhale when I see the determination back in his stature. I turn around and glance at Cat's door. There's no light underneath and no sound coming from inside. I hope she's okay, but I just don't have the energy to fix another person right now.

It's fucking draining being the voice of reason all the time. I just want to get back to Toronto and bury my dick in pussy.

Chapter Seven

It's been three weeks and six days since I've seen her. The morning after our blowout, I walked across the hall and stood at her door. The words I wanted to say were running on blast in my mind and my heart was pounding out a nervous rhythm. I knocked on her door and waited, my heart in my throat.

I thought of ways to win her over, maybe bringing her a plate of those breakfast sausages I always see her rushing for, and just maybe giving her that kiss she wanted.

But there was no answer at her door, and when I searched the compound, she was nowhere to be found. It was Trent who finally told me his daughter wanted to go back to Los Angeles and right into the dangerous hands of the mafia. Do you know what that tells me? Catalina would rather have her life on the line than be anywhere near me.

Cameron has been quiet since he's gone home and his texts have been abrupt. I know it sounds fucking crazy, but maybe they're talking to each other and maybe they're both realizing just how fucked-up I am. It sounds stupid, even to my ears, but I can't help but feel like I'm losing the people closest to me.

In seconds, everything I tried to keep tamped down came rushing to the surface, and four years of avoidance nearly ripped me inside out. Why didn't I just kiss her in that fucking bathroom? Why couldn't I just bury the hurt I had built up in four years and show her I actually fucking cared?

It's been nonstop training for me with Uncle Emmett and Aunt Ember. They rotate out the weekends, and I must admit, I've used the anger to improve. I'm in the gym each day, I'm pumping weights until my body screams, and then I collapse into my room, just to do it all again the next day. If I stop for even a few moments, I see her anguished face standing in front of me, and it makes me hate myself even more.

It makes me remember the very first day I met Catalina Costa.

"Hold your arm straight, but don't lock it." Uncle Emmett taps my elbow. "The kickback on any gun will jar your shoulder if your elbow is locked. You want to absorb the impact instead."

I nod and squint my eyes at the target.

"Eyes need to be wide open." Next, he taps my temple. "It's never just the target you're watching, and most of the time, they aren't immobile."

I nod again and open my eyes, settling on the dummy twenty feet ahead. Then I squeeze the trigger and the gun sends a jolt down my arm, but my shoulder absorbs it like he said. The bullet flies and finally hits the dummy in the chest. It's not the head, which is where the target is, but at least this time I got the fucker.

"Yes!" I grin and look at Uncle Emmett.

He smiles and nods, a look of pride on his face. "Keep practicing."

"Bro!" Cameron hollers from the other side of the glass. "You killed that fucker for sure."

I turn and beam at him over my shoulder, then my eyes land on Trent and a girl standing next to him. No, not a girl. She's definitely grown and she's fucking gorgeous. Cameron's eyes follow mine and then he's striding toward them, his hand held out to Trent. Cameron has always been the friendly one.

I watch him shake hands with Trent, clasping him on the shoulder, and then he's holding his hand out to the girl, her face stoic. She looks at his hand and back at his face, opting to give him a curt nod of acknowledgment instead. Who is she?

"That's Trent's daughter," Uncle Emmett says, making me wonder if I asked that out loud. "Catalina."

"Trent's married?" I ask him, my eyes never leaving her face.

"No." His voice becomes sad as I look at him. "She was his high school sweetheart."

"Was?"

"The mafia murdered her to keep him in line and then they raised his daughter, only allowing him to see her when they saw fit." His words send shock throughout my body.

"She lives with a mafia?" I breathe out.

"She's in training there. She's a soldier for them."

And that's when I really look at her, her arms toned and defined, her body thick with muscle but still feminine in curves, and her legs, revealed in the shorts she's wearing, are muscular and long.

My eyes travel upward and then to her face. She's looking right back at me. I don't look away. Instead, I show her I'm interested with a look, my mouth slowly curving into a smile. It never fails.

A single, perfectly arched brow raises on her face, and she looks away, completely disinterested. What the fuck?

Uncle Emmett laughs beside me, and I look at him in shock because I'm rarely rejected. "Is she not into guys?"

"She's nothing like those high school girls you're used to." He chuckles. "But you two have something in common. You both like to maim."

She smiles at Cameron and something inside me twists. I've never been one to succumb to jealousy. Especially over Cameron. If there's a girl we both like, then we both get a taste, and sometimes at the same time. There's nothing we keep from each other.

My stomach sinks even more though when he pulls his phone from his pocket and hands it to her, the smile still on her mouth. She types what I assume is her number and hands it back. I don't care. It doesn't fucking matter, I try to convince myself as my stomach tightens. Her eyes land back on me again and the smile slips off her face.

What the fuck is up with this girl?

Cameron has her number. The memory was vivid in its details. In all the years Cat and I have known each other, we never needed to exchange numbers, and a lot of that was because of our rivalry, but Cameron has it. Maybe they really are talking.

I take a deep breath and try to push down the sudden onset of jealousy coupled with the need to strangle him, making my way back to my room. I swear, I will drive all the way back to Toronto, drag him by his balls outside, and beat the shit out of him until I'm driving to California and dragging Cat back by her hair.

I get to my room and storm inside, slamming the door behind me. My phone is charging by my bed, and I open it to a few messages from Sabrina. My little sister is starting university in a few months, and she's been feeling restless lately. She's been thinking of deferring her first year and coming here to New York. She says Whitsborough is stifling.

I know that feeling, but the last place I want her is here, in the middle of a gang compound and full of guys looking for a quick lay. That's probably how I came to be, even though my mother says otherwise.

I skip her message and open my conversation with Cameron.

Me: I need Cat's number.

He reads it and then nothing. No three dots telling me he's typing, just nothing. I lay my phone down and decide to give him five minutes. That's more than enough to wipe his ass if he's on the fucking pot, or finish his meal. Tons of time. I watch the clock closely, and when five minutes are up, I grab my phone again. Nothing.

Me: You're not gonna want to ignore me.

There, that's threatening enough without being explicit. He should get the fucking clue it's important and not to play with me today. This time, I give him three more minutes to reply. That's fucking generous considering he's read every message and still chooses to ignore me. Fine, time for the big guns.

Me: Don't make me call your mother and tell her about you catching chlamydia in your first year of university.

Finally, those three dots appear, then disappear, and then reappear again.

Cam: Bro, will you relax?

Me: Number… now.

Cam: Look, maybe you should wait until she gets back? You guys left off on bad terms.

Me: Oh, you know when she'll be back?

Cam: No.

Me: Number.

My phone rings with Cameron's name on the screen, and I groan, running my hand through my damp hair. I don't want to talk to him, and it's weird he's calling now when we've barely spoken in three weeks.

"What?" I pick up.

"She won't want to talk to you."

"Are you talking to her?" I ask him straight up.

The silence that greets my question is answer enough, and my stomach tightens. Why are they talking?

"Sometimes she texts me," he answers, but he sounds hesitant.

"What about?" I try to keep the accusation out of my voice.

"You, mostly."

"Right." I roll my eyes. "About how much she hates me?"

"Sometimes," he admits, the vulnerable sound of his voice easing my suspicions. This is Cam.

"I just want to know if she's okay," I mumble.

"I can tell she's hurt, and I think she feels guilty about what happened, although she'll never admit it."

"You won't give me her number, will you?" I snarl into the phone.

"No." His answer is firm. "I really think you two need this time apart, and honestly, if you fight again, she may never come back."

"You really don't know when she's coming back?" The anger drains from my voice as my eyes sink closed.

"No, she can only leave with the family's permission," he states, and I nod, knowing that already. Cat is a member of the mafia. They own her.

"What's been going on with you?" I change the subject. "You barely talk to me anymore."

"I've just been feeling lost," he replies, and I can hear the dejection in his voice. "I don't know what to do with my fucking life."

"Your dad?" I press him.

Tommy, Cameron's dad, is a tough ass. He grew up rough and didn't have parents of his own. He was raised in foster homes and group homes most of his life, and he vowed not to let his child suffer like he did. It doesn't help that Cameron is an only child and expected to be something great. I have every confidence he will be, but I know the pressure that rides on his shoulders.

"Yeah, I need to have a life plan by midterm." His voice is quiet.

"That's why you've been distant from me?"

"I've just been keeping to myself." Sadness seeps through his words and I fucking hate myself for not realizing something was wrong before now.

"All right, I'm packing a bag. I'll be there in the morning."

"Wait, what?" His voice perks up.

"We'll figure out your fucking life plan and then you can find your balls again."

"Fuck you." He laughs, and the sound settles my worry for him. "Thanks, man."

"See you soon."

I grab my clothes and begin stuffing them into my duffel bag. I haven't been back home to Whitsborough in over a year because that town doesn't feel like home anymore. My family comes here on certain occasions to see me and we video call sometimes, but since I'm going to Toronto, I know I should also visit my family too.

Heading back there feels like I'm on my way to Hell, only this Hell is run by my very own family.

CAMERON

"What is it you like doing?" Carmelo is sitting across from me the next morning, and I'm thankful he brought me coffee.

"I don't know." If I fucking knew that answer, we wouldn't be sitting here. I look him over and notice he's bigger, more cut and muscles bulging. "You working out?" I watch him closely as he takes a sip of his coffee.

"Yeah." He shrugs.

I know what he's doing, and it makes me feel guilty for being absent lately. When Carmelo sinks into himself, he forgets the important things, like food and sleep.

"Are you sleeping? Eating right?" I question him, noticing the bags under his eyes. "It sucks you're there and your family is here, mostly."

Having Aunt Ember and Uncle Emmett there on weekends just isn't enough. Carmelo needs structure and supervision. Who's watching his training during the week and prepping him before fighting?

"Yeah." His eyes widen with excitement. "It sucks!" His mouth curves into a grin.

"That's not something to be excited about, bro." I shake my head. "Maybe I can set alerts and message you to eat and shit. Do you still have that nutrition plan I made for you?"

"No." His smile grows wider. "I don't. Anyway, I need a new one. I want more muscle."

"You need balance and flexibility; don't just bulk up."

He laughs and slaps his hand on the table. "You're right. I need someone there all the time. Not just weekends."

"Exactly." I nod. Maybe all the muscle is eating at his brain cells somehow because he's acting real simple right now.

"This is perfect." He keeps nodding and looking more and more like a simpleton. Maybe he needs to go on a vacation.

"Well, I'm glad you drove all the way here to figure your shit out, but I'm done with school in three months and my father is expecting a detailed future plan." I stand from the table and throw my empty coffee cup in the trash.

"We just made one." He's looking at me like I'm the stupid one now.

"What?"

"I need a manager and you're the one to do it. Fighting has paid me extremely well and I don't spend it on anything because I live at the compound." His eyes shine bright. "We can even get our own place and you can start a business managing fighters. I'll be the first."

Shock rushes through me and I fall back against the counter. I really am the stupid one. This is a great idea. Only thing is, would my family be okay with me in New York? And is this a suitable plan for them?

"We'll convince them," Carmelo assures me, reading

the concern on my features. "Let's make this plan, include yearly earnings and add on other fighter prospects. I know a few guys who need the same shit I do."

"Thank you," I say to him, my chest squeezing for the help he's giving me.

"Yeah." He waves me off and pulls his laptop out of his bag. "Will they require expenses and stuff like that? Do prostitutes fall into that category?"

"Oh my God." I grab his laptop as he chuckles. "Let me do this."

Finally, I feel the pieces I've been missing sliding into place and I'm more optimistic about my future.

"Carmelo!" Ivy yells as she bolts out her front door and toward my car.

"I'm happy to see her, but I hate Whitsborough." Carmelo shudders as he opens the door, preparing to meet Ivy.

I know what he means. Whitsborough is home, but it's also like stepping into another dimension, and it's like something dark settles over you when you pass that town sign. It's similar to that feeling you get when you enter a cemetery, almost as if the ghosts of Whitsborough's past are still here and haunting the shit out of us.

I get out of the car just as Neil steps out of his and Ivy's bungalow. It's small and cozy, just enough for the both of them. Ivy told us when they bought it, she wanted nothing to do with the upper side of Whitsborough, and this house right here instantly felt like a home to her.

It's near Neil's family and I'm excited to see Amelia. I told her I would be here. It's been fucking months, and she's one of my closest friends. Neil steps out on the porch and shields his eyes from the sun, watching Ivy as he always does. In the beginning, Carmelo and I would get irritated with how protective he was with her, but then considering everything she went through, we realized he just loves her and wants her safe.

I have yet to find a girl who makes me want to drop everything else and make them my life, the most precious thing I want to protect. As sweet as it is to see Neil do it for my family, I don't see that as something I want, and that's why I haven't settled down. I don't want to be shackled and spend my time with someone else. I'm not ready. Do I sound like an asshole? Maybe, but at least it's my truth. I need to sort out my own life first.

"Someone here is excited to see you," Neil calls out to me, and I laugh. I know he's talking about Amelia.

When I first saw her, I remember my breath getting lodged in my throat and thinking she was the prettiest girl I had ever seen. Her exotic looks and goofy personality were the perfect mix, but it didn't take long for us to establish just a friendship. I wasn't even on her radar, and I knew I valued our friendship more than that.

"Oh, yeah?" I grin as I clasp his hand and slap him on the back. "Maybe because we're ready to let the cat out of the bag about our relationship." I fucking love teasing Neil.

"Knock it off." She appears behind Neil and laughs, her curls bouncing around her face. "Everyone knows I want nothing to do with that thing between your legs."

I step inside and haul her into my arms. She feels like

home. "He's taken enough jabs lately. Don't hurt his feelings more," Neil reveals with a snicker.

"Do I want to know?" She laughs into my chest, and the sound flows through me, putting my insides at peace.

"Probably not." We move further into the house and toward the kitchen. "How's college?"

Amelia stayed close to her family and attends the local college. Her parents are still in the same house and she's been helping her mom out at the gym part-time. She seems content.

"So good." Her eyes brighten and a blush steals across her cheeks. So good indeed.

"Who is she?" I grin at her and watch as her eyes widen.

"Huh?" She tries to play it off and I let her. When she's ready, she'll tell me.

We sit at the table and the rest join us, chatting and laughing as they come in.

"Have you spoken to Saxon?" Amelia steals a glance at Ivy as she whispers to me.

"Not in a few weeks." I shake my head. "Things have been fucked-up."

"He got kicked out of Precious Blood."

"What? It's his final year. What happened?" I ask a bit too loudly, and the chatter stops.

"What's going on?" Carmelo cuts in as Neil clears his throat.

"Saxon got expelled last week," Ivy states with a huff as she sits down at the table with us.

"Aunt Adri couldn't prevent that?" I raise my brow.

"He has a few months until graduation."

"No." Ivy shakes her head. "This went to the board. Precious Blood Academy is a private school, and the final decision lies with them. He's already completed his GED. We all know he's already university-level smart and has been since he was twelve."

"Is no one going to ask what the fuck happened?" Carmelo glares at us like we're crazy.

Ivy looks at each of us, fear clearly on her face and indecision blatantly in her eyes.

"What is it?" I press her.

"It's bad," she whispers. "Even my mom and dad couldn't make it go away."

"I heard a bit, but it can't be the entire story. It never is," Amelia adds.

"We all need beers for this." Neil walks to the fridge and brings out a six-pack.

"Saxon got into a fight." Ivy runs her fingers through her hair. "He put the guy into the hospital."

"That's about all I know." Amelia nods.

"You won't hear the rest of it because we've covered it up." Ivy bites down on her bottom lip and I watch as anger flashes in her eyes. "I wish we could all easily come forward when terrible things happen."

"I'm sorry." I look from her to Neil. "I'm lost."

"Saxon says a group of guys jumped him at school," Neil explains. "He retaliated and almost killed one of them."

"What happened?" Amelia asks. "Who was it?"

"Brian Cox." Ivy's eyes darken in anger.

"Wait." Carmelo snaps his fingers. "That name sounds familiar."

"It should," Ivy sneers, her face looking a lot like Aunt Ember's. "His uncle was found shot in the head in his car right here in Whitsborough."

"Shit," I breathe out as everything comes together. "The murder they accused your mother of."

"And arrested her for." Her hand forms a fist on the table top.

They acquitted Aunt Ember for the murder of Andrew Cox with the help of her Grandma Jenna, but none of us have forgotten that one dark stain on our family name, and it looks like maybe others haven't either. It's an especially dark stain on my family name, being it was my grandfather who set Aunt Ember up.

My grandfather was Whitsborough's police chief and he was a fucking sadist. There's still so much about our pasts and our families we just don't know, but some secrets we found out the normal way—old newspaper clippings at the library.

"Did he do that to Saxon because of his uncle and the connection to Aunt Ember?" I question.

"Saxon isn't saying much, but it looks like he's been on Saxon's case for years," Ivy replies, her face dark with anger.

"I remember Brian being a shit to Saxon in elementary, but it wasn't much more than name-calling," Amelia chimes in.

"So, what now?" Carmelo asks. "Is Saxon going to be charged?"

"No." Ivy shakes her head. "The family was hushed

with money."

"Why didn't he say anything to me?" I'm unable to hold back the anger in my tone.

"Sometimes the shame from being a victim, whether it's sexual or not, clouds a person's judgement," Ivy cuts in, sounding like she knows all too well what that's like. "Even though they know it wasn't their fault, something inside them tells them it was."

"You're speaking from experience," Carmelo tells her, and Amelia gasps.

"The reason they sent you home from New York?" I interject. "The teacher thing?"

"No, not the teacher." She shakes her head. "There was someone in New York who hurt me and someone here in Whitsborough."

"Adam Van Dyke," Carmelo snarls, and Ivy nods.

It took months, but Ivy finally told us what happened to her and the role police officer Adam Van Dyke had in it. He was the one who ran her down in his car and then shot himself outside of Neil's house. All of it was strange, and the Greenes covered up as much as they could. It didn't matter though because the stigma of his suicide stayed with the Van Dyke family and they ended up leaving Whitsborough.

"Thank God he's dead because I'd be killing him myself," Carmelo growls.

"Yes, thank God he's dead," Ivy repeats as she grabs Neil's hand.

"I need to speak to Saxon." I push back from the table.

"Not yet." Ivy stops me. "Mom has him in therapy.

There's a therapist they found in New York. She's hoping it helps him. Let him come to you when he's ready."

"In New York?" Carmelo questions.

"Yeah." Ivy nods. "They start the sessions this weekend."

That means they'll probably stay at the compound and Carmelo can talk to Saxon. I don't know if Saxon will open up to him because they never had the chance to form a bond, and to be honest, they never had much in common.

Saxon is misunderstood mostly, and it's because people are put off by his personality. I'm hoping Carmelo can see past that.

Chapter Eight

Carmelo

One month and six days. That's how long Catalina's been gone. This isn't the longest she's been gone by any means, but it feels like forever this time, and I fucking want her back here so we can talk. After our last confrontation, we need to talk, and her avoiding me is only making it worse.

Cameron still refuses to give me her number and sticks to the logic that we need the distance. If she really hates me this much, it's going to be hard to convince her otherwise, and the longer she stays away, the more doubtful I become. California is far, but it's not impossible to find her, and I'm not opposed to unconventional methods of convincing her to come home.

Tomorrow, I have another fight and tonight, Aunt Ember will be here for Saxon's shrink visit. I didn't see him last week because I was training with Uncle Emmett and they didn't stay at the compound. This weekend is Aunt Ember's turn to train with me and I'm expecting to see Saxon. I also need to bring up what Ivy and I spoke about all those weeks ago. I haven't had a chance to yet, and with all that was going on, it never felt like a good time.

I can't go on any longer without answers. My mind has conjured up some fantastical scenarios that my aunt is a superhero and capturing bad guys. Then there's Saxon. If he's getting jumped, maybe it's time to teach him how to fight and defend himself. I can do that for him. He's done with high school now anyway. Maybe he could stay here with me, and I can teach him how to kick some fucking ass. It'll get him out of Whitsborough too.

There's a sharp knock on my door, and I get to my feet, opening it. Trent stands on the other side with his hand in his hair. His being here while his daughter is away is nerve-wracking.

"What's up?" I try to sound calm, but my mind is running with all the scenarios that could've happened to Cat.

"Your aunt has requested you join her for a meeting this evening." He looks stressed and slightly irritated. "Please dress appropriately as there will be important people there."

"What people? Why am I being summoned to this meeting?" I press him.

"I asked the same questions and was told nothing. I do not think you are capable of what she will ask you to do." He shakes his head. I don't take it as an insult because I can see he has no malicious intent behind his words, and that only makes me more curious.

"Where's the meeting?"

"Here in the compound. I will be by to pick you up at eight." Then he's turning abruptly and stalking back down the corridor.

It was on the tip of my tongue to ask how Catalina was and when she was coming home, but I didn't. I don't want it to get back to her. If she found out I was asking Cameron and her father about her? She would rub that shit in my face as soon as she got back.

I grab my workout clothes and head into the washroom to change. Might as well pump some iron until Aunt Ember gets here.

The knock on my door jars me from my thoughts, and I quickly glance at the time on my phone. One minute to eight, he's prompt. I open my door to a frowning Trent and step out into the corridor with him. He strolls down the hall, almost like he's prolonging the inevitable, and I start sweating.

"Trent." I stop walking and place a hand on his shoulder, forcing him to turn and look at me. "What is this?"

His face falls and he runs his fingers through his hair. "There's not much I can tell you, but you need to trust your aunt, and I guess so do I. She sees something in you I have not, which just means I haven't been looking hard enough."

"I'm confused."

"You won't be for long, I hope," he huffs out and continues to walk.

"Are we going to her lair or something?" I ask before I can stop myself, and he looks at me over his shoulder.

"What?"

"Never mind," I mutter.

We get to the conference room and it's eerily silent. I was told once a few years ago by Uncle Emmett that it's completely soundproof and you couldn't hear someone's screams through these thick panels. Now I am terrified of what I'll find when Trent opens the door.

"Keep an open mind and remember your last name," he warns me and knocks briefly before pulling on the heavy paneled door. I nod and walk inside.

Aunt Ember is sitting at the table with nine others. Mostly men, but there are a few women as well. When she pats the chair beside her, I send her a questioning look. I walk slowly, taking in each face and noticing they look like a gathering of mafia heads, something you would see in the Godfather movies.

She gives me a hard look when I sit in the seat.

"A lot of you never had the chance to meet my brother, Carm," she starts, and my heart kicks up inside my chest at his name. "But a few of you have."

A few heads turn and look at me closer, recognition plain on their faces.

"This is his son, Carmelo Torres." She squeezes my shoulder. "He will sit in on all meetings from now on and you will treat him as you do me."

There is a wave of nods around the table, and I am still as confused now as I was when I was first told about this meeting. Who are these people, and what do they gather here to have a meeting about? Are they mafia leaders? Are the DeRuccis here too?

"This is the opening of the Head meeting for May," Aunt Ember states and crosses her arms on the table. "Let's begin. Number One, where are we at?"

An older man with white hair begins, "This month, we have dropped the drug penetration in our region by almost thirty percent. We found a well-known distribution route and claimed it."

"Yes!" Aunt Ember slaps the table and a few excited murmurs circle. "That's great news. Number Two?"

"Drugs are down in our region too. We have helped dispose of a prominent drug distributor."

"Good news," Aunt Ember says with an enormous smile. "Three?"

This woman is large, easily hitting almost four hundred pounds, and her presence feels just as heavy. She looks like someone's grandma who you would never want to fuck with.

"Two known predators have been disposed of, and I would like to extend my gratitude to you and Trent for the help with the body cleanup."

Body cleanup? My heart slams inside my chest and my lungs grow heavy, making breathing difficult.

"I knew you would catch those fuckers," Aunt Ember growls. "You have saved many young women from their clutches."

What the fuck is happening? Does disposed mean killed? She said help with the body cleanup, right? I can feel sweat gliding down the back of my neck as I pull on the collar of my dress shirt. The room is suddenly too hot and my sight is blurring around the edges.

Aunt Ember continues down the line and it's more of the same. Drug sales down, gang leaders disposed of, predators disposed of, and officials are still firmly under all their thumbs. As the others continue their tallies, I can feel myself having what feels like an out-of-body experience. My father was a part of this?

"Region Ten." Aunt Ember folds her hands. "I had two predatory teachers a few years ago. They asked me to let them live as long as they leave Whitsborough." A few people gasp in surprise and Aunt Ember holds up her hand. "I just promised I wouldn't kill them in Whitsborough. I was monitoring them and was waiting for them to fuck up again. It happened. I've put a plan in motion to take them out."

This seems to placate the table and they all nod in agreement. Which two teachers in Whitsborough? What does she mean 'take them out'?

"Also, I have had an incident involving a young man who was once affiliated with a sexual predator in my region." She leans forward and looks at each of them. "He has assaulted another student based on that connection. The student retaliated and now that young man is in the hospital with swelling of the brain."

A few nods and the others continue to watch her closely. Then, the older man—Number One—speaks up. "It looks as though this young man may follow in the footsteps of his predecessor. Maybe watch and see if the student's beating taught him a lesson? When they are younger, there's always hope for change."

Everyone nods their agreement and Aunt Ember lets loose a breath. "Thank you for the advice." She nods. "This month has been a busy one for me. Whitsborough has been quiet, but here in Hunts Point, I've had to dispose of three cops under our payroll and then the rapists they saved from certain convictions. It looks like cops are becoming more easily swayed with money, so we need to once again remind them of the consequences."

Everyone around the table agrees before Aunt Ember taps on the table. "I think that's it for today." She looks at me and then back to the others. "I have a bit of explaining to do here."

They all laugh and rise from the table. "Your father was noble, and you will be too." Number One nods as he turns and heads toward the double doors.

Once they've all left, I sit quietly and wait for Aunt Ember to explain. Is this compound her superhero lair? Are all those people her sidekicks? What the actual fuck is going on?

"I brought you into this meeting without context because I wanted to see how you would react under the revelations." Her hand lands on my arm. "You did well. The people you met today are collectively known as the Head Corporation. It was a title my father gave to them, and it carried on through your father, and now me, although their purposes have changed. Ivy told me she let the cat out of the bag about what it is I do, and I decided it was always meant to be." She looks at me closely. "I desperately want to retire."

"Retire from what, exactly?" I whisper, my throat dry.

"From running the Head Corporation. When my father started this thing, it was a gang of criminals whose only purpose was to make money. They stole, laundered money, bought off government officials, traded in prostitutes and sometimes children, and they sold drugs and guns to street gangs." She looks at me with sad eyes. "While he was in prison, I worked for the Eastside Rampage as a collector. I would collect on debt owed, or I would teach lessons for lack of payment. Funny thing was, I didn't know this belonged to my father and that my half brother was running it at the time. I hadn't met either of them. My best friend Tommy, Cam's father, was running with the Rampage and offered me a few jobs to help me and my mother out with paying bills."

She stands up from the table and paces. "When I killed our father, Carmelo had no choice but to step in and take over everything in his place. Your father had a good heart, but they taught him that crime was the way of life and groomed him from a young age to take over. He understood as well as my father did that this was how the Rampage made money. At first, I was angry that he was caught up in all of it, but then I inserted myself and became a Head." She sits back down, but this time across from me, and leans in. "I decided I would not be the typical Head, and I didn't like the idea of gaining money by exploiting innocent people. I became a hit man."

"A hit man? So, not a superhero at all," I mumble and startle at her laugh.

"Did you say superhero?"

"When Ivy said you were getting rid of bad people, I thought she meant capturing them for the police," I explain around her loud laughter.

"Oh, no." She finally calms down and shakes her head. "I kill them, mostly." She gets a dark gleam in her eyes and I swallow thickly. "And I fucking like it, Carmelo."

"I–I won't l–like it, A–Aunt Ember," I stumble over my words as I try to spew them out. "Sure, I understand why you do it. I even will go as far to say I agree with what you do, but I can't do that."

"I know." She exhales and falls back into her seat. "It takes a special type of fucked-up to do what I do. I don't expect that from you. I will remain a Head until the day I find a replacement suitable for my regions, but you will take over the handling."

"The what?"

"I'm going to need you to run this." Her arms go wide. "Make sure everyone is on top of their projections, which you get reports on at the beginning of every month, and then you meet. You are to make sure they get a payout worthy of their efforts, and then you bank the rest."

"How do we make money?" I ask her.

"The events we have here, the capacity we bring in, and everyone gets paid for all the hits they make. Sometimes I am hired for my services and that money goes into a pot, same as everyone else, and then it's distributed. The leader of the Head Corp. takes a cut based on the protection they provide and the officials they procure in their pockets."

"This sounds well above my pay grade." I shake my head.

"I don't give a fuck what you think your pay grade is," she growls, and this is the first time I've seen my aunt vicious. The sight makes my skin crawl as I struggle to swallow. "You'll do well to remember your last name and who sat at the head of this table first."

"I don't think I'll be good enough," I mutter.

"That's what I'm here for." She stands and walks to the door. "Training starts Sunday. I know you have a fight tomorrow night, so let's get ready."

Her tone leaves no room for argument, and I decide to trust her because the alternative is too worrisome to contemplate. She seems to have it all fucking figured out.

CAMERON

There's a weird buzz in the compound tonight. I would attribute it to Carmelo's fight, but I've been to plenty of them, and tonight feels different. It's not coming from the ring. It's more in the walls of this place, and it's seeping out everywhere, like something vile has wormed its way inside.

This weekend, it's just me and Saxon. He's been quieter than usual. I have yet to speak to him about what happened or his therapy, and he seems in no rush to tell me either, which is very much like Saxon. I really don't want to push him about it until he's ready. Despite how quiet he is, he still looks unaffected and as cool as a cucumber. Maybe therapy is working.

"Does it feel weird here to you?" I lean over and ask him.

He side-eyes me. "No, not any more than usual."

"It feels like something is about to go down," I mumble.

"Okay, did you see that on your tarot cards after you read your tea leaves?"

I hate him.

The crowd cheers when Carmelo's opponent comes down the aisle. He's about Carmelo's size, before he forewent life and fucked a dumbbell or six a day. It surprised me with how big he had gotten, and I know all this drama with Cat is a part of it.

Speaking of, it's been a week since I have heard from her, and I can't help but worry. She said she was onto something there, and maybe it was the out she and her father needed. That was the last message I received, and I can't find Trent to subtly ask about her. It has been nice texting Cat again—she's actually hilarious and smart. We used to text years ago while she was training with the DeRuccis. She's also been someone I didn't realize I needed. She even pulled me out of my self-deprecating moments and told me what I needed to hear, even if it was harsh.

When Carmelo is announced as Malice, the crowd roars and chants his name. He comes down the aisle with Trent at his side, his hoodie pulled low over his face, and he really looks malicious.

"He's packed on muscle," Saxon states.

"Yeah, the last few weeks have been good for him."

"Or he's trying to forget Catalina while she's in Los Angeles," Saxon says matter-of-factly.

I lean over to ask him how he knows that when I hear the bell for the match to begin. I've always loved watching Carmelo fight. He moves with grace and is always one step ahead. His training over the years has really changed his fighting style, and I no longer worry too much about concussions.

I watch as Carmelo's strategically placed hits slow his opponent down, and as he dances around him, I can see boredom on his face. It looks like he's going to need more of a challenge. The last time I spoke about UFC, his face screwed up and he complained about all the fucking rules. I'll need to figure out something else for him.

"I heard about the proposal you gave your parents," Saxon reveals, his face stoic.

"What? How?" They haven't even spoken to me about it.

"Your father came to see my mother about it. He's worried you're getting too close to the Torres family business."

He gives me a look, his brow raising in question.

"Torres family business?" I press. "What? Fight rings?"

"Sure." Saxon snorts before my attention is once again on the ring.

Carmelo plows a hard uppercut against his opponent's chin, laying him out flat, and the guy is out cold.

"That was too easy." I sigh.

"Don't worry, his life is about to get interesting." Saxon once again snickers and I look at him with narrowed eyes.

"Do you know something I don't?"

"Yep." He stands and looks down at me. "A lot of things actually."

"What the fuck does that mean?" I call out to him as he walks over to his mother and Trent.

Of course I don't get an answer, and the more I think about it, the more I feel like I don't want it anyway. Our family has more secrets than the fucking CIA, and I'll be damned if I get sucked in now, because I'm about to be free of Whitsborough.

I get out of my seat and make my way up to the locker room, where Carmelo goes after his fights. It's a cramped space, but it's good to unwind there before seeing people. Unless he's waiting to deck me again… I mean, that's completely possible, and I slow my steps as I near the door. I should be good though. I did nothing wrong this time. Not that I did last time.

He must hear my hesitant shuffling feet because he calls out, "Will you just get in here?"

I walk inside and find him unwrapping his hands, his face filled with worry. I sit on the bench beside him and lean forward, resting my arms on my knees.

"What's going on?" I ask.

"There's so much shit, I don't even know where to start," he mumbles and tosses the tape to the floor. "I can't sleep, and I feel like the stress is going to consume me."

"You need pussy," I state.

"No—"

"Yes," I cut him off. "I'm serious. You need to find a girl and just have fun. You don't want to fuck her, then fine, but it's been a while and you are a fucking man."

He's closed off all romantic prospects when he started fighting, and I haven't seen him engage with a girl in a few years. That's a long-ass time, and it can do things to a man's psyche. I don't care what anyone says, you can release in your hand all you fucking want, but it's missing the connection with a partner.

"So…" He looks at me and smirks. "You're saying I need to stick my dick in a female?"

"Or a male." I grin wider. "Too bad we're a tad related, otherwise this new body you got going on would totally sway me."

We both laugh and Carmelo shakes his head. "I needed that. How long until you move here?"

"A few more months." I clasp him on the shoulder. "Let's unwind and celebrate that win, which looked like it bore you to fuck."

"I just have other shit on my mind." He looks at me. "We need to talk before you leave tomorrow. In private."

Trepidation flows through me at his words and the

intense look on his face. I can already tell this is going to be big. I nod and we leave the room. Carmelo heads to his room to shower as I enter the dining hall. It's boisterous, as is the usual after a Carmelo win, but when my gaze lands on a table filled with our family, I freeze.

Catalina Costa is sitting there, stiff and stoic, with an unfamiliar man beside her. Trent is also sitting there and looking like he's ready to explode, with Saxon and Aunt Ember rounding it out. Why wouldn't she tell me she was coming back? Why did she stop talking to me? Who the fuck is the dude? Anger, red and hot, bubbles inside of me at the sight, and I want to grab her by the throat.

I storm to the table and stand at the edge, everyone's eyes on me. Catalina's round in surprise and then narrow, as if trying to tell me something.

"Look who's back," I sneer, and she rolls her eyes.

"Hello, Cameron." Her husky voice is like a hit to the gut. Fuck, I missed her.

I look from her to the new guy and give him a once-over. He looks smug, a little older, and a lot mafia. Why the fuck did she bring the mafia back with her? Does she usually do this? Admittedly, I'm rarely around for when she comes and goes, and honestly, I never paid attention before.

"Cameron, this is Gionni." Her voice is slow with a bit of a warning.

"Her fiancé," Gionni states, and I feel like I'm about to vomit. Did he really say fiancé?

The air in the room changes, almost like being thrown into a freezer, and I groan before I can hold it in. I know he's here and I don't have the slightest idea how this is about to go down. I look over my shoulder and see him looking at our table, but no emotion is telling on his face.

"Carmelo needs a drink." Saxon pushes up from the table. "Nice to meet you, Gionni."

Then I watch as he heads straight for Carmelo before they both walk to the bar, their heads together. I don't give Gionni or Cat the same courtesy as Saxon and leave them there, quiet and awkward, to go to the bar.

I stand at Carmelo's side and can feel the tension coming off him in waves, wincing at his growl.

"Did you know she was coming back?" he asks me.

"No."

"Did you know about this fucking fiancé?"

"You know I didn't." I shake my head. "I would've told you."

"Seems like a good reason to hold back her number from me," he snarls, and I exhale. I can see how he would think that.

"I know," I agree, "but I swear I didn't know."

"Who cares?" Saxon slides us each a shot. "Fuck bitches, make money."

"What?" I look at him with confusion, then watch as they pound back the shots without me.

"That's right!" Carmelo slams his shot glass to the bar top. "Fuck bitches, make money!"

I don't know what the fuck they're saying, but I take the shot and slam my glass down too. "Fuck bitches, make money," I mutter as Carmelo laughs and slaps my back.

We do a few more shots and toast to the same line each

time, my confusion waning and the meaning clearer. Yes, fuck bitches and make money. New life motto. Carmelo has his eye on a group of girls, and I grin with excitement. If Cat is ready to get married, then Carmelo can dip his dick into something warm. It's only fair.

"Let's go talk to them," I suggest to him and Saxon.

Saxon looks the group over with disinterest but shrugs his shoulders, and Carmelo's grin widens, showcasing his white teeth.

"Fuck bitches." He nods.

"Damn it." I try to put on a stern face and hold back my laughter. "Just don't say that to them."

"Got it." He nods and we push away from the bar.

The girls are welcoming and sweet, but I think I'm fucking broken. I haven't been able to stick my dick in anyone since Saxon caught me that day in my dorm. I'm not interested, and neither is my dick, but I'm happy Carmelo is enjoying himself, and Saxon seems to be as well. I can live with a limp dick if it means they're not suffering. God knows they both need the distraction.

My eyes can't seem to stay put though. Every few minutes, they flick over to Cat's table, and I find her always in the same position. If she is newly engaged, why does it look like she's trying her best to avoid touching him? His arm is around the back of her chair, and she's pitched slightly forward, away from it. She hasn't smiled and the entire table just looks out of sorts.

Aunt Ember is the first to stand, and I can tell the yawn into her hand is fake. Trent follows soon after, and I watch as they both leave the dining hall, leaving Cat alone with her betrothed. He leans over and says something in her ear as her face hardens. That doesn't look like love at all. Then he stands and points a finger at her, and she nods, her eyes briefly catching mine.

I look away and find Carmelo has a girl in his lap, his tongue down her throat. It looks like a starving lion who just caught a fucking gazelle. Shit, is the girl enjoying that? When she moans and turns to straddle his lap, I exhale with relief. Then I look to my lap and back to the girl whose skirt has ridden up over the globes of her ass as she grinds down onto Carmelo. Nothing. My dick doesn't even twitch. I am fucking broken.

My eyes once again find Cat's table, and I'm shocked to find her alone, glaring at Carmelo. I look around the room, looking for her mafioso fiancé, and come up with nothing. Did he just leave her here alone? That's fucking rude. I turn back to her and her eyes are on me, fire filling their depths. She looks pissed, and I can't for the fucking life of me understand why. I raise my brow at her and startle when she stands abruptly, her chair falling behind her.

Her face turns back to Carmelo and then I watch as her full lips, glistening, pull back over her teeth. I follow her sight and cringe when I see Carmelo clearly fingering the girl in front of everyone, uncaring about his audience. When I told him he needed pussy, I didn't mean like this. I hear a low growl and turn in time to see Cat stalk over to Carmelo and the girl. I sit up quickly, but I'm not quick enough.

Cat's claws sink into the girl's blonde tresses and then she's yanking her off Carmelo's lap. The girl hits the floor with a screech and Carmelo is looking up at Cat, shock all over his face. He doesn't have time to recover as she turns on her heel and comes at me. I throw up both hands and try to defend myself just when she straddles my lap, sinking her claws into my hair.

"Cat, what the—"

Her plush, velvet soft lips crash into mine and my dick swells rapidly. Motherfucking traitor. Her teeth nip my bottom lip, pulling them open, and then her tongue is plundering inside my mouth. I can't stop the groan that works its way up my throat, and my hands land on her ass, hauling her in over my cock. It takes hearing Carmelo's shocked voice to pull me out of the lust haze.

"The fuck?"

My fingers glide up her back, and when I feel her hair, I snag it in my fist. Then I give her a firm yank, pulling her mouth from mine roughly, and stand up, forcing her to find her footing or fall.

"Are you fucking serious?" I don't know why pain slices through my fucking chest, but it does. "Is that what I am? Someone you can make him jealous with?"

I release her hair and her fingers reach up to touch her lips tentatively. "I don't know what—"

"Why don't you run along to your fucking fiancé?" I snarl at her and watch as her eyes fill up with tears.

She sucks in a sob before turning and fleeing toward the bathrooms.

"Harsh." Carmelo laughs as he stands.

"Whatever," I mumble as the pain in my chest intensifies. "I'm going to bed."

Before anyone can stop me, I am out of the dining hall and heading to my room. I refuse to be used in her games, no matter how much my heart and my body loved it.

Chapter Nine

I pick the blonde girl up off the floor and smile at her. "I'm sorry about that."

"It's okay," she purrs, her hand traveling down my chest.

The effect she had on me earlier has long faded, and looking into her eyes now, I feel nothing. I sit her down onto the chair I vacated and lean in to kiss her cheek.

"I'm sorry." She looks up at me, nodding.

Then, before I can talk myself out of it, I am stalking to those fucking bathrooms, chasing the woman who loves to stoke my fucking anger. I slam open the women's bathroom door, making two girls standing at the sinks scream.

"Get out," I snarl, and they quickly run past me.

Her sniffling sounds from the farthest stall as I stalk over to it and kick it open. She isn't scared or surprised. Cat can take care of herself, and it's the one thing that doesn't add to the hatred I have for her. The one thing that ensures I can be myself around her and not hold back.

"Engaged?"

"Jealous?" she sneers back through her tears.

I reach inside the stall and grab the front of her shirt, hauling her out forcefully, then I throw her up and against the tiled wall, her back hitting it with a resounding thud. The air whooshes out of her chest as I crowd in her face, watching as she fights to suck in another lungful.

"I fucking hate you." My voice is filled with vitriol.

"I fucking hate you too," she says back, hers wheezy and out of breath.

"Why are you dry humping Cam when you should be in your room fucking your fiancé?" Then I chuckle. "Or are you still a frigid little virgin?"

She struggles to get out of my hold, and I shove her back against the tile, grabbing her throat in my hand. I feel her swallow, the sinewy muscle contracting in my palm, and a rage settles over me.

"Why the fuck are you engaged but kissing on Cam?"

Her hand grips my wrist and I watch a tear slip out of her eye and over her cheek, settling on her full upper lip. The light from the overhead fluorescents makes it twinkle, and I can't help but lean in and lick it off her skin. She gasps, her mouth opening and her eyes becoming heavy.

"I did it because you were practically fucking that whore." There's no anger; it's more sadness lacing her words.

"You're jealous." I grin and press my hard cock against her stomach.

"You looked like a heathen," she snarls, but I don't miss how her body arches into mine.

"Why did you use him?" I drop my hand from her

throat and step back. "Why would you do that to him?"

"I admit at first it was to piss you off, but once our lips touched…" Her fingers graze across her mouth. "It was something else."

It pisses me off that she kissed Cam first, but not necessarily that she kissed him at all.

"So, you've become a frigid whore? All over three men and still a virgin? Soon you'll be carrying the next Messiah."

Her hand connects with my cheek and my head swings to the side. I should be thankful it wasn't a fist. She then slams her fist into my other cheek. I spoke too soon. I see red and feel myself begin to lose control as I once again grab her and throw her on top of the counter, the back of her head connecting with the mirror. I watch as it cracks, the fractures spreading quickly like a spider's web.

She groans as she tentatively touches the back of her head. "That hurt."

I pull apart her legs and stand between them, tugging her to the edge of the counter. She looks at me, slightly dazed, but that's quickly replaced with anger. Then I grab her chin and force her to meet my eyes, digging my fingers in until she winces.

"Has he fucked you yet?" I pull her face in closer. "In the month and a half you've been gone, has that fiancé of yours fucked you? Claimed what I know you've been saving for me?"

"You fucking asshole." Her attitude is back and I'm thinking she didn't hit her head hard enough. "Nothing was ever saved for you."

I flick my tongue against her bottom lip and chuckle

when she snaps at it with her teeth, my cock twitching as she does.

"Tell me you missed me," I whisper hoarsely. "Tell me how much you want me to kiss you right now."

The fight slowly leaves her eyes and her hands dig into my hair, yanking roughly on the edges. I drop my hand from her chin just as she crashes her mouth to mine, both of us groaning long and hard at the impact. Both of my hands grip her ass, pulling her along my swollen cock and rubbing it against her.

We're a frantic mess of teeth, tongues, and saliva. Four years of pent-up energy released in a single moment, and I feel like I'm about to explode. Thankfully, she's wearing a pair of those stretchy tights that girls like to wear, and I pull on the waistband so hard I can hear the rip of the fabric. Then my hand is gliding inside, over her soft skin, into her soaking folds, and teasing her hardened clit.

Her hands pull on my hair and she breaks away from my kiss with a gasp. "Oh my god," she rasps reverently.

"That's right, baby," I say against her open, panting mouth. "Call me your fucking god."

She bites down hard on my bottom lip as I sink a finger into her tight little pussy, and the taste of blood explodes in my mouth.

"So tight, baby," I praise as I lick the blood off my lip. "Feels like no one's been in here."

I slowly pump my finger in and out of her soaking wet pussy as she gasps and moans. As soon as I feel her tighten and her moaning grows louder, I press my mouth to her ear.

"Lucky me," I husk, her chest heaving against mine.

"Two pussies tonight."

Her head snaps back as she stares at me, first in complete shock, and then it quickly morphs into pure anger. I pull my finger out of her and hold it up between us.

"Wet pussy isn't rare, sweetheart. I can get it anywhere."

That's when her forehead slams into my nose, and I hear the crack of cartilage, the pain rushing between my eyes.

"I fucking hate you," she snaps, and my eyes are too watery to see as she storms by me and out the door.

I need to remember Cat doesn't fight like a fucking girl.

CATALINA

He's still there in the swell of my lips and the throb between my legs. I don't know what came over me in that bathroom, but it was the single most exciting thing that's ever happened in my life. I had let myself go, opened the floodgates of feeling, and let it wash all over us, but was it fucking worth it?

Now Carmelo Torres knows for sure I want him, and I'm fucking sure he's feeling smug about it. Who am I to him anyway? Just the second wet pussy he had tonight. I hit the wall with my fist and exhale as the pain snakes its way up my arm. It's the only way I know how to deal with shit I don't understand.

I stop as Cameron's door comes into view and feel a rush of guilt over what I did to him. Yes, I hopped on his lap, intending to make Carmelo jealous, but what I wasn't expecting was how much I enjoyed it. When our lips met, it was like nothing else existed as he soothed my tumultuous insides. Regardless of the outcome, I was wrong to do what I did when he's been nothing but a good friend to me.

The memory of his kiss is just as strong as the one I shared with Carmelo in the bathroom, and I can't deny I have feelings for Cameron too. What is wrong with me? Is it because I have denied myself for so long? Now I just want every male in my radius? No, I know that's not it, and I can't keep pushing down what I've been feeling for four years. I want both of them. How will that work?

I remember Carmelo saying something about them sharing girls before I left for Los Angeles, and even though I commented that it was gross, it actually sounded hot. Being between them, having them both worship my body and being completely caged in, turns me on more than I'd like to admit.

I find myself in front of Cameron's door, and even though he probably hates me right now, I can't stop my hand from knocking. After a few moments and no answer, I figure he's asleep and turn toward my room. Then I hear the click of the lock before he's standing there in his boxers. I give him a slow once-over, and he growls while stepping back, closing the door again.

"Wait." I rush forward, pushing on the door. "I need to talk to you."

"About what exactly, Cat?" he says, sounding exasperated, and I don't blame him.

"A lot of things," I answer. "Everything."

He stares at me a few moments longer and then rolls his eyes as he opens the door once more. "Make it quick. I was having a good meat beating session before you got here."

"Ew." I crinkle my nose and walk into his room.

He clears the clothes off the armchair and motions for me to sit, then he sits on the edge of the bed, waiting for me to begin.

"Sorry I ignored your messages for the past few weeks." I feel like an asshole, but seeing him here in front of me makes me want to tell him everything. "I had no choice."

"Cool." He nods as he brushes his fingers along his chin. "So you ignored me. Does your fiancé not approve of male friends?"

"My fiancé." I let out a bitter chuckle. "That was Gionni DeRucci you met, and he is certainly not my fiancé, although since I was a baby, his father, Don Julius DeRucci, always said we would be married."

"You're in an arranged situation?" His eyebrows crash together in disbelief.

"No." I exhale and run my hands down my face. "At least, I hope not to be. We were supposed to have brought them down by now. Don Julius is the godfather of the DeRucci Family, and Gionni is his youngest son, who is thirsting to take over the throne. Sometimes, Don Julius sends Gionni here to remind my father to stay in line, or else. They don't trust the Torreses, and they only keep my father here for the intel he feeds them."

"What intel?" I can glimpse the anger flashing in his eyes.

"My father and your aunt have been feeding the DeRucci Mafia bullshit for years, but I think they're catching on. The night I messaged you and said I found something was the same night Gionni caught me in his father's office. I barely got out of it by the skin of my teeth, and because of me, their suspicions are amplified."

"What did you find in the office?" He leans forward, now completely engrossed.

"Ledgers about shipments that are coming through New York, breaking the agreements they have in place with the Head Corp."

"The Head Corp?" he asks, and I groan. Of course Carmelo hasn't talked to him yet. I've known about this plan for years, which is why I stayed so far away from the man.

"That's all I can say about that. I would suggest you ask Carmelo." He nods and waves me on. "Gionni followed me back here, threatened my father, caused a scene with our engagement, and is now on his way back to Los Angeles."

"You could've given us a heads-up," he stresses, and

he's right, I could've, but why would I? We're not besties. I think a part of me wanted Carmelo to think I had gotten engaged though, but I'm not admitting that to Cameron.

"I'm sorry."

"Well, if that's all." He stands and walks toward the door.

"Wait." I stand and place my hand on his bare chest. "You know that's not all."

He looks down at my hand and then back at my face. "Well?"

"I shouldn't have kissed you to make Carmelo jealous."

His body relaxes and he lets out a breath. "Yeah."

"But I don't regret doing it."

His eyes snap up to mine in surprise. "What?"

"There's always been that zap of energy between us, but I never paid much attention to it. I was too busy training or being the perfect daughter." I lower my hand and let it skim over his abs, defined and protruding. "Once I kissed you, I knew I had feelings for you. There's no denying them."

"I can't do that to Carmelo." He shakes his head and grabs my hand, halting its descent.

"I know." I turn away so I don't have to look him in the eyes when I confess my feelings. "I don't know what's happening, but I have feelings for you both. He's just such an asshole."

"He's always been an asshole, and there's only a select few who can tolerate him," he agrees. "But I will never betray him, no matter what my feelings are for you."

"I won't ask that of you. I have a lot to figure out." He fingers the tear in my leggings and his brow raises in question. "Carmelo and I fought," I explain, and my hand lifts to the back of my head.

Cameron is around and behind me in a second, inspecting the bump. "What do you mean? And you have a fucking goose egg back here."

"I don't think he and I will ever get along. He's like the gasoline to my flame." My voice shakes as his fingers meet my skin, and I try to breathe to steady it.

"Sounds like an inferno," he mutters. "You need ice."

He starts for his bathroom, to the first aid kit every room has, and I turn and open his room door. I need to get away before I do something stupid… again. It's time to put some space between me and the two boys who seem to make me forget my purpose.

Chapter Ten

Carmelo

Every time she fucks up, Trent's jaw tightens, and right now it looks on the verge of snapping. It's been a week, and Catalina will not even spare a glance in my direction, but I can see she's suffering. Does that give me some kind of pleasure? You bet your fucking ass it does, especially since it's agonizing to endure her silent treatment.

"When's the next fight?" Uncle Emmett asks me as I line up the knife with the target.

I fling the blade and watch as it sinks in, perfectly centered on the target. "Can I ask you something?" I change the topic.

"Of course." He nods and hands me another blade.

"What was all this training for? Knives and guns? Endurance?"

"For your reflexes and stamina as a fighter," he answers quickly, like the line was rehearsed.

"Could it have been for when I take over the Head Corp by any chance?"

Uncle Emmett sputters while I try my best to hold

in the laugh that's creeping up my chest. "She told you." He finally rolls his eyes.

"Yeah," I say and chuckle. "I went to one meeting, and she said there would be more."

"That's your rightful place." His hand clasps my shoulder. "Your father ran it, but Ember made it worth something to be proud of. It's your legacy."

"She told me what else she does." I drop my voice and his eyes widen.

"Really?" His voice rises with surprise as I nod. "Well, that's not your legacy, so I wouldn't worry about it."

"Whose legacy is it?"

"It may be no one's." He shrugs. "Ember didn't make herself into that as something to pass on. She made it to feel better about the world around her. I'm sure if there's someone to take it over, they would need to share the same sentiment."

"I see."

"You just concentrate on the Head position and be proud she saw something worthy in you for it." He smiles, and his words warm something inside my chest.

"Fuck!" We both turn at a fuming Trent and a panting Cat. One looks on the verge of snapping and the other looks beat.

"I need rest." Cat shakes her head, and it's then I notice the large bags until her eyes.

"You'll rest when the DeRuccis kill us!" Trent exclaims, and Cat grimaces at his words.

"That's harsh," I mutter to Uncle Emmett.

"Yes." He exhales. "But unfortunately, it's true. Cat is our in with the DeRuccis, and if she fucks up at any point, we'll be facing a war we're not prepared for."

"Is that something she will have to do her whole life? To be our intel with the crime family?" I grumble as I begin to feel sorry for her.

"Yeah, unless we get them out, which we are always trying to do."

I watch as Cat storms off, away from her father, and Trent punches his fist into the bag.

"I'll talk to Trent, and you go talk to Catalina." Uncle Emmett winks at me, and I roll my eyes.

"She will not want to talk to me, trust me." I pick up another knife.

"Go find out." He grabs the knife out of my hand and slams it into the target, the force making the knife sink in past its hilt.

"Show-off," I hiss, leaving the room and his chuckling behind.

I'm not sure why I'm listening to him, but my feet really are taking me to Cat's room and most likely to my death. The last time we were alone, I was drunk, and I'm not using that as an excuse. I meant everything I said and did to her. She has the ability to both send me into a rage and make me forget every reason why I can't stand her. The tension surrounding us is saturated in sexual energy, but it's intertwined with pent-up resentment as well.

Her door is firmly shut, but I can hear her moving inside, and by the shuffling noise, I would assume she's pacing. I rap my knuckles on the door and listen as the shuffling stops, but they don't move any closer. I don't call out to her because the moment she hears my voice, she'll continue to ignore me and refuse to open the door.

"Who is it?" she calls out, the irritation clear in her tone.

I don't say a fucking thing.

I can hear her padded steps as she stalks to the door and then throws it open, her inquiring face becoming a mask of anger.

"Oh, fuck no," she snarls and tries to slam the door, only to have it bounce back open off my boot. "Go away, you piece of shit."

"Are you still pissed about last week?" I grin at her.

She steps up to me, chest to chest, and reaches out to tweak my nose. The pain is instant, and I hiss while she chuckles. It's still sore from her headbutt.

"Are you still tender?" she sneers and turns away.

"You look tired."

"What the fuck do you care?" All the fight leaves her voice, and the exhaustion is no longer masked when she begins to walk away.

"Caaat," I drag out her name. "Can we just fucking stop this shit for ten minutes? Tell me what the fuck is going on. Do you miss your fiancé?"

She turns abruptly and looks at me like I'm crazy. "Cam didn't tell you?"

"Tell me what?" Curiosity gets the better of me. I'll kill him for hoarding yet another secret.

"I'm not engaged. That was the youngest son of the Don coming here to spy."

Why do I feel immediate relief, then consuming guilt for how I behaved when he was here?

"You look confused," she says condescendingly.

"So…" I take a few steps toward her. "Why did you tell Cam and not me?"

"I hate you," she replies with a slight shrug of her shoulders. I know she's speaking the truth. We both have those feelings, and yet there's something else simmering just beneath the surface. "I really fucking hate you," she reiterates.

"Do you think that hurts me?" I growl at her as a grin climbs over my mouth. "That only tells me one thing."

"What's that?" She takes the bait, looking bored.

I grip the fabric of her sports bra and pull her against my body. "That you're feeling something at least, and Cat, feelings can change."

She's staring at my mouth, and her breathing hitches, then she licks her bottom lip. The moisture glistening there calls to me, and I do something that shocks us both. I lean in and kiss her softly. Just a brush of our lips, no teeth and no pain, just a press. She reciprocates and presses her lips to mine, a slight moan escaping her mouth. I pull back about an inch, and her eyes slowly open as a gorgeous blush stretches along her cheeks. She likes it soft and sweet.

"You liked that," I rasp as my hand releases her shirt and wraps around her back. "You want a sweet man, Catalina?"

I rub my hand softly up her back, bringing her in tighter, and watching as those chocolate brown eyes fall shut. She wants sweet, and she thinks she can get that from me?

Poor girl.

My hand reaches her hair and I grab a handful, pulling on the roots to angle her head back. She whimpers as her eyes fly open to narrow on mine, her mouth turning down into a frown.

"I can't be your sweet man, Cat." My teeth sink into her bottom lip and I pull, watching it bounce back against her teeth. "I hate you too fucking much for that."

She stumbles against the wall when I abruptly release her, her face now red in anger, and I laugh at her..

"Get out!" she screams, her fists clenched. I bet she wants to hit me, and the thought has my cock swelling. I love a good tussle with Cat.

I stalk toward her and cage her in, my hands on the wall beside her head. She could easily get out of this, physically move me and break a few bones if she really wanted to, but she doesn't. That's how I know she doesn't want sweet from me and doesn't really want me to leave.

Her head hits the wall and she exhales a frustrated breath that warms over my face. "I'm too exhausted for this game today."

I can see it, the pronounced bags under her eyes, lined in blue, and how her mouth is set in a permanent frown. She really doesn't have the energy for our usual banter. With the external stress of her training coupled with the internal stress of her predicament, it just wouldn't be as amusing as usual. Not today anyway.

"Meet me in the hall in an hour. We'll talk over the cook's chicken parmesan," I tell her as I push off the wall and out of her space.

"Fuck that," she spits, her exhaustion forgotten and her fire seeping back through her.

I shake my head and chuckle, knowing she'll show up. Catalina Costa may be all fight, but she's also curious as fuck, so she'll want to know what I have to say.

"I'll see you in an hour," I repeat as I close her door behind me.

Before I get back to my room, I hear a loud "Fuck!" and laugh as I stop to look over my shoulder. I knew she wouldn't be able to stay away.

CATALINA

I am not going to that dining hall.

The door clicks behind him and I stand there staring at it. What does he want to talk about? Maybe Cameron? Maybe he and I?

"Fuck!" I scream and kick my dresser. I need to go to that damn dining hall to find out.

I make my feet move and head into the bathroom, my body heavy with exhaustion but knowing I can't sleep. Sleep seems to elude me lately, and I feel like something bad is about to happen. I want to protect my father. I want to make sure he's safe here with the Rampage, and yes, I want to make sure Carmelo is safe as well. The hatred I feel for him is real, but I've also learned hate is exhausting.

I turn on the water and wait for the steam. I need hotter than hot right now. My muscles are screaming in pain and throbbing with the need to rest, but like Dad said, we'll sleep when we're dead. I strip down and step into the shower, resting my head against the tile. I need a plan that takes me out of the DeRuccis' clutches, and I need them to leave us alone. It fucking seems impossible though.

I have a sliver of hope and it rests with Gionni, or Gion, as I call him. We grew up together and I know he wants to marry me about as much as I want to marry him, which is not at all. We were raised like siblings, trained together and got into trouble together. He hates his father as much as I do, but he's also fearful and I can't blame him for that. Don Julius is a monster, and I know that all too well. I've heard stories over the years, and the one that sticks with me the most is how he killed my mother.

I was only six months old, my father was here in New York, and my mother and I were in California. He was looking for a home for us and trying to distance himself from the mafia, knowing he would never truly be free. He often lived half of the year in New York, and he wanted us to live here permanently, but someone in the crime family knew what he was up to, so Don Julius taught him a lesson he'd never forget.

They did just that when they brutally murdered my mother, writing messages on the wall in her blood for my father and then kidnapping me. I was raised thinking the DeRucci family was home and Don Julius was my fucking father. I was five years old when they allowed my father to visit me for the first time. They figured he had suffered enough and that his fear of them bought his loyalty, but they were wrong. It only made him hate them more, and now that he's combined forces with the Rampage, he's readying everyone for a war.

It wasn't until I met Ember that I thought we might stand a chance. She's brutal, trained, and she has this look in her eyes that begs you to fuck with her. I want to free my father from the clutches of the mafia, but at the same time, I want nothing terrible to happen to Gion. It's heartbreaking because there's no way I can have both. Gion would never go against his father because he's afraid of him, and I would never go against mine. One of us will just have to die trying.

I quickly wash up and get dressed. My ass needs to find out what the fuck Carmelo wants, because I need to sleep, and I won't be able to even attempt it if I skip on our meeting.

Chapter Eleven

Cameron

My phone buzzes on the table beside my bed and I put aside my textbook to grab it.

Saxon: Chill?

He's been more quiet than usual lately when I try to talk to him, so I sit up quickly, my thumbs flying over the screen of my phone.

Me: When?

Saxon: I'm coming up.

Okay then, he's here. I look around my room and shrug. He knows my dorm is never pristine. At least this time there isn't a girl in my bed and I don't have to look for discarded condom wrappers on the floor. My dick has been out of commission for weeks. I don't know what's wrong, but I've stopped stressing about it because I have a few weeks left here, and then I'm off to New York anyway.

The door opens and Saxon steps in, real quiet. If I didn't have my eyes on the door, I wouldn't have even known he was here, and that gives me a weird vibe.

"Hey," I say, and he pulls the cap off his head.

"Yo."

I can see bags under his eyes like he hasn't been sleeping and there's now muscle in places he didn't have before.

"You working out?" I ask him.

"Yeah, a bit." He falls against the wall.

"Is it because of what happened to you?" He has spoken little about it and I am always trying to push him without overwhelming him. I know people speak when they're ready to, but sometimes they need a little push to feel ready.

"That was the turning point, yeah."

"Any news on the Cox family?" I open the fridge and toss him a can of beer. "How's the kid?"

"They're staying quiet. Mom found out Brian had a bit of a record for aggravated assault and a couple B&Es, and now they know she somehow got her hands on a closed file. They're scared." He sits in the chair at my desk and stares down at the can.

"Good, the shit that kid pulled on you was fucked-up. You know you did nothing wrong, right?" I coax him.

"But I did." He looks at me. "I knew I was stronger than him. He knew it too. That's why he rallied a group, but I still attacked him when he was unsuspecting, and when I should've stopped, I continued until his face was unrecognizable."

"Saxon, what happened to you was traumatic. It's understandable why you did what you did." I want him to know that his reaction, as extreme as it was, was warranted. I can't imagine what it would've been like to be jumped by five guys while I was changing in the locker room. It's one thing to be alone, but naked? He was completely vulnerable.

"I had this sudden rush of anger. It fucking ripped through me as soon as I saw him, and I didn't snap out of it until the taste of his blood was in my mouth." He takes a sip of his beer and shakes his head. "When I told Mom, she said she was familiar with that feeling."

I open my mouth to ask about his mother but decide to skip it. I'm not sure I want to know. "And the therapist is helping?" I press him. He squirms in his seat and gives me a quick look out of the corner of his eye. "What?" He's hiding something.

"Damn." He rolls his eyes. "I need to tell someone before I fucking burst."

"You're fucking the therapist. Is she hot?"

He turns a weird shade of green and gives me a horrified look. "Bro, my therapist is literally my mom."

I choke on my mouthful of beer and laugh as I try to suck air into my lungs. "Your mom?!"

"It's not even funny," he huffs.

"I'm gonna need more info because last I heard, Aunt Ember was not qualified to be a therapist. A personal trainer? Yes, but a therapist? No."

"There was never any therapy, not in the traditional sense." He gives me a look, and the only way I can describe it is sinister.

"Explain."

"She's teaching me ways to control my anger, outlets for it, and techniques. I've gained muscle because I'm training." He smiles.

"Like Carmelo?"

"Similar." He nods, and I feel myself relax.

"That's not so bad, explains your new physique."

"Yeah, and I feel better, more stable in here." He points to his head.

"That's good." I clasp his shoulder. "Your wellness should be a priority. Hey! Maybe we could get you in the ring with Carmelo."

"No." He chuckles darkly. "I'd kill him."

Those words send a chill down my spine because I know Saxon isn't joking. He rarely does, and I question if Aunt Ember's techniques are truly working. I can't see Saxon getting the drop on Carmelo.

"I'm not training to be a fighter," he explains when he feels me staring at him.

"So, what is this training for?"

"Just to become the best version of myself," he answers quickly and chugs the rest of his beer.

"I'm headed to New York this weekend," I tell him. "Are you going to be there?"

"I will be." He nods. "I'll also be staying there for a while."

"Living at the compound?"

"Yeah, it's too fucking much of a drive to do it multiple times a month." He places the empty beer on my desk and crosses his arms over his chest.

"I'll be living there too," I reveal and laugh when a grin stretches across his face. "I'm going to be Carmelo's nutritionist slash life coach."

He leans back and belts out a laugh. "That is going to be sweet to watch, especially the drama with Cat."

"What drama?" I raise a brow.

"The fact that she wants the both of you. I watched her kiss you that night, and that wasn't just to make Carmelo jealous, she fucking wanted to do that."

My heart sinks at the fact that he caught on to our weird love triangle, and even though I'm trying to stay away from them there in New York, I also want to be there and see what's happening between them. Masochistic, I know.

I should've offered to drive Saxon to New York. I hate doing this trip solo, and he is completely right. It's fucking tedious. My parents got back to me about my future proposal, and even though they are skeptical, my father is at least comfortable with me being at the compound with Aunt Ember.

I'm looking forward to being out of Whitsborough and in a new place with new goals to focus on, but I'm not looking forward to trying to get over these conflicting feelings I have for Catalina while she's in my face day in and day out. I can do it though. My biggest fear? She and Carmelo end up being together, and I will have a front-row seat to that show too.

In the end, I will just have to suck it up, and knowing those two, I'll be breaking up a lot of fights, whether or not they end up together. I've never seen two people who hate each other so much, but when they're in the same room together, it feels like a lust bomb is about to explode all over us. If I can see it, I know others can too, and like Saxon said, there is so much drama wrapped up in the three of us.

I pull into the compound's lot and park my car. It's full for a non-fight weekend, and I'm wondering what the hell is going on when I spot Cat leaning against the wall. The garage door is open and she has her head tilted back, soaking in the sun's rays. I stay put in my seat and watch her, the way her black hair holds tints of blue in the sun, and her cheeks are a little rosy. She's gorgeous.

I exhale and pull myself out of the car. Time to lock down those thoughts and look at Catalina as nothing more than an acquaintance. I grab my duffel bag and head toward the garage door, hoping to get by her without saying much and avoid something awkward.

"Cam?" Her voice hits me and I stand just inside of the door. "Were you even going to say hi?"

"Hey, Cat." I give her a nod before continuing to the elevator.

When she comes to stand beside me, her eyes are on my face just as I hear the door shut behind me. "I didn't know you were coming this weekend. You have returned none of my texts."

"Sorry, I've been busy."

"Bullshit, you pussy," she spits angrily. "You've been avoiding me since I got on your lap in that dining hall and kissed you. You're a pussy."

I look at her in shock as the elevator dings open. She struts inside and holds her hand against the door. "Are you coming in? Or are you too pussy to stand in here with me too?"

I walk in, a little dumbfounded by her words and a little pissed that she thinks I deserve her attitude after what she pulled the last time I was here. The elevator lurches downward, and I cross my arms over my chest. I stand there watching as the lights on the top descend in numbers—which is stupid because there's only one other floor in this place—and avoid looking at her. I can feel her staring a hole into the side of my head.

"Now what?" she asks, the growl betraying her anger. "We're not even friends?"

"I don't know, Cat." I shrug. "Did you think about that when you nearly sucked my face off?"

"Sucked your face off?" she scoffs. "Are you serious?"

"Yes!" I scream, and she narrows her eyes at the sound. "I am! What did you think was going to happen?"

Her mouth opens and shuts as the door slides open, providing my escape. I rush out the door and hear her hurried footsteps behind me, so I take longer strides down the corridor and turn into the one that leads to our bedrooms.

"Will you wait?" she snarls behind me, and I roll my eyes.

"I'll probably see you around, Cat. This place is large, but never large enough to avoid you."

"I think we should talk. There are things we need to say." Even though I know she's jogging to keep up, she's not even winded.

"I've said everything I need to," I assure her.

"I haven't!" she retorts.

I stop abruptly and roll my eyes again when she slams

into my back. "This is all coming off a bit desperate," I tell her over my shoulder.

"Cam, I miss you." Her voice drips with remorse.

My heart melts, but I harden it as I think of Carmelo. I would never do this to him.

"I'll see you around, Cat," I mutter and get to my room.

"Fine," she replies, her voice back to normal.

I watch her turn on her heel and stalk back to her room, knowing I'm breaking my heart but protecting it at the same time.

CATALINA

So fucking frustrating.

My fist hits the drywall again, and the plaster falls, shooting dust into the air. I don't even know why I care. I shouldn't want either of them in my life because having them close would be dangerous, but after my dinner with Carmelo last night and then seeing Cameron today, my heart wants what it can't have.

Carmelo at dinner was frustrating enough, sitting there smugly while watching me stuff a chicken Parmesan into my mouth, hoping to disgust him. He looked anything but while he questioned me thoroughly about Gion and Don Julius, drilling me about what it was I was doing with them. By the end of the meal, he made me feel like I was on the DeRuccis' side or playing both for my gain. I dumped my diet coke over his head and came back to my room, only coming out today to take a breather. Just my luck, Cameron pulled up at that exact moment.

I don't know how I am so connected to both men, why each of them pulls me in opposite directions and then has the power to crush me into dust. My throat tightens as I feel the burn behind my eyes. I have cried more over these two men than anything else in my entire life. I was raised to believe showing emotions was a weakness, and every time I cried for my family, I was beaten. I was told that women are fragile creatures who think with their hearts and that's why they are the weaker sex, so I closed off my heart. I became a better soldier than most of their men and I fought with a brutality that lacked empathy. I was dead inside, and they reveled in that.

Until Carmelo showed up at the compound, all teeth with his smug grin and eyes like pools of tar. It was instantaneous how fast I felt sucked in with just one look from him, and I grew to hate him for it. He took a lifetime of training from me in that one moment and laughed while he seized my heart for his own. So I worked harder and suppressed longer, until I exploded in that bathroom with him.

Cameron, on the other hand, was a slow burn. The first day I saw his sweet, smiling face, he planted a seed deep inside me, and when it grew into a tree, I was shocked. It shocked me that he ever lived in my heart, and I never thought he belonged there. He is the perfect fit to soothe my tumultuous mind and internal anxiety. He's like the cooling balm after a vigorous workout. Then he has a way of stoking the fire inside me, gradually increasing the heat until I can't take anymore, and I want to suffocate him in my inferno.

Two vastly different men, and yet, each one consumes me and owns an equal part of my heart. It's funny that the moment I'm ready to risk it all, I fall for two men, and they both can't stand the fucking sight of me.

Tragic poetry for the blackened soul.

Chapter Thirteen

Carmelo

"You need clean carbs. I need to talk to the cook." Cameron is pacing my room and reading the menu. In a few short months, I will have him here full-time, and I can't wait.

He and I grew up inseparable. Best friends that shared some family… sort of… distantly, but that wasn't what cemented our friendship. Cameron was always that calming presence I needed when I was on the brink of an explosion. His bright blue eyes and bright wide smile always pushed back on the dam that was threatening to break. I have always wanted him near me and am always lonely when we are apart. Many people over the years have asked if we were romantically linked, and the answer is no, but I can see how they would confuse it.

We move and speak like one, like maybe we are two halves of a soul. The more I think about it, the surer I am, and I believe Cat is our soul's mate. Sure, she and I have this burning hatred for each other. We act irrationally and our outbursts are violent. Cameron does for her what he does for me. I can see it. He calms her and chases away the darkness that threatens to devour her.

I know this sounds crazy. How could three people ever be made for each other? But I grew up with a great example, and they love each other hard. My Uncle Emmett, Aunt Adri, and Uncle Travis. They need each other, all three of them, and it works. It works perfectly. Aunt Adri and Uncle Travis are filled with heat, always at each other's throats, while Uncle Emmett intercepts with humor and stands between them, absorbing the blows and showering them with love. Cameron is our Emmett.

Now, I just need to figure out how to convince them, and I have a tentative plan, although knowing Cat, this whole thing may just blow up in my face.

"Hey," I interrupt Cameron's pacing. "I think Catalina has serious problems with the DeRuccis."

"Yeah." He stops and looks at me with a shrug. "What else is new? She and her father both do."

"Catalina is not actually engaged." I want to see if he'll continue to hide this from me.

"Yeah, I knew about that for a while now." He doesn't even have the decency to look guilty.

"And you didn't tell me. Why?" I can't help the feeling of betrayal that washes over me.

"I figured you would find out on your own, and it wouldn't hurt to have you two talk about it instead of using me as a middleman... again." He's got a point.

"What if we just killed that guy?" I ask nonchalantly.

"What?" His eyes blink rapidly with confusion as he slowly shakes his head.

"Yeah, the next time he comes here to check on Cat, we kill him." I shrug my shoulders and tip back the disgusting green mixture he made me to drink.

"I think you are losing brain cells because of the lack of fresh air down here. Do you jog around the block at all?"

"Jog around the block?" I fall back on the bed and laugh. "Do you know where we are?"

He hums in thought as I continue to laugh, and then he kicks at my foot. "Why do you want to risk the wrath of the mafia? And for Cat?"

"Not just Cat, but my whole fucking family has a stake in it, and obviously I have a lot to figure out. I just thought I'd let you in on my secret. You know, the ones I don't keep from you."

He rolls his eyes, but a smirk plays around the corners of his mouth. "I don't think murdering the guy is a good idea."

"Right. I'll think of something." I waggle my eyebrows at him. "Have you seen Cat yet?"

"Yeah." His answer is short and clipped.

"Still fighting?"

"No." They are. I can see it in his eyes, and it's killing him, but I know he's keeping his distance from her for me.

"You feel something for her, right?"

"Can we not do this? I know where this will go, and I'm not willing to lose our friendship for it," he huffs and begins to pace again, avoiding looking me in the eyes.

"So, you're okay to lose hers?"

"Are you on drugs?" He spins and stares at me wide-eyed. "Are you saying I should consider losing you to keep her?"

"Who said you would ever lose me?" I sit up and lean

forward on my knees as I sit on the edge of the bed. "When did I ever say that?"

"I know what's between you two. Anyone can see it. Hell, we can all feel it. I wouldn't want to be the one who gets caught in the middle and loses everything." He tosses his arms up with frustration as irritation laces his words.

"What if we all got what we want?" My tone is saturated with suggestion as his brows come together in thought.

"Are you seriously suggesting what I think you are?"

"Well, why not?" I throw my hands up, mocking his earlier action. "We've shared before without issue. Our balls have rubbed on several occasions."

"You mean like a one-time fuck?"

"I mean like a relationship. You with her and me with her," I correct him.

"We share her? Like a throuple? Like your Uncle Emmett has?" His face gets green. "Dude, I love you, but I'm not gay. Like at all."

"More like two separate relationships, but with the same girl. I think it's doable." I fall back onto my elbows on the bed while nodding.

"And what if one of those relationships breaks up? What happens to the other who's so used to being in the picture?" His hands hit his hips as an arrogant smirk lines his mouth. He thinks he's got me.

"We act like adults and move on. You'll always have me."

"And she's cool with this?" His brow raises.

"I haven't told her yet." His head tips back with a laugh

while I try to speak over the noise. "I have a plan for that too. Now, are you in? Do you want her?"

"I do." He exhales heavily. "But I can only see this ending badly."

CATALINA

There's a knock at my door, and I look down at the towel wrapped around my torso.

"Who is it?" I call out.

"Cam."

My heart thunders inside my chest as I press my hand to it, hoping it'll slow. Then I do a full circle, looking for clothes before shrugging my shoulders. Fuck it. I open the door and stand there in my towel, my hair dripping water. Cameron gives me a slow once-over that instantly heats my skin. Until I remember how he treated me this morning, and then I'm trying to slam the door in his face.

"Wait!" He shoulders inside my room, and like the idiot I am, I let him.

I turn to scream at him to get out when his fingers suddenly tangle into my wet hair and his mouth lands on mine. All thought escapes as I turn myself over to the feelings that rush through me. He's not gentle, but he's not near as rough as Carmelo, and I like that. I want them to be different.

His tongue pushes inside my mouth and I open on a moan, feeling hands tugging on the towel I'm wearing. When I finally clear the lust from my brain, I realize Cameron's hands are still in my hair. I pull away as I hear the door to my room shut and look over my shoulder to find Carmelo.

"What the fuck—"

"Kiss me." Cameron's finger pulls my face back to his, and he's once again clearing the intelligent thought from my brain. I feel the tug on the towel again and try to figure out if this is insanity.

I guess not, because my hands release the fabric and it brushes down my legs, pooling at my feet. Cameron's hands become rougher as he tugs my head to the side, allowing better access, and Carmelo's fingers glide down my back. Is this really happening? Are they saying they want a threesome? Is this a prank?

My heart throbs as I pull away from Cameron to force air into my lungs, and he immediately moves to my neck while Carmelo steps in, pressing his front to my back.

"Kitty Cat," he purrs. He literally purrs. "Do you like this?"

"Why are you guys doing this?" My voice shakes with trepidation, but I don't move from between them.

"Because we both want you," Cameron murmurs against my skin. "Is this okay?" His hands glide down my sides as Carmelo's snakes into my curls.

"Tell him yes, Cat." His voice is raspy and deep. "Tell him you want the both of us too."

I nod and Carmelo yanks my head back with a growl. "Say it."

"Yes." My voice comes out husky and no longer my own.

My head is snapped to the side next, and then his mouth is on mine. Just like the memories I replay every day, his kisses are rough and aggressive, his teeth biting into my lips. Then I feel Cameron's mouth seal around my nipple, and he nips it between his teeth, my gasp getting lost in Carmelo's mouth. Cameron's hand skims over my stomach, which shakes in anticipation as he hits my mound, the feel of his fingers rough against my soft skin.

I pull away from Carmelo's mouth and look down at Cameron just as his lips follow the same trail his fingers did. When he presses a kiss into my folds, I moan loudly, my head tipping back against Carmelo's shoulder.

"Open her legs." Carmelo's breath tickles my cheek as he instructs Cameron. "Prop her foot on your shoulder."

Cameron looks up at me with a grin and lifts my right foot, placing it on his shoulder. "She's fucking soaking for us," he moans and lightly runs his fingers through the wetness.

"Show me," Carmelo husks, and I moan as Cameron sinks a finger inside me. He pumps it in and out twice, then pulls out the glistening digit to show Carmelo. "She's definitely soaked for us. Let me taste that." Cameron extends his arm and I watch with rapt attention as Carmelo sucks his finger, soaked with my juices, into his mouth. He slowly releases Cameron's finger and moans. "So fucking delicious. Taste her."

Cameron wastes no time dipping his mouth between my legs and sucking my clit into his mouth. I scream out his name just as Carmelo's hand tightens around my throat, and breathing becomes difficult.

"I think I'm going to need you to be quieter." He sounds so fucking dangerous, and I can feel the flood of moisture collecting at Cameron's mouth. "Do I have to stuff your mouth?"

I shake my head, but as Cameron lashes his tongue against my clit and then combines his fingers, I can feel how explosive this is about to get. My stomach tightens and heat pools in the lowest depth of my stomach, my foot shaking on his shoulder.

"Looks like she's going to come." Carmelo chuckles into my ear. "Make sure you're quiet, or else."

I clamp my teeth shut just as my pussy clamps around Cameron's fingers, and the orgasm that steals over me is earth-shattering.

"Fuck, she's so tight," Cameron whispers, his knees still on the floor.

Carmelo's cock is pressed into my ass, and I grind against it as I ride out my orgasm into Cameron's hand. Once I'm spent, Cameron drops my foot back to the floor and stands up in front of me, our chests touching. He holds up his hand, and I am shocked to see how much fluid is on it, some drops rolling down his palm. Carmelo wraps a hand around his wrist and tugs it to his face, running his tongue over the droplets, catching every one.

Then they simultaneously take a step back from me and grin at each other, my head twisting back and forth.

"Time to get your ass in the gym," Cameron tells Carmelo, who nods and reaches to open my door.

"Huh?" That's the only thing I can muster to say as Cameron walks out the door and Carmelo looks back.

"We'll be seeing you."

The door clicks behind them, the sound loud in my now silent room, and I can't help but wonder if any of that was real.

Chapter Fourteen

"This raging fucking hard-on won't go away," I groan into my arm that's flung over my face.

"Go back to your room and pound one out." Carmelo sounds disinterested.

"Why didn't we fuck her? Why did you think it was a good idea to leave after that?" I sit up and ask him.

"Because she hasn't had one dick yet. You want to give her two without warning?" He laughs, and I want to punch him in the face for starting this whole thing.

"How are you so unbothered?" I wave my hand at him.

"I've had a bit more time to deal with the aftermath of Cat." He chuckles. "You'll get used to it until she pisses you off and it restarts the cycle."

"That might be your cycle with her, but I don't want it to be mine."

"That's noble." He hums, and I'm pissed again. "Let's get your dick off your brain and go eat some dinner. She'll be there and you can woo her."

"I don't woo," I scoff. "I just need to get her under me.

Do you know how long it's been?"

"Shut up your whining." Carmelo snickers and gets up. "Let's go get food, and no more of that green shit. It gives me the runs."

"You're disgusting," I mutter and follow him out toward the dining hall.

I slow down as I pass by Cat's room and listen for any noises coming from inside. I'm a fucking asshole, because with her, I don't just want to get laid. Catalina Costa has a tough exterior that she uses to fight Carmelo, but I can easily see her soft insides that she's used to win me over. She's closed off and cold on the outside but complex and emotional on the inside.

"Let's go." Carmelo shoots me a look over his shoulder. "That's creepy as hell."

"I'm not being creepy." I'm being creepy as fuck, and I need to snap out of it. This isn't me, and I don't know what it is about Cat that has me so fucking twisted.

We get to the dining hall and I scan the room, looking for her. She's not here yet, so where is she? Was she sleeping in her room? Did the orgasm I gave her knock her out? Because I am so fucking ready to do that again, multiple times a day, and every day.

The line is small, and I see a good choice of vegetables and meat that I set on a plate for Carmelo. He grumbles about there being brownies and how he can't have one, but I ignore him. He better get used to me breathing over him at every meal. We sit at our usual table, and I sit with my back to the door. If I face it, I will be constantly watching for her, looking like a heartsick fool.

"Please tell me that brownie on your plate is for me," Carmelo growls as he sits. "It would be awfully cruel of you to give one to yourself and not to me, especially considering I was just moaning for one."

"Why would I put a brownie on my plate for you?" I raise my brow and chuckle when he growls again.

His fork clashes with his plate as he angrily stabs an asparagus. "This shit makes your piss stink," he mumbles, and I choke on my chicken.

"Will you just eat without complaining?" I continue to laugh.

A few minutes later, the air inside the hall changes, and I know she's there. I know it before Carmelo's eyes lift and narrow behind my head, the irritation in his gaze comical considering what we did with her not too long ago. I think he will always be like that with her. It's ingrained in him to dislike her, no matter how much his body disagrees.

"Your lover has arrived," he murmurs.

"She's yours too," I snap, and he laughs. "That doesn't even sound right."

"Regardless of what it sounds like..." His eyes follow her across the room. "She needs to agree first, and her screaming your name in orgasm doesn't count." He's right. "Why is she sitting over there?" He stands. "Oh, Miss Costa! You're sitting in the wrong spot."

Everyone's eyes are on us, and the weight of their nosy stares has me staring down at my plate instead of looking at her like I want to. I hear her low grumble and smirk at how similar she sounds to Carmelo. No wonder they're always at each other's throats. She sits beside me and her scent washes over me, hardening my cock once again. I turn and look at her and find her chocolate gaze already on me, her cheeks turning a delicious pink.

"Hey." I smile at her.

"Hi." She ducks her head and scoops her hair behind her ear.

"You two look ridiculous." Carmelo snorts. "He was just sucking on your pussy juice like a Slurpee. No need to be coy."

"Will you shut the fuck up?" I snarl at him, but that only causes him to continue.

"What did it feel like, Virgin Kitty? To find yourself between two men?" he teases. "Most virgins only get one."

"Carmelo Torres." I slap the table. "Enough."

I look at Cat and groan when I see her face reddening in anger. This is going to end up badly. Why is it every time these two are near each other, there tends to be some kind of blowup? If this is going to work, Carmelo needs to stop taunting her, and Cat needs to rein in the violence.

"I guess I need the both of you to make me feel like there's almost a whole man with me," she retorts, and I snap my head toward her.

"Hey!" I lightly shove her arm. "Don't bring me into this."

"I didn't! He did!" She shoves me back harder.

It's like being at the playground with children. I take a deep breath and tamp down my need to join in. "Eat your fucking food." I toss the brownie onto Carmelo's plate. "Shut up."

He shoves it in his mouth and grins around it at Cat as she huffs, stabbing her fork into her asparagus much the same way Carmelo did earlier. So fucking similar. She pops it in her mouth and I can't look away. I never thought the sight of someone chewing could be so attractive. I'm fucking losing it.

"Be careful." Carmelo's words are muffled around the brownie in his mouth. "Neither of us like the taste of asparagus pussy."

Before I can chastise him, she has her plate off her tray and in her hand, throwing it into his face. The force of the blow has the porcelain cracking down the center as it falls into his lap and the food drips off his face. Then, before I can react, she has the tray in her hand and slams it across the side of his head, sending food flying down the table. I sit there in fucking shock, but Carmelo is quick to retaliate, and he scoops the food off his face, throwing it back into hers.

"I should make you eat everything you just threw onto the floor!" he roars at her. "Then force you to lick it off me."

I finally come to and shove him back down as he stands. "You two look like children! Is this how it's going to be? Will you never grow the fuck up?"

"If he'd kept his mouth shut—" Cat begins, but I cut her off.

"And if you didn't react in violence. You're both to blame."

"I hate you." She fists her hands and screams into Carmelo's face. "I really fucking hate you." Then she's storming toward the doors.

"But you're feeling something, sweetheart!" he calls out to her.

"Is this how it's always going to be?" I shove up out of my seat. "How is this normal?"

"Normal? You want normal?" he scoffs while licking

the potato off his cheek. "This is a three-way relationship. There's nothing normal about it."

"And this is how you want it to be? Chaotic and violent?"

"There's something that drives me wild when that girl gets going." He grins maliciously and stabs another asparagus on his plate. "I'd still slurp her asparagus pussy."

"It's always going to be me who calms you both, isn't it?"

"Looks like it." He nods, looking ridiculous as mashed potato slips off his jaw. "You're like our safe place during the storm."

That's going to be one hell of a job, and I don't know why it feels like something I want to do as long as it means we're all together.

CATALINA

Oh, my God. I fucking hate him.

I pull another chunk of potato out of my hair and growl at my reflection. I want nothing more than to punch my fist through his chest cavity and rip out his tiny black heart. Why does he feel the need to goad me? And honestly, Cameron is right. Why do I feel the need to retaliate? I am never this emotional about anything else or with anyone else. There's just a nerve that Carmelo plucks inside of me, and I turn into the fucking Hulk.

I start the shower, fuming about having to take another, and rip my food-crusted clothing off. My hands are vibrating with anger and it's taking everything in me not to smash my fists into the nearest breakable object. My anger issues are nothing new, and while I was training with the DeRucci Family, they taught me how to keep it under lock. I never let emotions or words affect me, and I was never prone to violent outbursts until that piece of shit Torres. I step into the shower and blast myself with cold water, needing to cool down.

Once I've calmed down some, I turn the dial to warm, then grab the shampoo and scrub it into my hair, making sure to get all the food bits. Each time I feel something, my anger ramps up further, and no amount of breathing it out is going to work. I'm going to need to take myself to the gym and punch it out.

I hear a click and stick my head out of the shower curtain. Did I lock my door when I came in?

"Hello?" I call out but don't get an answer.

I must've locked the door; I always do. At least, I think I did. I step back under the spray and tip my head back, washing out the shampoo suds. As the water slides down my face, I hear the shower curtain rings grind against the curtain rod, and my eyes open immediately, ignoring the sting of the shampoo. My fist lands square on Carmelo's jaw.

He hits the counter as another pair of muscular arms wrap around my waist, hauling me out of the shower, and I fling my leg out, satisfied when it connects with Carmelo's stomach, his grunt like music to my ears.

"You're both dead." I lock down my feelings and hear the deadened sound of my voice. They're in so much trouble right now. Carmelo better hope his training has been adequate.

My head snaps back, connecting with Cameron's chin, and he releases me, staggering back with a moan. Carmelo's hand comes up, trying to halt me, and I grab his wrist, twisting it painfully to the side. His other hand comes up, and he's quick, I'll give him that much, but I've always trained to be the best. I had to be better than anyone I would come up against, and right now, I'm about to show them. I chop my hand to the inside of his hand coming toward mine, the other wrist firmly in my grasp, not moving as I kick into his solar plexus. He bows forward, and even though we are in the small confines of my bathroom, I use the counter to slide over his back, bringing his wrist with me.

Just as Cameron gets his wits about him, he steps into the bathroom once again and holds his hands up. "We were coming to say sorry."

"By cornering me in the shower?" I squeeze Carmelo's arm up higher and he hisses.

"Take it easy." Cameron swallows thickly. "Let him go."

I feel my anger wane slightly, so I release his wrist, shoving Carmelo forward into Cameron, but not before giving him a sharp kick in the ass. They both stumble out of my bathroom, and I grab a towel to wrap around my torso. I am still naked and fucking soaked as I rub at my eyes to chase away the sting.

"I told you this was a bad idea," Cameron groans as he shoves Carmelo away from him.

"And I told you it would be fun." Carmelo chuckles.

My fist flies out and slams into Carmelo's cheek, the pain snaking through my fingers. It feels so fucking good. His head whips to the side and I can see I've split open his cheek. Poor baby. He turns on me so fast and I begin to feel giddy inside. Let's fucking fight, asshole. I can hear Cameron yelling at us, but at this moment, it's just me and Carmelo, and this has been brewing for years. He does exactly what I expected he would and grabs my throat, slamming me against the wall. My head bounces with the force, and I let out a humorless chuckle. My hand runs up and under his hoodie, scraping over his abs. His eyes narrow, but other than that, there's no reaction.

I fist the material inside the sweater and yank him closer to me, our chests now pressed together. Then I lean forward and lick the bead of blood that's run down his cheek from my assault and moan exaggeratedly.

"It always tastes so much better when the damage is caused by me." Then I slam my forehead into his chin and watch as he falls backward into Cameron's arms. "Did you really think you could come into my fucking room and attack me?"

"For the last time…" Cameron grabs an advancing Carmelo. "We were coming to say sorry."

"While I was in the shower? In a compound filled with men who are rough and lack respect for women?"

Cameron has the sense to look remorseful, but Carmelo just looks plain angry, and I can't help but grin at him, blowing him a kiss for good measure. His hand comes up to touch the cut on his cheek and the smeared blood from where I licked him, bringing his fingers in front of his eyes.

"You made me bleed, Capo." His voice is so dangerous and deep. "I think it's only fair if we return the favor."

"No, Carmelo." Cameron tugs on him. "Stop this nonsense. All of this was a bad fucking idea and I just keep listening to you like an idiot."

"You ready to bleed for us, Capo?" I know what he's alluding to, and my thighs clench, my throat suddenly dry. Am I ready? And with both of them?

Cameron is looking between the both of us, and when it dawns on him just what Carmelo means, his eyes widen on mine. I'm twenty years old and have never thoroughly enjoyed a man. Yes, I've kissed and fondled a few mafia soldiers, but it never got far. Gion would always send the guys on different routes and I wouldn't see them again. My virginity was meant for him. Even though both of us never wanted to be together, he still felt like that part of me belonged to him, and he coveted it like a trophy.

I don't want it to be Gionni's though.

These two men, standing in my room and waiting for my response, are who I want to give it to. With my heart pounding inside my chest and my throat constricting in apprehension, I drop my towel to my feet. There's no better time, and the perfect moment will never be because Carmelo and I will kill each other by then. Cameron drops his hold on Carmelo, his eyes trained on my body, and Carmelo comes forward, his finger brushing the underside of my right breast.

"You have a beauty mark right here." His voice is soft, and even though we were ready to kill each other moments ago, I can hear the reverence in his voice.

Then his hands wrap around my waist and I'm hoisted into the air before I'm tossed onto the bed. My back bounces a few times, and then Carmelo is pulling my legs apart, crawling up the center.

"With the little taste I got earlier,"—he sucks in a deep breath—"I've been craving for the real thing." He looks over his shoulder at Cameron, who's watching us with hooded eyes and a pronounced bulge in his pants. "I think you'll need to keep her quiet. Fill her fucking mouth."

I should feel anger at those words because he's so fucking disrespectful, but instead, I feel my thighs dampen with arousal. Coming from anyone else, I would've knocked their teeth out, but these two? They can say whatever the fuck they want if it means I'm going to be pleasured.

Cameron approaches the side of the bed, one knee propped up on the mattress, and slowly undoes his pants when I feel the first swipe of Carmelo's tongue. I cry out at the contact, and he looks up from between my thighs to tsk. "Cam, I gave you one job."

Cameron chuckles beside me and drops his pants, the glint of metal hitting my eyes. Is that a piercing? And what was all this talk about being small? He's a fucking monster. He laughs, and I pull my eyes away from the beast to look up at him. "I told you I was a grower."

Carmelo's chuckle into my folds has me moaning again, and I reach up to wrap my hand around Cameron's cock. I give him a few pumps and cry out again when Carmelo sucks my clit between his teeth. He bites it sharply, a warning about my noise, and I drag Cameron's cock down to my mouth. I really don't want my father walking by or anyone else hearing the noises either. The metal moves to the side when I flick my tongue against the ring at the tip of Cameron's cock. I flatten my tongue and run it over the head, paying special attention to that ring. His small whimpers and his cock jerking have me opening my jaw and sucking him deep into my throat.

"Holy fuck, Cat," Cameron whispers, and I feel Carmelo look up from his meal.

"I think she can take more than that, don't you, Cameron?" Carmelo taunts, and I feel Cameron pull out a bit, then push back in, farther than the first time. He hits the back of my throat and continues to work past the gag. "Now that's fucking beautiful. Make her cry."

Make me cry? Just as I'm about to knee him in the face, Carmelo dips back down between my legs, his fingers spreading me wide as he attacks my clit. Cameron pulls out once more, and then with a bit more force, pushes himself in, a little farther than the last. I can feel myself tightening, and I know I'm about to make a mess of Carmelo's face, which makes me more satisfied. I hope he drowns down there. That's a win all around for me.

"Capo is about to come, and those tears on her cheeks are gorgeous," Carmelo says as two fingers slip inside me to work that special spot. "Make sure she can't breathe."

Cameron, ever the good boy, obeys Carmelo's orders and stuffs his cock down my throat. I squeeze around him as I struggle to suck in a breath, and my pussy constricts at the same time around Carmelo's fingers. I squeeze my eyes shut and watch as stars explode behind my lids, my body shaking with the force. Every sensation is heightened because my lungs are struggling for air, but I feel no panic, and my orgasm continues to drag out.

Cameron finally pulls out, and I suck in a breath so hard, choking and sputtering. Carmelo crawls up my body and grabs my chin in his hand. Luckily, I'm too drained to fight him. "I want to be the first to fuck this tight pussy, Cat." He punctuates his words with a sharp thrust of his groin against my pussy. "But I will hurt you and make you scream with pain. As good as that sounds, I don't hate you that much. Cam will make it enjoyable, and he's gentler. Besides, I want to watch him stretch you for the first time."

His words both scare me and make me ready for orgasm number two. Then he crushes his mouth to mine, and our tongues tangle in a flurry. This is how it is with Carmelo. Everything we do is bordered on the extreme, and when we're finished, at least one of us is left wounded. He pushes up off me, and Cameron is removing his clothes, his body now having my full attention. His chest and stomach look like something chiseled from stone, all the muscles rippling as he tosses his clothing.

I hear the scrape of a chair over my carpet and look to see Carmelo placing it at the foot of my bed. "On your hands and knees, Kitty Cat." His devilish smirk is heating me up.

My legs are still spread and I'm slow to obey his command. I'm not used to following orders, I'm used to giving them. A hard sting courses through my pussy and the sound of a slap has me looking at Cameron in shock.

"Did you just slap me?" He slapped my pussy. And yes, it hurt, but now it's throbbing with need.

"Are you gonna do as you're told, or do you need another one?" Cameron asks, and that's when I see the sinister glint in his eyes. He's not always the sweet one.

With my arousal once again rising, I turn over and prop myself up on my hands and knees, my pussy on perfect display for Carmelo. I look over my shoulder and our eyes connect. His tongue runs along that swollen bottom lip of his and I feel mine doing the same. Then I feel the mattress dip at my feet and turn to look over my other shoulder just in time to watch Cameron slip a condom down his length.

This is it. I'm finally losing my virginity, and nothing about it is conventional.

Chapter Fifteen

Her pussy is red and a bit swollen from Cameron's slap, but soaking with her arousal. She likes it on the rougher side, and that soothes my worry. I'll be too much for her first time. I've always been known as the guy who likes sex more on the painful side, and I have held myself back with other girls, but the strength inside Cat calls to me, so I know she can take it. She'll be able to take all of me. I just don't want her first time to be like that. I know how special it's supposed to be for a girl, and I don't want her memories of this moment to be of pain, even though the pleasure would be that much more.

Cameron finishes rolling the condom down his length and runs a finger up her center, causing her to gasp, then shows me the finger with a grin. It's fucking soaked. She's ready. He nods at me before angling her a little to the side, spreads her legs a bit more, and then lightly pushes her between her shoulder blades, forcing her chest closer to the mattress. I am so hard it fucking hurts, and I decide to relieve myself of the pressure of my jeans. I pop the button and pull down the zipper, opening my jeans wider, then flip down my boxers and groan at the relief. Cat's eyes land on mine once again as Cameron lines himself up. I watch hers widen at the feel of him nudging her entrance, and I stop everything, time slowing down to this one moment.

He breaches his head inside her, and she pants, looking slightly overwhelmed, her eyes never straying from mine. He slowly pushes in another inch, and those chocolate brown eyes lose focus as she lets herself get lost in the sensation, a completely new experience. I'm so lucky to be a witness, sitting here in the front row and watching her be taken for the first time. The noises she's making, the facial expressions, and the way her body is reacting. I can see her nipples are pebbled, her skin has a sheen forming along its surface, and her thighs quake. This is my first time too. I have never watched a woman lose her innocence.

"Cat." Cameron's voice is rough, filled with restraint. "This part will pinch. I'm going to be quick about it."

She nods, still watching me, and I wrap my hand around my pulsing cock. Cameron slams himself in with a grunt and Cat releases a sharp cry, her eyes wide with pain. I can see the tears building against her bottom lid, and I can't help reacting to that, my balls tightening and ready to explode.

Cameron pulls out a few inches and then pushes back in, all the way to the hilt. A tear escapes her eye and slowly rolls down her cheek, her bottom lip sucked between her teeth. I stand and lean over, gathering the moisture on my finger, then pop it into my mouth and suck it off, the salty flavor bursting against my tongue. Cameron hasn't moved again, giving her time to adjust and looking slightly worried, but he needn't be. Our Kitty Cat is so fucking strong. I pinch her chin between my fingers and press a kiss to her trembling lips.

Then I pull away and look at where Cameron is completely lost inside of her. The need to see him move is overwhelming.

"Let me see," I tell him, my voice husky.

He pulls out slowly, and the condom is covered in her juices with a bit of pink and red mixed in. She whimpers from the discomfort, and I brush my hand along her hair. She's still trembling, so I reach out as she turns her head and looks over her shoulder, my two forefingers sliding along Cameron's length. I collect her fluids as Cameron slides back into her, stretching her tight hole. Her whimper becomes a moan, and I know the pain is subsiding. I hold my fingers in front of her face and her mouth opens in shock. It's not a lot of blood, but it is a lot of her juices. She may be in pain, but she is completely enjoying it.

I suck the two fingers into my mouth and moan around the tangy taste. I've now tasted the end of a woman's innocence and it's fucking delicious.

"Fuck," Cameron grunts as he watches me suck my fingers clean. He picks up the pace, unable to control himself, and Catalina hisses, the pain still there.

I pump my cock in my hand and she watches, transfixed by the motion. "Need a distraction from the discomfort?" I grin down at her.

She nods and opens her mouth for me, nearly making me explode all over her face. I take a few deep breaths and ease my cock into her mouth. She moans around my girth and the force of Cameron's thrusts has her bobbing on my cock beautifully. The slapping noise intensifies, and Cameron's face is a mask of pure bliss. I know it'll be over soon. She moans more around my cock, and I look at Cameron with my brow raised.

"Cat," he pants, slowing down his thrusts. "Play with your clit. I can feel your pussy squeezing my cock."

I want to watch her come, to see the rapture on her face, and then feel myself come because of it. She reaches her hand down between her legs, and I pull out of her mouth, content to stroke myself. Cameron increases his rhythm as Cat's full breasts swing from the motion, my balls tightening with the sight. I pick up the pace of my strokes too, timing them to match his, and then Cat's eyes roll into the back of her head, her mouth opening in a wordless scream.

"Fuck!" Cameron groans and slams into her one last time, throwing his head back.

"Come in my mouth," Cat says, looking up at me, her face euphoric.

Her words send me over the edge, and my head makes it just past her lips in time to explode. I groan loudly as I continue to spill myself into her mouth, and her throat works to swallow every drop.

Then all three of us collapse to the bed, and I look to the ceiling, my mind completely void but for one thought.

There's no going back now.

CATALINA

I wake up to the sound of my phone buzzing with a text message and look around the room. The burning sensation between my legs tells me that everything was real and I wasn't dreaming. I stretch for my phone and groan through the stiffness of my muscles. This is a different feeling than after I work out.

I open the screen and see a text from Gion, making my heart stop inside my chest.

Gion: See you tomorrow.

My fingers fly over the screen in a flurry of anxious fear.

Me: You're coming back so soon? Why?

He doesn't answer me, and I fly off the bed in a panic. Does he know what I've done? No! I shake my head, hoping to dislodge some sense, and pace. Gion knows nothing. I need to be logical and lock down the stress threatening to dissolve me into a puddle of terror. I'm not so much afraid of Gion as I am of Don Julius, and I know he pulls all Gion's strings. So why is he sending his son here again?

There's no way I'm sleeping tonight, and now I'm filled with energy that needs to be depleted. I get dressed and throw my hair up in a bun as I fly out of my bedroom door. I need to give my father a heads-up as well.

Hurrying down the corridor, I make a right, thankful he's far enough away and making it impossible to hear anything from my room. Fuck! I can't think of that right now. I need to prepare for Gion. When I bang on my father's door, he opens it in less than twenty seconds.

"Cat, what is it?"

"Gion will be here tomorrow." My words come out rushed and I sound like I can't get enough air. "I barely got a warning this time. Have you heard anything?"

His eyes widen, and I know he's taken by surprise, my trepidation warranted. "No." He shakes his head brusquely. "Nothing."

"Fuck," I growl and pace the hall outside of his room. "Why so soon?"

"Maybe he has heard about Carmelo Torres taking over the Head Corp?" His fingers snare into the goatee on his chin. "Ember and I have always wondered if we have a rat in our numbers."

Carmelo? I can feel my skin become damp with fear and the realization that if they have their sights on him, then there's no dislodging it.

"Papa." My chest heaves rapidly. "They won't like that."

The DeRuccis were fine with Ember Torres-Greene heading the Head Corp, because like I've said, misogyny is still prevalent within their ranks. They believed her to be easily manipulated if the need ever arose, but now, to put a Torres male back into that position, one whose lineage screams psychotic and unbalanced, would mean war.

"I need to call Ember." The crease between his eyebrows worries me. "She'll know what to do."

"Papa, Carmelo… nothing can happen to him." I know I sound weak, and it grates on the teachings that have been forced on me, but I can't help it.

"I know." He nods, giving me a sympathetic look. "That boy means something to you, always has."

I don't know how to answer him, and I feel like screaming in frustration. This is not what needs to be discussed right now. We need a fucking plan.

"Please let me know what Ember says." I muster up as much calm as I can find and turn on my heel, heading back to my room.

A rat in the Head Corp? And Ember still put Carmelo up for bait, knowing the mafia could be watching? What the fuck was she thinking? I can feel the anger inside me rise. I need to punch my fists into something before I explode. How could she put her nephew in danger like that? The DeRuccis will not think twice about killing him. They do not want another Raphael Torres running the Rampage and Head Corp, and then they'll kill my father for not telling them himself. He is a spy here for them. Little do they know, he's a double agent. Then again, I would assume by this shit, they know.

My one saving grace is it's Gion coming and not Don Julius himself. Maybe I can convince him not to start a war and that everything they heard or think they know is not correct. Maybe I can twist it just enough that he'll believe their own rat is a double agent. I run my hand through my hair and let out a shaky breath. I haven't been this scared in a long while.

The truce between the Rampage, Head Corp, and the DeRuccis is tempestuous at best. At first, when Ember stopped the illegal distribution of drugs and human trafficking, they were ready to level the compound. That was until I convinced Don Julius this was better because the Heads weren't loyal to the family, and they sold other products as well, so at least this way, the competition's product wasn't moving either. But this? He will see Carmelo as a direct threat, no matter what the Head Corp says they're doing. He accepted Ember and her soft, womanly proclivities. But a man? That's a formidable opponent. He has balls after all.

I find myself in front of Cameron's door and rest my forehead against the wood. Of course I would come to him first, our levelheaded and logical thinker. He uses his head before his fists and that's what I need right now. I rap my knuckles on his door, soft and light, and wait for him to open it. He doesn't keep me waiting long, and when the door opens to him in his boxers, I almost forget why I came. I give him a slow once-over, and when I reach his face, he's smirking and shaking his head.

"No longer sore?" Smug bastard.

"We need to talk." My hands drop as his brows crash together at my words and the tone of my voice, catching on that I am here for a whole other reason than his dick.

I push into his room and sit on the chair. He comes in and opens the small fridge, throws me a bottle of water, and sits on the end of the bed, waiting for me to begin.

"Gion is coming tomorrow." His brow raises in question and I shake my head. "My fiancé?"

"You have a pet name for him?" I can hear the jealousy in his words.

"We grew up like brother and sister. He also calls me Catty sometimes." I roll my eyes. "That's not the only problem."

"I'm guessing when he finds out I was balls-deep and taking your maidenhood, he'll want to duel?"

"Can you listen to me for two minutes? Did I come to the wrong room?" I throw my hands up as he tips his head back with a sigh.

"You're right. I'm jealous and acting irrationally. Tell me everything."

"I think the family knows about Carmelo being trained

to take over Ember as Head. My father admitted that he and Ember feared there may have been a rat in their ranks."

"Okay, so what?" He shrugs. "Ember can't do it forever. Someone would have to take over eventually. Who better than the man who has the Torres last name?"

"That's the problem, the man with the Torres last name. They were fine with a weak woman in that position, but another man could mean war."

"Oh." It finally dawns on him. "They're afraid of retaliation for you and your father."

"Yes." I nod empathically, happy I don't have to explain further. "They never thought Ember could lead an army, and even though we all know differently, they would never suspect a woman to amount to much."

"They trained you!" he exclaims, and I shake my head with a sigh. "Do they not know you're a woman?"

"To be strong enough to marry the son of the Don."

"So, we need to get Carmelo out of here." He stands, and I swear I can see his heart pounding through his rib cage.

"No!" I stand too. "That would be proof Carmelo is up to something. They know he lives here, and he has to be here when Gion arrives. They will hunt him down for the rest of his life otherwise."

"Let me get this right." He holds up his pointer finger. "If he goes on the run, they will hunt him down and kill him—"

"If he's lucky, they'll kill him quickly," I cut him off.

"Or he stays here, and they kill him anyway."

"Gion won't kill him tomorrow. I think he's here to

observe, but I need Carmelo to not be his usual self, and to keep his mouth fucking shut. If he even says one thing to Gion—especially about me—he will sign his own death warrant."

Cameron lets loose a sigh filled with fear. He knows as well as I do that keeping Carmelo quiet is going to be no easy feat, and after what we've done, the three of us, he's going to be even more unpredictable.

"Please, Cameron." I'm not above begging, not when it comes to either of their lives. "Please convince him to behave, and no matter what he sees, not to react."

"You know we're all dead, right?" He looks at me, dead serious.

Yeah, I know it's the most probable outcome.

Chapter Sixteen

"Say what?" I look at Cameron like he's lost his damn mind.

"It's only for a few days, and he'll be watching you the most. You're a threat now." I can't help it, but I like the sound of that. I'm a threat now.

"So let him watch me." I grin and crack a few knuckles. "Especially while I'm with his fiancée."

I'm sitting on the edge of my bed, watching as Cameron paces in front of me, his hair sticking off in all directions from his stress pulling.

"That's the shit that's going to get you killed." He points at me as he passes by.

"No one's killing me," I scoff and let out a sarcastic laugh. I'd like to see that guy try.

"What about me, or what about Cat? If you show possessiveness toward her, they'll know she's your weakness. Do you want her to die?" No, of course I don't want them to die.

A sharp knock sounds throughout the room, which

startles us both, and my gaze snaps to Cameron as he stops pacing, a high-pitched gasp leaving his mouth.

"Is he here already?" Cameron whispers, and I roll my eyes.

"He wouldn't be at my door, jackass." I get up and stride to my room door, opening it wide.

"Hey, ladies. Heard you might need some help." Saxon is leaning against the doorframe with an arrogant look on his face.

"We need your mother." I chuckle as I give him a shake of my head. "What the hell are you gonna do?"

"He'll bore the Don's son to death," Cameron retorts behind me, and I laugh.

"Hey." I reach my thumb out and swipe it through the scruff on Saxon's cheek. "Is that blood?"

"Must've done it while shaving." He shrugs and pushes his way into the room. "Just don't put it in your mouth. I might be diseased."

"The fuck?" I shut the door and wipe my thumb off on my pants.

"Where have you been?" Cameron questions him. "You were supposed to be here yesterday."

"I was." He sits on the bed. "I was running errands. Now, start talking."

While Cameron fills him in, I walk the length of my room, trying to think of a way to get us out of this, and no matter the scenario, it always ends up with someone dead.

"You may need to pledge yourself to the DeRuccis." Saxon's voice cuts through my thoughts.

"No." I shake my head and stop to stare at him. He's colder now than he's ever been, even his eyes conceal his thoughts, looking as dead as his emotions.

"Yes," he continues. "Then the four of us—because I'm assuming you've all pulled your heads out of your asses and realized your feelings—are going to come up with a fucking plan."

"To do what?" I toss my hands up.

"To sever ties with the fucking mafia." Saxon scratches at the hair on his chin. "See, everyone is always trying to plan on how to take them down, but who gives a fuck what they do in California? It's the shit they do here that fucks with us. So, we think of a plan to sever ties, and I think the answer lies in that pretty girlfriend of yours."

"Watch it." I point at him, not liking that he's calling my Cat pretty.

"Her fiancé is a son to the Don of the DeRucci Family. It needs to happen with him," Saxon explains, his tone sounding a little more blase. "And the only way to get to him is through her. So you fucking watch where you're pointing that finger. Besides, it's either join them or let things get a bit… messier."

There's something different about Saxon I haven't noticed until this exact moment. He's broader across the chest, his face is harder, and he appears tougher. I would assume his mother has been laying the training on him since his incident at school, not wanting him to be in the same predicament again and to help him gain a sense of confidence.

His words are ringing in my head with reluctance. He's right, we need to take down the DeRuccis, and it needs to happen with Gionni DeRucci, starting with Catalina.

"She can't get hurt," I growl, and Cameron nods.

"I think I'd have to worry more about you two getting hurt. Cat can handle herself. She was raised there. Or did you fuckers forget?" Saxon gets up and shakes his head. "I'm starving, and it looks like I won't be getting much sleep. I will watch your every interaction with him, and I'll also have my eye on him with Cat. You two stay away from me and don't draw too much attention to the fact that I'm even there." He opens the door and looks back. "Also, try to keep your temper in check. They're looking for any way to start shit." The door shuts behind him and I look at Cameron.

"He's different," I murmur to him as I scratch my temple.

"Yeah," he agrees. "There's more going on with him than we know about, but we don't have the time to figure it out right now."

He's right, but I can't help but stare at the door where Saxon just exited, wondering what path he's taking and if it's going to be a problem in the future.

It's a few hours later when a loud knock sounds on my door, and both Cameron and I eye it warily.

"Let's get this over with," I groan as I stand from the bed.

I open the door to Cat's worried expression. "He'll be here in minutes. I have to go up and meet him, but I wanted to stop here and remind you two I never planned on marrying him. I see nothing in him. So, behave."

I grab ahold of her T-shirt and haul her in against my chest. "Kitty Cat, that's going to be a tough request, but I'll do it to keep you safe." And then I crush my mouth to hers and swallow up the moan she releases.

"My turn," Cameron growls and shoves me out of the

way.

I chuckle as I watch him devour her much the same way I did, and nothing but contentment settles inside me. This is exactly how we were meant to be. I won't let the DeRucci Mafia fuck it up, because I know this is my only chance at love, and I will find no one who will understand me more than Catalina Costa.

"I have to go," she whispers and steps away, her face filled with anxiety. "Please don't draw attention to yourself." She says the last part to me and I roll my eyes.

Then I watch as she shakes off whatever emotion she's feeling before heading down the corridor to the elevators, gaining her usual stride.

"They'll go to the dining hall first," Cameron mutters beside me.

"And I'm suddenly famished." I look at him with a grin and am shocked when I find a similar expression on his face.

"Same."

Both of us know Cat will bring Gionni to the dining hall. That's where almost everyone who visits goes first while someone sets up a room for them. I know she wants us to keep our distance, but I can't leave her alone with him, knowing he's here under suspicious circumstances. Besides, the dining hall is large enough to watch and still be unseen.

We grab a plate of pasta each and sit in the far corner, both of our eyes on the door. Aunt Ember and Saxon walk in a few moments later as my chest squeezes with a bit of worry. She wouldn't have come this fast if this was just a random visit.

"Ember is here," Cameron mumbles around a mouthful of food.

I don't answer because obviously I saw her, and right now, speech is impossible. If this Gionni asshole does anything to hurt Cat, or if she looks even a little uncomfortable, fuck the DeRuccis, I'm going to war. Aunt Ember and Saxon sit at their regular table and without a plate in front of them, so I know they're there to talk to him too.

Finally, those doors open, and Cat walks in, Gionni coming up behind her. There's nothing remarkable about him. He has thick, wavy hair, the ends falling down across his forehead. His eyes are dark brown and his full mouth has a permanent sneer on it, one you would imagine on a privileged kid in a candy store. He's tall but not very built, lankier, and he's wearing a pair of baggy pants and a polo top.

"He looks like he thinks his shit doesn't stink." Cameron snorts and I nod. "They're going straight to Ember's table."

"That's who he's here to question after all."

He pulls out a seat right across from Aunt Ember and leans across the table, though she's not even slightly bothered. If anything, she looks excited. Saxon looks bored as he picks at his nails, and Cat sits, her spine straight with her eyes on Gionni. The way she's looking at him is with a mixture of worry and frustration. She cares about him, that much is clear, and like she told us, it doesn't look romantic.

Gionni is talking to Aunt Ember, but she looks to be answering him in one-word answers while Cat stays quiet as Saxon grows more and more bored. If he's actually interested and playing bored, his acting skills are superb. Well, his parents studied acting in school, so it makes sense.

"Hey, Carmelo." I look up at a slightly familiar blonde and raise my brow.

"Fuck," Cameron groans.

Oh! It hits me that she's the chick I was fooling around with the last time Cat was here with Gionni and I thought he was her real fiancé. Fuck, what was her name? Did I even ask her for it? She sees the confusion on my face and sits down beside me, and curiosity has me turning toward her slightly.

"Fuck," Cameron groans again.

"It's Serena." She holds out her hand. "We were too busy last time to exchange names."

"But you know mine," I point out, ignoring her hand.

"Who doesn't?" Right. I give her a small smile and then freeze when her hand lands on my thigh. "We should go out sometime." Her voice lowers and becomes husky. "I really had a good time with you."

"Listen…" I struggle to be nice, but wanting to tell her to fuck off.

"I know Catalina has this jealousy thing, but really, I heard she's like an ice queen," she sneers, and we both look at Cat across the room. Gionni stands and holds his hand out to Aunt Ember, who grips it in hers. "Besides, I heard that's her fiancé."

"Word travels fast down here," Cameron snaps, anger blooming red on his cheeks. He doesn't like the sound of that any more than I do.

I toss Serena a smile and a nod, hoping she gets the clue I'm not fucking interested. Then I continue to watch as Gionni leaves the dining hall before finding Aunt Ember leaning across the table, saying something to Cat. Cat's face is a mask of indifference, but she nods her head, hearing everything being said. But what's being said? I should know. Why the fuck does Saxon get a front-row seat?

I feel Serena's hand land on my cock and I snap my head to her, staring at her, dumbfounded. Then I'm shocked to hear Cat's voice, almost like she flashed her way to me.

"I would suggest you get your hand off him." She sounds like a lioness readying for the kill.

"Aren't you getting married?" Serena asks and gives my exceptionally soft dick a squeeze.

"Yeeeeeah." I grin at Cat, deciding to tease her a bit. "Aren't you getting married?"

Her face hardens and she turns to leave, her back heaving with each breath. I feel bad, so I sweep Serena's hand off me and stand to stop her. Cat spins, her face determined, as her fist flies out, hitting me square in the jaw. I fall back into my seat and Serena jumps up to run back to her table of friends.

"You deserved that." Cameron grins as he stuffs a forkful of pasta into his mouth.

"You want to fuck around, Carmelo Torres?" Cat snarls and grabs the front of my shirt. "Go right ahead." She releases me and stomps off toward the bathrooms. That's her place she goes to when she knows I'll follow.

"Go fix that shit." Cameron juts his chin in her direction, then grabs my plate. "I'll finish this."

Fucking bastard. I was enjoying that pasta. It's not every day he lets me have cheesy carbs.

I throw myself out of my seat and head to the bathrooms, rubbing my jaw. She has a mean right hook, and I'm going to need to make her understand that hitting me isn't a good idea. I fucking retaliate most of the time, and although I don't want to hit a woman, she needs to not be hitting me either.

I throw open the bathroom door, expecting to find her in a stall crying again, and instead get another hard right hook into my jaw.

"I fucking hate you, Carmelo!" she screams, and my vision becomes red.

"You hate me?" I scream back at her and grab her around the throat. "Am I the one flouncing about with a fucking fiancé?"

I hold her at an arm's length so her nails can't reach my face and then turn her around, throwing her against the wall. Her back hits it and she's panting as she stares me down, murder in the dark brown depths of her eyes. She flies at me and I grin, waiting for the hit, but instead she's up in my arms, legs around my waist, and her mouth hot on mine. My fingers dig into her ass and my tongue forces its way into her mouth. Then her teeth clamp down, and when I taste blood, it only amps me up further.

I wanted to wait to make love to her in her room, maybe some candles and take my time, savoring everything, but fuck that. This room, this bathroom, has seen the precise moment our spark ignited. So why not let it see me claim her as my own? This right here is Cat and I, no candles, no flowers, and certainly no making love. We run hot or inferno, there's no in-between, and me treating this relationship any differently would just be a lie. I drop her ass on the counter and pull away, just enough for us to catch our breaths. The mirror behind her catches my eye and I grin because it looks like someone replaced the broken one. I kind of want to slam her head into it again. I'm still fucking angry, so I decide to take it out on her tight pussy.

"Take those leggings off," I command, and her eyes

narrow at me. I raise a single brow and she huffs as she lifts her ass, allowing me to pull them down.

She's wearing no fucking underwear, and when her bare ass hits the counter, she gasps from the cool surface.

"Cat, did you meet your fucking fiancé with no panties on?" She swallows thickly at my question and I watch as her cheeks turn crimson.

"I was in a rush," she whispers hoarsely.

Thank God I'm wearing track pants because I need to be inside her while her cheeks are still burning and my cock is still twitching. This has been building inside of me for four years, and I want it to last longer than two pumps because I know I'm about to lose the last piece of my heart to this girl. I pull down my pants just enough to free my length and she moans at the sight, a bead of pre-cum appearing at the crown.

"I'm fucking you raw, Cat." I yank her to the edge of the counter and my cock bumps her center. "I haven't needed condoms in four years, so be fucking prepared."

Her mouth opens, ready with a retort I would imagine, but I'm plunging my length into her pussy, her sheath squeezing me at midpoint. I can't push in any farther, and she feels like a fucking vice around me.

"Fuck, Carmelo," she pants. "It's too big." Her head drops back and she moans as I pull out.

"Then we just need to stretch her, now, don't we?"

I do a few shallow pumps and watch as her breasts heave with the motion. I can already feel my balls tightening. It's been too long since I've fucked someone, and never have I done it without a condom. The feeling is completely different. The heat radiating on the inside is even more intense against my sensitive flesh. I push forward again, almost all the way in.

"It won't fit," she says with another moan, looking down between us to where we're connected.

"I'm going to fit, even if it fucking hurts."

I pull out a few inches and then slam it in. Finally, her pussy sucks me in to the hilt, and we both moan at the feeling. She clenches around me, and I press my forehead to hers, willing my body not to let me down. I want to last long enough to hear her scream my name and come undone. I need that so fucking bad.

"Fucking move," she snarls, and I huff out a laugh.

"Think I can get you to scream loud enough to make your fiancé hear you?"

"He'll kill you if he sees you taking what he thinks is his." She flutters her lashes and an evil grin appears on her face. "So yes, I fucking hope so."

Is that right? My hands slide around her waist and her breath hitches, like she knows she's in for a punishment. I know we both get off on the words we slice each other open with and the actions that bruise our bodies, but our souls are demanding to be set free. The anger that bubbles just under the surface is coating something else altogether, more powerful, and it's threatening to swallow us whole.

I pull almost all the way out and then I tighten my hold on her waist, slamming back in. Her head flies back on a scream and the fucking mirror cracks once again. She's going to have a concussion one of these days. I set a punishing rhythm and fuck her the complete opposite from Cameron. This is rough and fucking depraved. She gazes down at my cock pounding into her pussy and she whimpers, tears flowing down her cheeks.

"Carmelo," she whines, biting down on her bottom lip. "Fuck, I'm going to…"

"I know, Kitty Cat." Unfortunately, my arrogant tone is lost on her as she climbs the crest of her orgasm. "Let me hear just how good it feels."

I reach down just as she tightens around my cock and flick her clit with my thumb. The second I do, she combusts, her screams shaking the fucking walls around us. My name mingled with God and loud wrenching sobs are music to my fucking ears. I don't last another two thrusts before I'm slamming myself in so fucking hard and coming deep inside her. She continues to pulse as my cock jerks in tandem, my seed coating her insides.

"I'm not on birth control." Her voice is hoarse from screaming. "That wasn't fucking smart, Torres."

"So what?" I suck her lip into my mouth and release it with a pop, my cock still deep inside her. "You'd look good swollen with my baby."

"I don't want to have children right now," she moans as I pull out. My cum mixed with her release seeps out and drips to the counter.

"Oh well." I shrug, completely nonplussed. If I had my way, Cat would be dripping with my cum every day.

"I need to get back to my fiancé. He must be so worried." She smirks as she hops off the counter.

"He better not be in your fucking room, Cat, or else I'll be fucking you while he lies bleeding out from a slash to the throat."

Her eyes widen on mine as she discovers I'm speaking the truth. Then she pulls up her pants as I pull up mine, my cock sticky with our cum.

"You can't say shit like that, Carmelo. You'll be killed."

I brush by her and open the bathroom door, giving her a look over my shoulder. "It's getting old how often you say that."

Chapter Seventeen

The sounds of Gion's chewing through his mannerless open mouth is getting to me. After he spoke to Ember, and she assured him Carmelo was only acting as Head leader, I thought he would be leaving. He's still here though, which only means one thing. He didn't believe a word she said, and a part of me thinks Ember wanted just that. Why though?

The more she taunts the DeRucci Family, the hotter the water will be that boils around her nephew, and then she'll have to deal with the fact that he's dead. I look at him again, sitting in his usual spot with Cameron and laughing at something that's being said. That mouth, so plush and perfectly shaped, the dimple in his right cheek, and the bruise that's blooming on his jaw, all remind me of what we did a few hours ago.

"Father has finally realized that Rocco won't be returning home." Gion's statement has my eyes snapping back to his face with surprise. Hopefully his keen eyes didn't catch me watching my boys for too long.

"What do you mean?" My heart begins to pound inside my chest as sweat forms along my brows. If the heir to the DeRucci throne is gone for good, then that means Gion is next in line, something Don Julius would despise.

"Rocco ran away from his responsibilities and now my dear father is threatening me with handing the throne over to my uncle."

"Dante?" Gion's Uncle Dante is the best option as the heir to the DeRucci Family because that means I won't be marrying the son who will be taking it over. Not to mention, Gion is not fit for such a task.

"Yeah." He exhales and shoves another mouthful of food into his mouth, annoyance creating lines around his eyes. "But marrying you will sway him my way, I'm sure."

My eyes flick back to the table where the two loves of my life sit, and my heart sinks into my stomach. He's right. Don Julius would be more inclined to give him the reins if I'm Gion's wife.

"You keep looking in that direction." Gion's matter-of-fact statement sends a bucket of cold water down my spine.

Fuck.

"Huh?" I turn back to face him slowly and plaster a look of confusion on my face.

"I've known you since we were babies, Cat. I know when you're feeling any type of way. You're looking at one of them"—he points his finger at Carmelo and Cameron—"like you did with Leon when you were thirteen."

"Leon was like one of those Greek statues your father has in the garden. Those guys?" I nod my head in Carmelo and Cameron's direction. "Are nothing but assholes."

"So that blush across your cheeks and the squirming in your chair is because you hate them?" The intensity of his possessive glare has my heart kicking up speed. We may not want to marry each other, but make no mistake, Gion thinks

I'm still his.

"See the bruise on his jaw?" I ask him and then hold up the knuckles on my right hand. "I hate him."

I mean, it's pretty close to the truth.

"Make sure you're remembering what's mine, Catty."

I want to reach over the table and smash his face down into it, but I know I need to grin and bear it. "I haven't forgotten." He seems mollified with my words, chomping back into his food.

I'm fairly sure I just fucked up royally.

CARMELO

I just ate enough to feed a small village, and I did it to distract myself from walking over to that mafioso motherfucker and introducing his face to the table. My fists still twitch whenever I think about him talking to Cat like he owns her.

I throw open the door to my room and stop mid-stride, because sitting at the end of my bed is none other than the DeRucci piece of shit himself.

"You got two seconds to explain why you're in my room." My voice is level, though my insides are anything but.

"Catalina Costa." He stands and walks over to me, his voice filled with curiosity. "Why is she so affected by you? Is there something I need to be forcing out of my woman?"

We're standing nose to nose, and if it weren't for the underlying threat toward Cat in his words, I would kick the shit out of him.

"I hate that bitch, and just the sight of her makes me fucking sick," I sneer at him. "If she's your woman, why don't you take her back to California where she belongs?"

His eyes narrow briefly and then he lets loose a laugh that sours my stomach with the need to break his fucking neck. "Cool," he hums and walks by me and out the open door. "Looks like she gave you a couple of good hits." He nods toward my jaw.

"Yeah, and I warned her if she did it again, she'd have a few to match."

He opens his mouth to say something, but I slam the door in his face instead. I know that probably didn't win me any points with the crime family, but I don't care. It was that or kill the fucker.

The anger is ripping through me and I'm barely holding it together. I send a text to Cameron, asking him to head over to Saxon's room and find out what the fuck was said at that table. They seem to be tight, and Saxon is acting peculiar. More than usual anyway. I want to know what this plan is that he's cooking, and I need to know if it's actually feasible.

The urge to go to Cat's room is nearly overwhelming, but I don't know if that asshole will be there or if he's waiting for me to do just that. I wouldn't be able to come up with a lie believable enough to explain why I was there.

An hour later, Cameron is opening my room door and slipping in. He has frustration written all over his face and I prepare to hear some more bullshit.

"Saxon says that Gionni guy is here until your next Head meeting. He wants to see just how involved you are," Cameron starts.

"Perfect, I'm not at all. I had one prior meeting." I shrug, not feeling too worried about that.

"Yeah, that's what Ember and Saxon were saying, so that's not an issue. Ember thinks there's more to why he's here though. She said something feels off because of the shit he was questioning her about and how easily he accepted your little involvement."

That is weird. Why come all the way here for that? He could've easily been told the same shit over the phone. No, Saxon and Aunt Ember are right. There is something more and we won't know unless we turn the tables and question him, which will be impossible for us, but would it be impossible for Cat?

"Do you think Cat could find out his true motives?"

"How?" Cameron questions me, and when I say nothing, he jumps to his feet. "Like seduce him? Are you fucking crazy?"

"Or make him think she's seducing him? She obviously wouldn't act out anything because she knows I would kill her," I state like that's the most natural thing to say.

"You think Cat has a seductive bone in her body?" His eyebrows shoot up. "She'd be better to torture it out of him. Besides, she herself said they see each other as brother and sister."

"Yeah, but would you care about your sister keeping her virginity for you?"

"The fuck?" His face turns to disgust as my words penetrate his thick skull.

"Exactly. He cares for her, and I would go as far as to say wants her and she doesn't have a clue."

"He would also be onto her if she suddenly showed interest." Fuck, he has a point.

I sit on the bed with a huff and scrub my hand down my face. "Why the fuck is this shit happening now? We've had a happy balance with the DeRuccis for years."

"The only change is you."

We sit in silence, our heads hanging and our minds at work. What did they think Aunt Ember was going to do when she got older? Everyone has someone they train to take over their positions. That's only natural.

Unless...

"Hold on." I look up at Cameron. "Do you think the

DeRucci Family thought they would eventually take over the Rampage?"

Cameron's eyes widen and his mouth curls up. "That would seem like the most likely scenario."

"I think we need to go talk to Aunt Ember."

CAMERON

"The Eastside Rampage has never been offered to the DeRuccis nor would it ever be," Ember says as she paces back and forth in her room.

According to Carmelo, they once held her captive in this very room while her father forced her to fight multiple times to the death, and it was in this room she decided to kill him. It's amazing she even wants to continue to stay in here.

"Right, but what if they just assumed once you were too old to run it, they would step in to take over? Your family is in Whitsborough and so was I until a few years ago," Carmelo states.

She looks contemplative as she continues to pace. It seems like the most likely scenario, and with her children living in Whitsborough, they may have assumed she'd have no heir willing to stay here. Maybe they had the intention of turning it back into what it was before, a system to push their drugs through the United States and even into Canada. Then it would be oh-so easy to jump to the Head Corp after that to add human trafficking back on the table.

"I think this is a possibility." She nods as she stops pacing and runs her fingers along her chin. "Maybe they were so quick to accept my changing the rules for the Head and Rampage and figured there was always an expiration on that deal."

The room falls silent and Ember continues to pace, her mind at work. Saxon is sitting in the chair quietly, flipping an ornate blade in his hands, and from here, he looks dangerous. I don't know when he went from being the weird kid to someone worth fearing.

"Maybe I'll say I've changed my mind and pulled out from the position?" Carmelo suggests, but Ember is quick to disagree.

"They are cunning. Regardless of your position from now on, you are still a threat, and without the Rampage behind you, easier to kill. The second we say you've stepped down, you will be taken and disposed of."

"There's nothing we can do right now," Saxon interjects, his voice dripping with boredom. "We need to just play it out. He's not here to kill you himself, and the DeRucci Family wouldn't just send one man to do it, especially not the son of the Don. No, he's here to observe and report back."

"Yes." Ember nods. "That is my assumption too. I think we need to make you look like an ass in front of the Heads tomorrow."

"That shouldn't be too difficult," Saxon retorts, and I snort.

"We have a meeting tomorrow?" Carmelo looks around, shocked.

"Mission accomplished," Saxon pipes up, and once again, I chuckle.

"I sent you a notification about it two weeks ago." Ember lifts her brow at Carmelo.

"Right," he mumbles, looking chastised.

"What do we tell Cat?" I ask Ember, and she looks at me in thought.

"Nothing," she replies. "I know you have something going on with her at the moment, and I am all here for it, but they will torture her for that information one day if they even suspect she knows. It's better you continue to act like you want nothing to do with each other."

"No more fucking in the bathroom and breaking mirrors," Saxon cuts in as he tosses up the knife and catches it by the sharpened blade. "What do you have now? Fourteen years of bad luck?"

"Something like that." Carmelo smirks and I snicker.

"At least wait until Gionni DeRucci is back in Los Angeles." Ember shakes her head. "And I expect you to be paying the bill for those mirrors." She slaps the back of Carmelo's head.

Carmelo and I get up to leave when Ember calls Carmelo's name. "Tomorrow, I need you to sit quietly and keep your mouth shut, no matter what we say. Understood?" Her tone is firm, and I can see why everyone looks to her as the head of the family.

"Yes, ma'am." Carmelo nods.

Chapter Eighteen

My heart is in my throat as my fists land on the leather-encased punching bag. Right at this moment the Head meeting is happening, and this will decide if Gion leaves without issue or calls his father for the next step. He was hoping the Rampage would belong to him when his father stepped down and his brother, Rocco, took the throne. He said as much to me and my father, and he didn't like the prospect of having to deal with 'another Torres scum,' but now with Rocco out of the way and Gion gunning for that position, he'll probably want it all.

Carmelo's great-grandfather, Antonio, was the man who first joined ranks with the mafia and moved here to New York to widen their reach. It was his son, Raphael, who made relations a bit more difficult, and then Carmelo Senior brought Ember into the fold and she changed everything. They thought this was the end, that the Torres' hold in New York ended with her, and were angry when they found out that wasn't the case.

The worst part? They're beginning to suspect my father is the double agent he is and has plans to marry me off to Carmelo. No matter what goes down in the Head meeting today, I will be called back to California soon and they will force me to marry Gion. He's said as much, and even though it's not ideal for him, he'd rather it happen than for me to be married off to 'the sewer scum.' I didn't realize the DeRucci Family hated the Torres as much as Gion has said in the last few days, which puts a damper on any plans my father and I had to free us from their clutches.

The thought of having to go to Los Angeles and marry Gion, then live the rest of my life under their thumb, makes me sick. To have to do their bidding and pretend I love it or else be killed is not a life goal of mine. What's worse is if Don Julius gives him the throne, then I'll be trapped for sure. Regardless, I knew it was a likely outcome the longer it took for my father and Ember to actually cut ties. There's at least one thing I can take with me when I go, and that's the memories I have with the two men who own my heart. Once Gion leaves, I will be free to make more memories, and I won't waste time fighting with them. Or Carmelo, rather.

I can no longer avoid what my future will be, so I will have to just live my life in the last few moments I'll have here, then leave with no regrets. I will have to face the fact that when I leave, my heart will be left here too, and I will once again be the frigid Catalina Costa.

"Sweetheart." I turn toward the sound of my father's voice and find him leaning against the wall. "The next time you are called back to California, I will come with you."

He's never said that to me before, never just accepted we may never be free, and I can't help the tear that escapes my eye, trailing down over my cheek. This is further evidence that we will never be free.

"No, Papa." I shake my head. "You can't come with me. Ember and Carmelo will need you here."

"We have spent enough of our lives apart. I will come with you." His determination shines from his eyes and the sight of it only breaks my heart a little more.

I agree with him. We spent too much of our lives apart, and I would love nothing more than to have him in California with me, someone there who would care about my well-being and ensure that I am safe, but that could never be. They would just use him to keep me in line and make sure I stay the well-behaved little puppet. He can't come with me, and when the time comes, I will tell Gion that one stipulation. There's no point arguing with him now though, and besides, I want our time left together to be as peaceful as it can be.

"I have to tell you something that's changed." My mouth dries out a bit as his eyes narrow.

"What is it?"

"Rocco is gone for good. He doesn't want anything to do with the family and he's relinquished his right to the throne." Just saying the words out loud makes my stomach sour with trepidation.

"Julius doesn't trust Gionni, he wouldn't just hand it over." He straightens as his throat works on a swallow.

"You're correct. Gion told me Don Julius has been threatening to hand it all over to his uncle, Dante." Dad looks relieved, but I shatter that expression with my next sentence. "But there's a good chance he'll give it to me."

"Shit," he growls as his hands form fists.

"So, I guess that's it then?" I look at him. "There's no escaping them." I just want to hear him say it.

"Not in our lifetime." His voice is filled with pain and it breaks my heart.

Just when I was feeling the most optimistic I have ever felt, life took its final shit on my dreams.

CARMELO

"Let me get this straight." Gionni leans on the table. "You all go running around and kill all the bad guys in your cities? Like vigilantes?" He slaps the table. "Such an American notion."

I want to rip his fucking face off, but I can't deny I thought the same shit not too long ago. Anyone new sitting at this table would feel the same way, a bunch of men and women fighting crime and killing criminals. It sounds fucking funny.

I snort into my hand but make it loud enough so Gionni can hear it. I have a fucking plan of my own, and I know just how a man my age thinks. He looks at me in surprise and then humor lines his features.

"It's not a simple job being a pest exterminator." I think it's Head Two who sneers at Gionni.

I shake my head, making sure I keep the amused look on my face. "Honestly though, you ten against, what did you call it? Pests? I would say they multiply faster than you're killing them, no?"

Aunt Ember's jaw clenches and she avoids looking at me, but I can see she's pissed. She told me to sit here like an obedient little boy and listen, but I don't see how that would really take the heat off me. I think if I line my 'interests' up with the crime family's, then maybe I will stand a fucking chance.

"Yes." Gionni points at me, his eyes filled with pleasure. "He's right."

"Our reputations keep these kinds of people out of our cities," another Head answers.

"Oh, I see." Gionni nods condescendingly and waves

the table on.

The rest of the meeting is much of the same, and just to tighten Aunt Ember's noose around my neck, Gionni almost always asks for my opinions. I make sure I sound just as cold and calculated as he does. By the end of the meeting, I'm no longer feeling the cold, dismissive shoulder from Gionni, and I'm seeing some light at the end of the tunnel.

"Carmelo," Gionni says to me as the last Head leaves the room and it's him, me, and Aunt Ember left. "I will go back to California for a month. I have a wedding to plan, but I want to come back before then and maybe discuss some things with you…" He pointedly looks at Aunt Ember. "Alone."

I swear I hear her jaw crack as it tightens some more, and it takes all my efforts not to wince.

"Sounds good." I nod.

He holds out his hand and I give it a firm shake, then watch as he rises. Aunt Ember remains quiet until the door clicks shut behind him.

"I know what you were attempting to do there." She sounds calm, but I can hear the tremor of anger in her voice. "You may have fooled him, and I say may because they are raised to be master manipulators, but I can assure you his father will believe otherwise, and they will reward you with a knife slicing open your belly, only to watch your own intestines hit the floor."

I am shocked by her descriptive words, and speech abandons me as she leaves me alone in the boardroom.

A few hours later, I am sitting in Cameron's room waiting until Cat comes back from dropping Gionni off at the airport.

"Do you think it was stupid? My trying to play to his interests? He doesn't know me," I mumble to Cameron.

"No, I don't think it was stupid." He shakes his head, but he's deep in thought. "I get why you did it, but it's a risk and Ember is right. It all really depends on what his father believes anyway."

The door slams open and Cat's angry eyes land on me, fire spilling through their depths.

"You stupid fucking idiot," she growls and stomps over to me, her hands in fists, just waiting to pound into my face. "Did you think if you won Gion's favor, he would... what? Let me stay here? Save my father?"

"Cat..." I shake my head in confusion.

"Cat," she mocks me and fists her hair in her hands. "I have to marry him! And now he has this grand idea that he'll become the next Don because we'll be married! His brother is missing and doesn't want the title. He wants to run the Rampage with you as his second! You have got to be the stupidest motherfucker I know!"

"I won't let it get to that. We have a month..."

"To do what?!" she screams, and the noise makes both Cameron and me wince. "The same thing my father and I have been trying to do for my entire life?!"

Her chest is heaving and her face is red, the sight making my stomach sink with dread. Did I really fuck everything up? I wanted to take the heat off us, to give us some time to think up a plan, and without a death warrant on my head, I really thought we could do this. But now, hearing her say they've been trying for twenty years makes my blood run cold and my heart sputter inside my chest. I really fucked up.

"I just wanted to set their sights elsewhere for a while. Give us space to think up a plan." I sound so fucking stupid.

"I have three weeks and five days before my wedding." She sounds calm again, but it's deceiving. She's anything but. "And my wedding gift? To become the leader of the DeRuccis with my husband… and help run the Rampage with my two lovers!"

I can feel the pain in her words, and when she looks at me with tears in her eyes, it breaks my fucking heart. I can't stay in this room and be surrounded by her pain, feeling it heavy in the air and letting it drown me. I have enough of my own. Standing slowly, I walk up to her, her chest still rising and dropping, and those tears threatening to spill at any moment.

"I promise you, I won't let any of that happen." I grab her chin and press a chaste kiss to her lips.

I won't break my promise to her, and I know if I fail, I will gladly kill Gionni, forfeiting my life, because I know I'd rather be dead than to ever see her marry that piece of shit.

I leave Cameron's room, and both of them inside, hoping without me, she'll calm down. I have some fucking planning to do.

I don't head to my room though. It's Saxon I want to talk to.

CAMERON

"Fuck," Cat moans as she sits on my bed.

I have been frozen to this chair ever since she came in, and I still don't know how the fuck I'm feeling.

"I feel like everything I come into contact with just explodes, like I destroy everything," she whispers, the agony clear in her voice. "Maybe I'm just destined to be forever alone."

"Not if I can help it."

She looks over at me with tears streaming down her face and they stop, sitting precariously along her jawline. I can see the storm raging inside her, but I know she's afraid to let it go, fearful of the destruction it'll leave in its path.

I get up out of my seat and kneel in front of her, brushing my fingertips along those tears. "Carmelo is headstrong and impulsive, but he would do nothing to harm you intentionally. He's quick to anger and he thinks his ideas are foolproof, but he's passionate and I can see how crazy he is about you. Maybe his idea will work."

"How do you put up with us?" Her voice quivers as she fights against crying some more.

"You guys are crazy." I smirk as my thumb glides along her bottom lip. "But you set something in here ablaze." I tap my chest. "My life was a mess before and I had no direction. Carmelo gave me that. I was teetering on the edge and fucking random girls, trying to fill a void. Until you came along."

Her hands cup my face and she looks down at me with affection shining in her eyes. "I don't know how we got so lucky to deserve you, Cam. Carmelo and I are not easy people to love, and without you, I'm sure we'd never find balance." Then she bends down and kisses me softly.

Her eyes pop open when I pull her lip between my teeth. Then I release it and grin as her eyes darken with lust. I know I don't have a temper like Carmelo—my fists don't do my talking—and I'm not an aggressive person, but I love my sex rough, and Cat is about to find that out. I took it easy on her for her first time, but all bets are off the table now. I stand up and look down at her, the bulge in my jeans level with her mouth, and raise a brow.

Her eyes flick to it and then back up to me, a slight blush forming across her nose and cheeks. Her hands work at the button on my fly, and I hold in the chuckle as they shake. I'm about to show her just what balance she fucking needs.

She finally gets the zipper down and pulls down my boxers. As soon as my dick pops out, she eyes the piercing through the top, and I moan when her thumb brushes along it.

"Did this hurt?" she whispers, her thumb rubbing back and forth.

"Not as much as it's hurting for your mouth right now."

She licks those gorgeous plump lips and bends forward, wrapping them around the head. Her tongue comes out and flicks the ring, making me gasp at the contact. As much as I'm enjoying the tentative exploration, I need more, so I plunge my fingers into her thick black hair and bring her head forward, grinning when she gags.

"I want that throat working just as hard as that mouth, understand?" I demand and smile when she looks up at me in shock.

I tighten my hold on her hair, forcing her once again to my dick, and she moans as she swallows me down. The vibration and clenching of her throat makes me tip my head back, her name escaping my lips. This is what it's supposed to feel like, the connection and the soul-warming feeling of loving the person you're meant to. Sure, meaningless sex feels good, and coming is amazing, but nothing tops wanting to do that with the person made for you.

As I fuck her throat, I groan when tears soak her cheeks, her gasps for breath pushing me to the edge. I pull out of her mouth, not wanting to waste it there, and grab the condom from my jeans. I need to pound into her tight pussy, stretch it out, and make it squeeze the cum out of me. The overwhelming need to claim her and own her is just too much to ignore.

"Take your clothes off," I growl, and she stands.

We're both tossing clothes aside, and finally she's standing in front of me, her skin glistening as I roll the condom on. I cup her breast in my hand and bend forward, nipping at the hardened tip. Her nails dig into my back as she arches, enjoying the attention. Her tits are the perfect handful, and I press my cock against her stomach as I move to the other, sucking it into my mouth.

"Cameron," she moans. "Please."

I release her nipple and reach around her to grab her ass, and when the head of my cock bumps her entrance, she wraps her legs around my waist, gasping. I turn us both around and then lay back on the bed, keeping her on top. Her eyes widen as she sits up on me and her hands land on my chest.

"Cam, I've never done it like this," she pants.

"Obviously." I grin.

"I don't know…" She sucks her bottom lip into her mouth.

I grab her waist and lift her, clutching my cock in my hand. Then I line myself up and guide her to sink down over my length, the grip of her pussy killing me slowly. Our centers finally meet, and she wiggles forward, her gasp one of surprise.

"Cam." Her voice is hoarse. "You're so deep."

I guide her hips in a back and forth motion, making her moan. Her pussy floods around my cock and I grit my teeth as I try to keep it together. I want to last long enough to watch her let go around me. She finds her rhythm and I release her hips, folding my arms under my head. Her smooth motion is mesmerizing, and the way she circles her hips feels like heaven. It's when she lifts slightly, then plunges my cock inside of her over and over, that I lose my fucking cool. She increases the speed and I grab her hips just so I can hold it together.

"Right there," she rasps as she slams down on me. "Oh, fuck."

Her inner walls clench around me, and I know she's about to come. Thank fucking God. I press my thumb against her clit, and she detonates, screaming to the ceiling. The grip she has on my cock has me following right behind, her name rushing from my throat.

She collapses forward onto my chest, my cock still buried deep inside her, the last few pulses making us both groan. Our sweat sticks our skin together and our heartbeats become synchronized. When we finally breathe normally again, Cat leans up and looks down into my eyes. She looks sated and relaxed, making my chest swell with pride.

"Thank you for giving me balance," she whispers and kisses me softly. "I'm so glad I kissed you that night."

I roll my eyes and lift her off me, moving to the side of the bed. "That was a messy night."

"But so are the three of us, messy but perfect," she breathes out as she stretches. "I can see how sex can be so addictive. I can understand why you were fucking everyone."

"Excuse me?" I say as I toss the condom into the wastebasket.

She looks at me and flutters her lashes. "It's like test-driving until I find the right vehicle, right?"

I flip her over onto her stomach, and she squeals, trying to wiggle out of my grasp.

"Test-drive?" I clap my hand down on her ass and watch as my print blooms red against her skin.

"Cameron!" She looks over her shoulder with a shocked expression.

"You're lucky it wasn't your pussy again, although that's sounding like a good idea." I get off the bed and gather my clothes.

"It's just a joke," she huffs and rolls off the bed.

"I wouldn't play that joke on Carmelo," I warn, then laugh when I envision his rage.

"Yeah." She smiles and shakes her head. "I'd have a concussion for sure."

"You belong to us now." I turn and grab her chin. "Not to Gionni and not to the DeRuccis. Mine and Carmelo's. It's fucked, but so are we, and it'll work."

"Yeah, it will."

Chapter Nineteen

Carmelo

It's been three weeks now and everything is quiet, feeling almost normal—if you don't count the looming wedding date drawing nearer. In eight days, Cat will have to fly to Los Angeles and marry that fucking asshole, but it's never going to happen because if all else fails, it'll be me on that plane to greet her supposed husband and she can be safe here with Cameron.

Everything has been going smoothly and the three of us have found our rhythm. Cat and I still explode on each other, but Cameron is usually there to knock our heads together. When we spend time and hang out, it feels like this was always meant to be, and the connection I've had to Cameron our whole lives now makes sense.

"I don't want to watch Bad Boys," Cat whines and throws popcorn at Cameron.

"Too bad." He shrugs.

"Wait." She looks over at me. "We should vote, Carmelo. What do you want to watch?"

I know the three of us are trying to be normal and trying not to think about the impending fucking doom, but I don't want to waste time arguing over a fucking movie.

"I want to watch you stand right there"—I point to the middle of the room—"and take your clothes off."

"Carmelo." She rolls her eyes.

Cameron takes a seat beside me and quirks his brow at her. "I don't think he was joking."

She looks back and forth between our faces, a smile creeping over hers. "Fine." She drops the popcorn bowl to the floor and gets up, her long, toned legs striding to the center of the room. Today, she's dressed in a pair of short shorts and a tank top, showing just a hint of stomach between them. Her hair is down around her shoulders, and her face doesn't have a hint of makeup, just the way I like it.

Her hips circle around as her fingers curl into the hem of her top, gently pulling it up over her belly. Her red, lacy bra is on display as she tosses her shirt to the far corner, and her tits are pushed up to her fucking chin. Both Cameron and I shift in our seats and look at each other quickly. I bet we're both as hard as fucking stone. Her hands cup her tits, and she gives them a rough squeeze, making my mouth fill with saliva. I want those tits in my mouth.

Then her hands skim down over her stomach to grip the waistband of those shorts. I lean forward, not wanting to miss a thing and hoping to see if those panties match that bra. She doesn't disappoint as those shorts slide down her legs. I catch a flash of red lace, and my dick pounds against my zipper.

"Jesus fucking Christ," Cameron mumbles, and I nod in agreement, the motion slow.

She stands up straight, and we watch, entranced, as her hands run back up her sides, then around to her back, unclasping her bra. The straps fall from her shoulders and the fabric is pulled away from her breasts, her nipples hardening into points. She pinches both between her thumbs and forefingers, giving them a twist and moaning at the feeling.

I'm up out of my seat in the same instance as Cameron and we both advance on her. She continues to assault her perfect tits, and I move behind her as Cameron steps to her front, her ass round in my hand. I run a finger up between her ass cheeks and she gasps, clenching them tight together.

"Do you think it's time I explored this ass, Kitty Cat?" I ask her, and she shudders.

"I don't..."

"At the same time, I plunge my cock so far into that tight pussy," Cameron finishes, and she becomes a panting mess.

"At the same time?" The sound of her fear has my mouth lifting into a grin.

"Yes." I lick along the column of her throat. "Both of us fucking you so hard."

Cameron grabs her face and devours her mouth while I slip out of my jeans, rubbing my boxer-clad cock over her ass. While they are engrossed in each other, I head over to the table next to my bed and pull out the tube I bought a few weeks ago, anticipating this very moment.

Cameron backs up toward the bed, bringing a moaning Cat with him, and falls back with her landing on top of him. Their mouths are still fused when I walk around and stand in front of them, pulling her thong down over her ass. Once I have it off and on the floor, I groan at how wet her pussy is glistening in front of me, and I know I need a taste.

Bending forward, I pull her ass cheeks apart and run

my tongue from her clit to the tight rim of her ass. She pulls forward a bit with the contact, but I hold her still, my fingers digging into her globes. She tastes so fucking good, and there's been nothing as sweet as my Cat's cream. I suck her clit into my mouth and bury my face into her wet heat, moaning as her juices sluice down my chin. I release her clit and move back up to her ass, running my tongue around her puckered hole. Cameron shucks off his boxers and mine isn't far behind. Reaching over and into the drawer, I grab two condoms, one for him and one for me. Since that one time in the bathroom, Cat has been adamant we wear protection until she's on birth control.

I roll the condom down my shaft as Cameron lowers Cat's tight pussy down over his length. They both groan as I pump my cock and grab the tube of lube off the bed. I open the cap and squirt some onto my fingers, working it over her hole, making sure it's well lubricated. As soon as the head of my cock touches her rear entrance, she stills and looks back at me over her shoulder.

"Relax," I soothe her as I nudge forward, the tight ring of muscle giving under my onslaught.

"Oh, my God," she breathes out as Cameron halts inside of her.

I thrust again and finally breach the entrance, my cock slowly moving inside. It's almost unbearably tight as I work my way to the hilt, feeling Cameron on the other side of the thin barrier, and then both of us move together.

"Fuck, that's so hot," she whispers.

As soon as I bottom out, Cameron pulls out, and as he pushes back in, I pull out.

"Holy shit," Cat pants as she turns herself over to the

pleasure we're giving her.

I can feel Cameron rubbing against me on the inside and Cat tightening around me, the sensations driving me closer to the edge.

"Fuck," she moans, and I feel her pulsing, gripping us both through her orgasm.

"Yes," Cameron grits out as he slams up into her, his cock throbbing against mine.

I get a better hold on her hips and pull almost all the way out, watching as her asshole tries to suck me back in. She screams at my brutal thrust, her orgasm still rippling through her. I yank on the back of her hair, pulling her head back and sinking my teeth into her shoulder.

"Tell me what it feels like," I demand as I pull out and slam in harder.

Her mouth is open on a soundless scream as I tighten my hold on her hair, making her whimper with pain.

"It hurts," she whispers just as I slam inside her again. "It hurts so fucking good."

"Play with her clit," I instruct Cameron, and he grins at me.

"I can't again." She tries to fight against the hold I have on her hair without success. "It's too much."

"You will come again," I say as I grunt and grind against her ass, my cock so fucking deep inside. "And your asshole is going to milk the cum out of me."

I let go of her hair, grab both of her ass cheeks in my hands, and spread her open, watching my cock disappear inside her. Cameron is still working her clit as a few sobs escape

Cat. Her head shakes back and forth, her cries making me stop moving to keep from coming.

"Is she crying for me?" I ask Cameron, who chuckles and nods. "Give me some."

He takes the same fingers he was just stroking her pussy with and runs it down her cheek, collecting those tears. Then he holds them out for me, and I suck his fingers into my mouth, tasting the salt mixed with her pussy.

"Get back to work." He slips his hand back down between them, doing as I command.

She moans, and her pants increase as I begin my punishing rhythm once again. I can feel the tingle as it works its way up my balls, spearing into my shaft. I need to come, but I refuse to until she's a sobbing mess and clenching around my cock.

"Please, Carmelo, no, I can't." Her breath hitches as she whines, her pussy pulsing softly.

"You're almost there."

"No, it's too much." Her words end on a sob as I pound into her.

Regardless of her cries and tears, she does indeed give me what I've been demanding. She lets loose a scream and her ass clamps down on me, making thrusting impossible. I grind into her until she is reduced to snivels and thrust into her once more, coming so deep my vision blackens.

Cat falls forward on Cameron and I pull out of her, watching as her rear hole shrinks back down. I'm almost tempted to play with it some more until I'm hard again, but when I hear Cameron chuckle, I look up as he points down at Cat on his chest. She's snoring softly as the tears dry on her cheeks and her hands are folded under her face. She looks like an angel.

Cameron lifts her off and I turn around to get dressed, hearing him do the same.

"I have another Head meeting tomorrow," I reveal as I pull my sweater on.

"I have to go back to Toronto tomorrow," he replies. "I have finals." He's been here more than there, and I know he just wants to pass those exams and move here permanently. "Has Ember figured out who the mole could be?"

"If she has, she hasn't told me." Aunt Ember is still pissed at me for the stunt I pulled during the last meeting and hasn't really been back since. Except to see her son.

"What about Trent?" he presses as he grabs a bottle of water out of my fridge.

"I think he's just as much in the dark as I am." I shake my head. "He's just accepted his daughter will marry that piece of shit and they'll just move on."

"That's what he's projecting anyway," Cameron mumbles, then takes a few gulps of water.

"Yeah." I look back at Cat and feel my heart twist inside my chest. I would do anything for her. "No one's taking her."

"Is this the position you plan on making a permanent one?" Head Four asks, his wrinkled hands folding together. "Or do you still want to be a fighter?"

"This position was entrusted to me by my aunt, and I am honored to carry on under my family's name. Fighting is a hobby, which I will continue in my own time."

"What are your plans for us? What should we be expecting under a Carmelo rule?" he continues, his questioning unsettling me.

"I will not be changing the course of what my aunt has sent forth. I believe in this cause, and this isn't a Carmelo rule, it's a Torres rule. As it always has been."

My answer seems to placate my aunt, who has a slight smile on her face. Maybe she's been waiting for me to stand up for myself, be the leader she appointed, and show I can have a backbone when I need it. What pissed her off the last time was my giving in to the DeRucci Family and acting like Gionni was higher than me. I can see where I fucked up. I won't let that impression last much longer though. It's time I take the helm and relieve Aunt Ember of the burden.

"I would like to reconvene this meeting in three weeks' time. I believe we will have a serious discussion about current members and possibly new ones." There's a gasp that runs through the room, but it's the pride in my aunt's eyes that's telling me this is what she was waiting for.

I wave my hand, dismissing the table, and watch each of them carefully as they leave, seeing if anything stands out. The door shuts behind the final Head, and I turn to look at my aunt.

"There's a mole, that much we are sure of, correct?"

"Mm-hmm." She nods.

"By the questions alone, I had my eye on Four." She nods again and waits for me to carry on. "But what I really noticed was Three, and how her facial expression hardened when I spoke about the Torres line continuing. It was slight, but I saw it."

"I'm impressed." She reaches out and ruffles my hair. "We've had our eye on Four at first too, and it was a waste of time. He wasn't the problem, but recently Three has been lacking slightly in the communication behind the scenes. I'm impressed you deduced a suspicion from our two-hour meeting of what we gathered in a year of extensive digging."

"Sometimes, when you are around a person for so long, you don't pick up on the little things anymore. Maybe with them all being so new to me, I could see it."

"Yes, most likely," she agrees, giving me a tap to the cheek.

"What's the plan?" She knows I'm asking about Cat and Trent's situation. If we continue to do nothing, we won't only be losing Cat, but Aunt Ember will lose Trent.

Her face falls, and she looks at me from the side of her eye. "We need a bit more time."

"Cat gets married next week."

"Yeah." She nods and says nothing more.

"So, that's it? Let her be sacrificed?" I ask, astonished.

"There's this great thing called divorce, and even though it can be frowned upon, many people use it."

"It's not about that, it's about handing her over to them!" I grab a fistful of my hair.

"Carmelo." Her hand rests on my arm. "She can take care of herself, and she knows the ins and outs there. She was raised by the Family and Don Julius himself."

"I can't let that happen to her." I can feel the burn of

emotion behind my eyes and try to breathe.

"You have his savior gene," she mutters, and I'm shocked to see tears building in her eyes.

"What?"

"Your father and I didn't have the greatest relationship. It started with me hating him, and for most of it, he didn't trust me. But he was raised that way, not to trust anyone, and having the father we did only proved that to be true for family as well. He never knew his mother and was made to believe she was a prostitute, who died shortly after he was born." Aunt Ember sits back in her seat and rubs her finger across her chin. "Then he learns his mother might be alive, but she's working to take down his very new sister."

"You."

"Yes, me." She frowns as her eyes gain this faraway look. "The woman's name was Jennifer Talia, and Carm wanted a mother so badly, he did everything that was asked of him. I almost died during a fight because of it. My aunt and uncle…" She swallows thickly. "They died because of it. Then we learn this woman was actually my grandmother, Jenna, and that she was in fact not Carm's mother."

"Jenna? But why would she do all that?" I press her.

"A lot of it was another's influence." She waves her hand. "It's a long story, but most of the things that happened were done by Carm, and what he thought were the right things to do. He felt badly about it and confessed his involvement in a letter he left in my mailbox the day he died. I believe he went into that situation knowing he would die so I could live, and I can see that same quality in you."

I would do that for Catalina in a heartbeat. I would die if I knew she'd live a long, happy life because of it, and I can't help but feel a connection to my father for the first time in my life. I know he didn't just make that decision because of the guilt he felt. He made it because of the love he felt, and he knew his life wouldn't be as fulfilling as his sister's.

It makes complete sense to me.

Chapter Twenty

Catalina

It's been quiet today, and it's the first day that I've really been alone in the past few weeks. Cameron had to go back to Toronto for finals and Carmelo is in a Head meeting. I look at the clock beside my bed and my forehead crinkles in thought. It should've been done two hours ago. I guess his Aunt Ember wanted to talk to him, but it feels like a rock is settling in the pit of my stomach because she probably wants to discuss my upcoming nuptials.

Gion has been messaging me all week, and now whenever I hear the ping of a message, I feel like throwing up. It's even more disturbing how often he asks about Carmelo and wondering if he should invite him too. I have maintained I hate Carmelo, but I think that only intrigues Gion more, so I wouldn't be surprised if he does indeed invite him just to see the hatred. He feeds off people's discomfort and loves to watch drama unfold.

I roll out of my bed—which is another place I haven't been in a few weeks—and decide to pass my time in the gym. After working out almost every day and then slacking for a week straight, my muscles are screaming at me with the agony they want to feel. I don't know what Carmelo is doing, and besides, he'll know where to find me if I'm not in my room.

There aren't many places to be down here in the compound anyway. I dress in some short shorts and a sports bra, then tie my hair up into a high bun. Before I get to the gym, I put my earbuds in. I need the extra kick-start.

Thankfully it's empty, and I start with a light jog on the treadmill. A little warm-up is all I need and then I jack up the speed, getting lost in my run and the music blasting into my ears. I forget the worry about my wedding and having to go back to California, and I bury down deep the sorrow I'll feel when I leave the people I love behind. There's nothing I can do to stop this shit from happening, but I can hope Carmelo and Cameron move on. I don't want them to ever feel like they failed me, because in reality, it was me who failed them. I failed my father too. He wanted his only family to be here with him, not in California playing a warrior for the DeRuccis and constantly worrying about me, but there's nothing I can do now.

I hate feeling helpless, and the thoughts running through my mind are only fueling my anger. I wanted to find a way out, and maybe if these past few weeks were spent planning instead of fucking, I would've. No, I can't think like that, because the two men who have been worshipping my body and loving me completely are exactly what I needed before I had to start my life of servitude.

I can feel the tingles of someone watching me run down the back of my neck, so I slow down the machine to a jog once more, doing a quick look over my shoulder. Carmelo is leaning against the wall just inside the door, watching me run, a thoughtful expression on his face. I turn off the music and continue to jog, waiting for him to say something. Anything.

"I think I know who the mole is," he finally speaks.

"Oh, yeah?" I don't want to hurt him, but it's on the tip

of my tongue that it's kind of too late.

"Some old lady."

I say nothing because hearing that maybe the mole was found is going to do nothing for the situation we'll find ourselves in this time next week. I nod and continue to jog, the sweat sliding down my back in rivulets.

"Don't you care?" He sounds angry, and that only ignites something inside me.

"I cared from the moment I learned my mother was killed because of the DeRucci Family!" I scream and jump off the moving treadmill. "The past ten years of my life I dedicated to training and avenging her, and I cared for the last month when I should've been figuring this shit out instead of fucking you!"

His lips thin out as he pulls it back against his white teeth and growls, "Instead of fucking me?"

"Yes! Look now! I'm still going to Los Angeles, and I'll still be a good little soldier for the Family. Fucking you got me nothing but memory loss."

He stalks forward and grabs the front of my sports bra, his chest heaving with angry breaths. I immediately regret every angry word I've said when I see the hurt flash in his black eyes. I know my mouth can run on sometimes and I can't control the things that rush out of it, but this time I really used them like weapons.

"You don't know what I've been doing while you just enjoyed our dicks these past few weeks!" he roars, and once again, my regret is swept aside at his words, being quickly replaced with red fiery anger.

"Oh, yeah?" I scream into his face. "Was it fucking that

blonde bitch? Because I don't see any changes for anything else!"

I'm thrown against the wall, and the color red pulses in my vision, my muscles tensing and readying for a fight. I throw my foot back and connect with his knee, his grunt of pain egging me on further. His front pushes against my back, and my face is pressed into the wall, not an inch of space separating us.

"You want to say anything else?" He rips down my shorts, the waistband settling under my ass cheeks.

"No," I grit out and try to squirm out from between him and the wall.

"Nothing else?"

"Oh, I have a lot to say, but I don't want you touching me," I snarl, then gasp when his hand cracks on my ass cheek. "No!" I scream, and his hand covers my mouth.

"No, what?" he taunts against my cheek. "No to this?" He presses his hardened cock against my ass. I want him, I always will, but I don't want this right now and not in here.

I shake my head, his hand moving with it, and struggle against his hold. His hand moves from my mouth to wrap around the nape of my neck, pressing me harder into the wall.

"Shhhh," he coos directly into my ear. "Someone might hear and then they'll see me defiling the virgin Cat."

"Stop, Carmelo, I don't want this." I push my ass back against him, trying to create some space, and feel the velvet smooth skin of his cock.

"You don't want this now? Oh? Is it because you're getting married soon?" He runs the head of his cock along the seam of my pussy, and I hate myself for being wet.

"You're going to rape me?" Maybe hearing that will get him the fuck off me.

"We both know this isn't rape, and you could get out of this if you wanted to." He pushes inside me, and I bite my lip to stop the moan. "I'm about to fuck you so hard, your new husband will know I've been here."

I could get out of it, but that would be injuring him in the process. As fucked-up as this moment is, I don't want to hurt him.

He releases my neck and grabs my hips in his hands, propping up my ass, then pulling my shorts down more. I don't fight him, but it feels shameful, and I can't even fight the tears that run down my cheeks. He's completely given up on me and this is his final farewell fuck before I'm handed over to the DeRuccis.

He shoves himself all the way in, and luckily, I'm wet enough to nearly enjoy it. I'm too caught up in my feelings of anger and sorrow to fully like what he's doing though. There's no discomfort, but it's not exactly enjoyable either.

He continues thrusting into me, my cheek scraping along the wall and his grunting loud in the otherwise quiet room. I pray it's over quickly just in case my father comes looking for me, because this is where he'd check first.

"Nothing?" Carmelo spits out. "Have you already forgotten what my cock does for you? Anticipating the new cock you're going to be riding?"

Fuck, that burns. Those words seep through my skin and turn my heart to ash. How can he be this cruel when he's inside of me? Does he feel nothing for me? Was everything a fucking lie? My throat tightens, and I can tell I'm on the verge of sobbing, but I just don't want to give him the fucking pleasure.

His thrusts slow and he slams in forcefully once more before pulling all the way out.

"Fuck you," he sneers before I hear him pulling up his pants. "You're not fucking worth it." The pure vitriol in his words breaks my fucking heart, and in the next instant, sets my blood to a boil.

"I hate you!" He walks to the door and I scream at his back, "I never want to see you again!"

"It's all good, Kitty Cat," he croons. "I'm gonna go find me that blonde. Maybe she can finish me off."

It's like the final nail in the coffin as I'm standing here in complete shock with my shorts down around my knees. The door shuts behind him, and I finally release the sob that's been festering inside my chest. That's it, it's over, and then I feel my heart completely incinerate.

I pull up my shorts and feel my phone vibrate from the holder strapped around my arm. I pull it out, my hand shaking, and swipe open the message.

Gion: There's a flower delivery guy waiting upstairs. One more week, fiancée.

He's becoming more obnoxious as we get closer to our wedding date. It's annoying and becoming harder to tolerate his fiancée digs. I shove the phone back into its holder and pull myself together. People have been through worse than this. People get stronger from shit like this. I wipe the lingering tears off my face and take a few deep breaths. Carmelo is the least of my worries. I have to go upstairs and receive flowers sent by the man I don't want to marry and pretend I'm happy about it.

The elevator ride is as rickety as ever and I decide to tell my father when I get back down to look into fixing it. I open the garage door and look into the parking lot. The sun's glare cuts into my eyes, and I try to shield it with my hand. Downfall of living underground.

Hands come around my waist and another set to grab my own. I'm shocked and frozen for about two seconds, and then I'm into action. The first thing I do is snap my head back to catch whoever is behind me in the face. My hands are released, and I turn to my side to see the guy grabbing my waist, looking shocked just before my fist slams into his nose.

The blood sprays, and I turn on the guy behind me, my fist hitting his stomach. They're both backing away from me, but I follow them, not quite done with releasing my aggression.

"Cat!"

I turn abruptly at the sound of Gion's voice and once again shade my eyes. "What the fuck?" I call out. "Did you try to kidnap me?"

"I wanted to see if I could get the drop on you." He grins like this whole thing is amusing.

"I could've killed them!" I thumb at the two groaning, useless sacks of shit behind me. "That's a great way to start a surprise visit before our wedding."

"That's why I'm here." He holds out his arms. "Let's go." He nods toward the blacked-out sedan.

"What?" I crinkle my brows in confusion.

"I came to get you early! Surprise! Now, let's go."

I look down at my attire and back up at him with my brow raised. "Gion, I need clothes and to tell my father."

"Text him in the car, and I have closets of clothes for you in Los Angeles. Let's go."

I look back at the garage door and the elevator inside. There's really nothing that's keeping me here, and I did want to leave without giving my father a chance to come with me, so I walk to the door and reach inside, hitting the switch to close it. Why not get the fuck out of here?

Then I walk to the car and punch the guy, whose nose I broke, in the side. "Never think you can take me. I'll kill you next time."

He hobbles to another car parked around the corner as the second guy gives me a wide berth on his way there too. Pussies.

I stand in front of Gion, and he pulls on the ends of my hair, something he's done since we were kids. I can feel myself choking up. Maybe marrying him wouldn't be so bad, and at least it's someone I know.

Suddenly, Cameron's face runs through my mind, and I swallow back a sob. He doesn't deserve this, but I know if he had to choose, it would always be Carmelo. He said so from the very beginning. Besides, I don't want to be the one who tears them apart.

Gion bends and gets into the backseat, sliding all the way over. I give the compound one last look and then I'm climbing in after him, closing the door behind me. They lock right away, and I get a weird feeling. I turn to look at Gion, who's staring at me intently.

Then he holds out his hand. "Phone."

"What?"

"Give me your phone."

I curse and hand it over to him, trying to keep the peace while figuring out what the fuck his problem is. He opens my phone and I watch as he brings up my father's contact, sending him a goodbye text. I would've liked to do it myself, but that's fine. I'll just call him later.

"Ready to go, Kitty Cat?" The last part is an angry whisper as his fist slams into my temple.

Just before everything goes dark, I have one thought.

Did he just call me Kitty Cat?

CARMELO

Fuck.

I have a fucking defect.

I turn to leave my room and head back to the gym. I don't know how that got so out of hand. The guilt is eating me alive because I know she doesn't deserve what I did.

The gym is deserted, the silence suffocating me. Of course it is. Why would she still be here? I turn and look straight ahead at the elevator and see it's lit up on the top floor. Would she go up top? Or back to her room? It could literally be anyone up there, but something is telling me to go check.

I hit the button to call the elevator down and suddenly have an anxious feeling, like it's moving too slow. My vision tunnels as the doors open and I rush inside, slapping the top floor button frantically. Something bad is happening, and my heart feels like it's going to jump out of my fucking chest. I hope I'm wrong and came up here for no reason and my Cat is down in her room, crying over my behavior. I will go right back down there and beg her to forgive me, then spend hours showing her just how much I care.

My fist hits the button and I scream in frustration at the panel. Why the fuck do we still have this slow-ass elevator? My first actual change around here will be a new fucking elevator. The doors squeak open, the metal scraping along the track at a snail's pace, and I squeeze through the opening just as the garage door hits the concrete floor. Someone is out there. I run to the door opener and slam my palm against the large red button, watching in agony as the door slowly rolls up. The next thing after the elevator is a new fucking door.

It finally opens enough for my body to bend and slip

outside, and I catch two blacked-out sedans turning out of our parking lot. This isn't strange because the Rampage owns like ten of the same cars, the same color and tint on the windows, and I know it could be anyone leaving on a job, but my gut is telling me it's not just anyone. My feet buzz with energy, making me want to chase them down, and my heart is still beating out a quick rhythm. The cars turn out and I watch until their taillights disappear down the street.

Then I step back inside and shut the door, watching it slowly roll down. My heart breaks like I've lost the most important thing in my life, and I know I won't be able to shake that feeling until I go back down and see Cat. I press the button for the elevator and the ding sounds right away, the doors opening at what seems to be a faster rate than when I came up here. Once I'm in the elevator, I press the button for the bottom floor, the anxiety inside my chest still making me feel like I'm on the edge of a breakdown.

The doors slide open, and I waste no time running down the corridor to Cat's room. I slide in front of her door and open it without knocking first. It's empty. Her bed is still rumpled, looking like she just rolled out of it, and her pajamas are thrown over her chair. I open the small closet and see her suitcase, her clothes still hanging on hangers. My speeding heart calms a bit at the sight, and I head into her bathroom next. Her creams and shampoo are still lining the counter and inside her shower. She hasn't left.

I exhale all the anxiety and now just feel an overwhelming feeling of guilt. After walking back into her bedroom, I curl up on her bed, covering my face with her blankets. I breathe in her scent and decide to wait here for her, taking the risk of being killed on sight.

"What are you doing in here?"

I open my eyes and groan, looking around a room that's not my own. My eyes swing to Trent, who's leaning against the doorjamb, his eyebrow raised and jaw clenched in annoyance.

"Where is she?" I sit up and realize Cat didn't come back to her room.

"I would imagine almost in California by now and getting ready to marry the heir to the DeRucci Family."

"What?" I jump out of her bed and stride toward him. "What did you say?"

"I received her text about five hours ago saying she was on her way to California to marry Gionni DeRucci. I tried calling a few times, but she's not answering."

"But all her stuff is here." I look around the room, something nagging at me and my brain working hard to put the pieces together.

"Probably because they plan on coming back and figuring out how to run this organization with you. Or have you forgotten that little detail?" He sounds pissed, and I understand, but right now he's the least of my worries.

I hit my hands against my pants pockets, feeling for my phone, and remembering I left it in my room. I push by Trent and quickly cross the hall.

"I thought you and Cameron would've convinced her to stay since you made a woman out of her and all," he continues as he follows behind me.

Ignoring him, I grab my phone and search through messages and call logs. Nothing. Cat hasn't even tried to contact me. I sit on the bed and hang my head. Why would she? But maybe she would call Cameron? I pull up his contact and hit send, knowing it's a busy time for him, but this can't wait.

"Bro." He sounds tired. "I had just fallen asleep."

"Have you heard from Cat?"

"What?" He sounds like he's awake now. "What the fuck did you do, Torres?"

"Listen." I take a deep breath. "We… Ah…" I look up at Trent. "Look, did she call you or message you?"

"No," he snarls, and I can hear the rustle of his blankets. "Where is she?"

"California."

"I knew when I left that you would fuck it all up. I just knew it. Why are you like fucking children when I'm not there? Is this the way it's always going to be? I have an exam tomorrow." I listen to his rant, absorbing it and taking it in because I deserve it.

"How many exams are left?" I ask in a quiet voice.

"It's the last one. I'm going to call her and then I will see you the day after tomorrow." He hangs up the phone, and I lower it from my ear, staring down at the screen.

"Nothing?" Trent presses, and I shake my head. "I didn't think so. I guess we'll all see her when she's a married woman." His words pierce my heart, and he gives a quick rap on my door before he disappears down the corridor.

I call her number and clench my teeth when it goes straight to voicemail. She turned it off. I throw my phone down on the bed and fall back with it, watching the ceiling fan rotate. It's irrational and I know I deserve everything that's happening, but I am fucking pissed. Why does she always run off when we fight? It's what we do, doesn't she realize that?

This is us! Maybe it's better off though, maybe this Gionni asshole can give her stability I will never give and maybe they will live out their days in a passionless marriage of convenience while I fight my way through my emotions.

Fight.

That's exactly what I need right now. I text my Uncle Emmett quickly and ask him to set something up here for tomorrow night. He gets back to me with a thumbs-up and I feel a smile stretch over my face. I feel bad for my opponent because he'll be taking the brunt of my anger, but I can't muster up an ounce of pity for it.

Chapter Twenty-One

I walk out of school for the last time and curse when her voicemail sounds in my ear. Thirty-seven times I've heard her voicemail, all the while hoping she's turned on her phone and is reading my twenty-one messages. I don't know what Carmelo has done and I don't want to hear about it until I'm in front of his face, in line with my fists if need be.

Me: I'm heading there now. I'll be there around ten.

Saxon: Perfect time for Carmelo's fight. See you then.

Fight? He lined up a fight for tonight like nothing happened? Like he didn't just chase our girl off to California to marry some mafia maniac? I am going to kill the motherfucker when I get there. He better pray I get there after his fight or else he won't be able to stand, let alone beat the shit out of someone.

The parking lot is filled, so it takes me ten minutes just to find a place to park. I am exhausted and running on fumes.

After studying and barely sleeping, then finding out about Cat, I might've slept two hours in the last twenty-four. I can feel the exhaustion in my bones, but I know sleep won't be coming for me until I have some answers. I text Saxon to come up and let me in, waiting beside the garage door.

A few minutes later, the doors open, and he stands there with a small smirk on his mouth. "His fight is just starting."

"Then he's lucky," I growl and step inside. Even from up here, I can hear the dull roar of the crowd. Sounds like a big turnout. "What do you know about this?" I ask him as we step into the elevator.

"I know Cat is in California with her fiancé and Carmelo is blaming himself for it," he answers quickly as we descend.

"As he should," I snap.

"Perhaps." Saxon side-eyes me. "Perhaps not."

"What do you mean?"

"I don't know what happened between them, but I know Cat was always supposed to marry Gionni. So this isn't a surprise."

"We were working on a plan to get her out," I inform him.

"Yeah, you didn't have one though." He's right, so logically, we should've known this was always going to happen.

"Right," I murmur and follow him off the elevator.

We head toward the ring and the screaming crowd, which only makes my already pounding head worse. I wanted to be done with exams and get back here to be with Cat and plan the rest of our lives. I thought we still had time. We enter the arena and people are on their feet, screaming for Malice. I don't see the cage at all until I'm halfway down, and when I do, I roll my eyes.

Carmelo is bleeding from a gash in his cheek and he's a bit wobbly on his feet. "Did he drink beforehand?" I press Saxon.

"Yep."

Would explain the excessive blood and unsteady stance. Maybe his opponent will do us both a favor and kick his fucking ass.

"He's been staring at the bottom of a whiskey bottle since last night. Talking about how the three of you were perfect and he ruined it." We sit in the front row just as Carmelo takes another punch to the face. "Were you and him together also? Because that's like, illegal, maybe?"

"First off, we are only like a smidge related, and second, no."

"Should've just led with the no part, defending how little you're related sounds really sketchy. Like kissing cousins, ya know?"

"You're fucking sketch," I retort and roll my eyes.

He shrugs and we both settle in to watch the bloodbath. Well, Carmelo's anyway. He's got another cut through his lip, and every time he smiles, blood runs down over his chin. This is reminiscent of our high school days when he would take a beating before snapping and beating his opponent into the ground. Although right now, it doesn't look like he's anywhere near snapping. Honestly, this looks like a fucking punishment.

"He wants this guy to kick his ass!" I yell into Saxon's ear as the crowd boos. Carmelo is knocked to the mat, his back bouncing.

"Yeah." Saxon nods, a crease forming between his brows. "Someone should let him know he still has a chance to get Cat back."

I look at Saxon closely and let his words penetrate my sleep-fogged brain. He's right. Even if she marries the shit, it's not a life sentence, and when she gets back here, we're claiming her. I get up out of my seat and head to the cage. Carmelo's opponent is leaning against the wire, and he looks down at me.

"Hey!" I holler to him, and he crouches to hear me, his eyes on a laughing Carmelo who's still on his back. "He's drunk and not in any shape to fight. How about a rematch when the win will be worth it?"

He seems to mull it over and finally looks back down at me. "I take the money though."

"Yeah." I nod. Seems reasonable.

"Cool."

I walk over to Emmett, who's standing at the door of the cage, screaming at a hysterical Carmelo, and I nudge his shoulder.

"It's over." I stare him down. "This was a fucking stupid idea. Let the guy out and give him his money."

"Fuck." He slaps his hand against the cage. "This is going to fuck with his streak."

"This should've never been planned," I fire back. "This is the problem with you being his coordinator but living in Whitsborough. With all due respect, you're fired. Stop wasting the time you could have with your family by dealing with this asshole." I point at Carmelo, who is now on all fours.

"I didn't know he was this fucked-up."

"Because you're not here." I shrug, the anger leaving me. "Open the cage and head home. I got this from here."

He gives me a once-over and nods. "Yeah, looks like you do."

The cage is opened, and the opponent steps out, giving me a quick nod. The crowd is booing, and I send word up to the emcee to clear the place out, promising a full refund at the door.

I step into the cage and find Carmelo standing in the center, swaying on his feet. He looks pissed, and I'm hoping he tries to deck me because I really need to kick his ass. His temper, his words, and his fucking attitude have always gotten us into situations over the years, but I'm at my fucking end. I walk up to him and we stare at each other eye to eye, his jaw working. Then, shockingly, his arms are around my neck and his weight is thrown against me.

"She's gone," he moans, and his body shakes with the force of his cry. "I drove her away."

The anger I have is still there, but I can't ignore his pain because it mirrors my own. I know he needs me, so I wrap my arm around his waist and help him to the cage door. Saxon meets me there and grabs Carmelo's other side, both of us half walking/half dragging him to the back room.

"Should've let that guy coat the mat in my blood," he groans as his chin falls against his chest.

"Yeah, we should've," I retort.

We get him up to the room and drop him down onto the bench. He moans and drops his head back against the lockers, blood still running off his chin.

"I'm just like him," he mumbles, and Saxon looks at

me.

"Like who?" I ask.

"My father, the real one."

"How so?" I press him.

"He fucked everything up, destroyed people's lives, and even caused deaths." He takes a shuddering breath. "And in the end, he fucking paid for it willingly."

I don't know what mistakes he's talking about, and from what I know, his father was killed in a shoot-out. He's not making any sense. Saxon grabs a towel and cleans his face while I grab the butterfly bandages. Once we have him cleaned up, he looks better, and I can notice the deep dark circles under his eyes. He hasn't slept either.

"Let's go to the hall and see what there is to eat," Saxon suggests.

Carmelo stands on his own, and even though he looks a bit more sober, his melancholy is worse. We head toward the hall, noticing there's not much of a party tonight since Carmelo threw the match, but there are some die-hard fans who scream his name when we walk in. Carmelo waves at them as we head to the line.

I grab him a salad and a chicken breast, much to his disappointment. Although, I let it slide when he grabs a brownie. The asshole needs some joy right now. We sit at a table and Saxon brings three beers with him. This place really needs to start carding and stop giving alcohol to minors. It'll make no difference though because he's the boss' son.

"Do you think we need those right now?" I ask him with my brow raised.

"Yep," Carmelo says just before he tips the bottle to

his mouth and chugs the whole thing back.

"Great," I grind out. "At least eat too."

Saxon leans on the table and looks between Carmelo and me. "How are we getting her back?"

"What?" I look at him, and Carmelo's eyes narrow.

"We would need an army, or a fucking group of assassins, to sneak into the place," Carmelo grits out, lifting his hand for another beer.

"What if I said the second option is a possibility?" Saxon leans forward, lowering his voice.

"I think I heard you wrong." I shake my head. "Did you say assassins are a possibility?"

"You didn't tell him what my mom does." Saxon looks at Carmelo with annoyance.

"How was I going to start that conversation?" Carmelo snaps.

"Hold on." I put my hand up between them. "What about your mother?"

"Aunt Ember is a hired hit man," Carmelo reveals, sounding slightly bored.

"She's an assassin," Saxon corrects with an excited gleam in his eyes. "She wears skull makeup when she's on a job too. It's fucking sick. A Sugar Skull to be exact."

"Sugar Skull?" I feel like my brain is swimming with the information, but I'm too tired to fully absorb it.

"More decorative than a normal skull." Carmelo takes a swig of his beer. "It sounds like it would be creepy to see."

Saxon nods eagerly and looks between the both of us.

"Let's send assassins!"

"First off…" I rub my hands into my eyes. "It's assassin, as in one, and second, Ember won't be able to do this on her own."

The table falls silent, and Saxon gets up, meandering over to the jukebox. Carmelo props his head up on his hand and stares at me, waiting for the shit he's suspecting I want to give to him.

"You knew that about Ember and didn't tell me?"

"Yeah." He nods. "I was meaning to, but shit just keeps happening. I didn't know about the makeup part though. That's fucking scary."

"Bro, she is scary."

He hums in agreement as the music in the room switches and I'm suddenly assaulted by an Elvis Presley song. What the fuck? I turn and find Saxon on his way back, his shoulders bouncing as he sways with the rhythm.

"Why are you playing Elvis?" I growl at him, and he snorts.

"It's called 'Kissin' Cousins'." He points between me and Carmelo.

"Lame," I retort, but I can feel a smile taking over.

"I can't do this right now." Carmelo stands from his seat and scrubs a hand down his face. "I just need to be alone."

Saxon and I watch him leave the hall, his head hanging in defeat.

"This is a terrible fucking song." I give him a look and he begins to snap his fingers.

"I think it's catchy, actually." He whistles along with the tune, and I crinkle my face in disgust.

Fucking weirdo.

CARMELO

I let the scalding hot water hit my head and roll down my back, watching the water drain with a tinge of pink. I can feel my sobriety coming back, and with it, the fucking overwhelming guilt. Everything is my fucking fault. My actions, the things I thought to be true, and the words I used to hurt her were all my fault.

I miss her.

I run my bloody, swollen knuckles under the water and then tip my face up, letting the sting of pain remind me of what I deserve. There's something inside Cat that twists around my anger and coils it out of me. I know I do the same to her, and no matter how hard we try to fight it, we will always end up the same way. But there's no denying the pull, the need to be with her, around her, inside her. I have felt nothing like it, and I know I will feel nothing like it again. She was my one chance at passion.

Passion that burns so intensely I leave with wounds after. Wounds of blistering heat and pain that are almost unbearable until I'm with her again. It's dangerous, explosive, and lethal, but I can't live without it. I would rather be subjected to the agony of her love than to live my life without the pain. Who wants their days to be boring routines? When she denies me, I want to fight her and I want to love her. I don't deserve it, but I want to. I want to be the man she turns to when she needs that fire and the man she holds onto when the blaze is too hot.

I get out of the shower and wrap myself in a towel. No amount of wishing will bring her back. I have to wait it out and meet her and her husband, then congratulate them by stealing her back. She may have run from me for the second time, but there won't be a third, and if Gionni is smart, he will leave without a fight.

My room is dark to help stave off the headache I feel forming. Eating and sleeping weren't priorities, just drinking and getting my ass kicked. The effects are now taking hold. I drop the towel and throw on a pair of sweats, then lay across my bed. I watch the ceiling fan overhead spin and I try to think of what I should do.

My phone pings beside me with a message and I open the screen to see it's from Cam.

Cam: You left me here with a drunken Saxon who's on an Elvis high.

Me: Sorry, man. I wouldn't have been any fun.

Cam: She's coming back, and I don't care if she's married. She's still ours.

Me: Yeah.

He's right, and it feels good to hear I'll have him on my side when I force Cat back to where she belongs. Her husband can go back to California and find his own woman to marry. He can't have ours. My phone goes off again and I grab it to see what Cameron is saying now, only to see an unknown number. I open the message and it's a link to a video. What the fuck? I click it and I see an amazing skyline of reds and oranges. The sun is setting. It could be California because the person taking the video is standing on a porch of some type and I am looking at palm trees as well. There's a beach off to the right with white sand and the ocean is so blue, it looks like a crystal. To the left is a cobblestone driveway that bends and weaves around trees, then stops in front of the porch.

The camera moves and we are now facing what looks to be a large mansion, the colors bright orange and red. The double front doors have stained glass windows and the details are astounding. It's decadent. I'm led into a foyer and it's large with columns, the ceiling high. The walls are painted all bright colors of orange and peach and the floors are a terracotta tile. There's no mistaking this is California, and if this is Cat showing me her marriage home, I may just fly there to break her neck.

The video moves to a large steel door, industrial by the looks of it, and sorely sticking out of place in this beautiful mansion. A hand reaches out and opens the locks. It's a man's hand. The sight of his hand has my heart pounding. This isn't Cat, and I don't know any other person in California who would want to contact me. I watch with bated breath as the door opens and I see a set of large terracotta tiled stairs. I can't see the bottom and the stairs look steep as we descend. My stomach tightens and I can feel something isn't right. While still keeping my eye on each step downward, I grab my bag and throw in my clothes. Something is telling me I need to get my ass to Los Angeles.

At the bottom of the stairs is a concrete floor, cracked veins running along its surface, and a pair of expensive-looking leather loafers taking impossibly slow steps. I can't see anything else because the camera is kept firmly to the ground, and there's no noise. I know this isn't some friendly video showing me the beautiful sunset in Cali or the luxurious mansion on the coast. This is a video showing me what's lurking just beneath.

The camera stops moving and I see another set of feet just inside the screen, delicate toes with the red paint chipping around the edges. I know those toes. I've been worshipping them for the last month, and my breathing speeds up with anxiety. Why are Cat's toes in this video and why is she in a cement basement? The picture gradually pans upward, up her shins, and stopping at her knees, which are badly scuffed and bleeding. The camera moves again before her thighs come into view, muscular and strong but riddled with fingerprint bruises and teeth marks. The grip on my phone is tight and my knuckles are lined in white, my breathing long ceased.

Now the camera is up over a pair of red bikini bottoms and over her toned stomach, also peppered with teeth marks, some red with blood. Her ribs are bruised, and I can see her breathing is accelerated in pain or anger. Could be either with Cat. Her breasts are covered by a red bikini top, but the swell of them over the fabric is showing the same abuse the rest of her body is littered with, and her neck is covered in hickeys. There's no mistaking the handprint marked on her throat and her jaw is bruised like she took a few hard hits. Her plush lips are split but they are healing, a dark red instead of fresh blood, and wrapped around a ball gag. Her teeth bury deep into the hard rubber as she angrily clenches her jaw, and I find I'm doing the same.

The picture zooms out, and I can see she's tied to a chain hanging over her head, her arms crossed above her. There is another bruise on her cheek and a deep purple goose egg on her temple. She doesn't move, doesn't make a sound around her gag, and even though she's being complacent, I can see the fire in her eyes. She hasn't given up. I just need to get to her.

The sound of delicate metal tinkles in the background, and I hold the phone closer to my face. The picture is so dark and I don't want to miss anything. The hand reappears, and it's holding what looks to be a collar and leash, made from thin metal links. It gives off a shine, and from here, it looks sterling silver if not white gold, and the collar is made of the same metal, but it's solid with **Costa** engraved into the surface. He made her a fucking collar? Was this always his plan? To deceive her for their entire lives and then to own her like this?

He wraps the collar around her bruised neck, then clicks it into place, her head moving away from his touch. He yanks on the leash and her head is snapped forward, the pressure on her shoulders obvious. She doesn't make a single noise though, and pride swells inside me. My girl is so fucking strong, and I'm going to get there to set her loose, then sit back and watch her decimate them all.

Finally, the camera turns, and I am looking into the black eyes of Gionni, their inky pools filled with mirth. He holds up the end of the leash, giving it a little shake, and a chuckle escapes his throat.

"Come get your Kitty Cat."

Then the video goes black. How the fuck does he know I call her that? I've only ever called her Kitty Cat in this very room, so there's no way he could know about that.

Unless…

I look at the foot of my bed and the wooden slope of the footboard. He was sitting here once. I walk to it and my teeth grind as I think about everything he could have been listening to if what I'm suspecting is true. Running my hand along the bottom board, I feel a bump, like something is taped there. I rip it off and look at the tiny metal bug, my eyes crushing closed. He was in here. Why didn't I assume he'd do something like this?

I stalk to my bathroom and toss the offending metal into the bowl, watching it flush down the drain with some satisfaction. My phone pings from my bed and I rush to it, quickly swiping open the message. It's a single address, and even though I know it's a trap, I'm out the door in the very next second.

I'm ready to sacrifice myself if it gives her a chance to

get away.

CARMELO'S Malice

get away.

CATALINA

"Sorry, Cat." Gion winces as he removes the leash and pulls the gag out of my mouth. "You must've known this had to happen. There is no way my father will let him live."

"You still haven't told me why you're calling me Kitty Cat," I growl at him as he unties my hands from the chain. I want to hit him, to keep hitting him until his face is mincemeat, but he has his men lining the walls, and the last time I hit him, they laid into me as he watched with rapt attention.

"Would you believe someone gifted me clips of audio from the very bedroom that piece of shit was stealing what was supposed to be mine? You were supposed to save your innocence for me." His eyes change from apologetic to rage-filled. "I got to hear the whole thing." I've seen Gion mad before, but never was it jealousy-fueled.

"Your mole was in Carmelo's room?" I ask, but he ignores me.

"To think most women lose it to a man they love and plan a future with, instead, you lose it to two men." He looks at me with disgust.

"Great espionage." I roll my eyes.

"It wasn't a mole of mine." He grins, and I'm suddenly cold with fear. "It was someone close to you guys, probably someone you trusted."

As much as I hate Gion right now, I know when he's telling the truth, and he certainly is right now. If he says we have a traitor in the compound, then it's in fact the truth, and that makes me worry about the men I care about. My father who works every day to exhaustion to get out of the mafia's clutches, then Ember and her men who work for the same thing, and then there are my men, the two who mean everything to me. They're all being watched. Now I'm left wondering how much of those plans the DeRuccis know about and just how close is my family to danger.

He tosses me a robe and I wrap up my bruised and sore body. I haven't been harmed in any way that's lasting. It's all skin-deep and was meant for the video he just made. I didn't fight it or else it could've gotten worse. The bruises I have on my face and ribs are because I used my fists on the beloved Don's heir. I knew what the consequences would be, and I still did it. It was worth it.

He watches me, expecting some sort of aggression, and as much as I want to kill him, I won't give him the satisfaction of seeing it on my face. The DeRuccis want to be feared and I know their tactics. I refuse to be afraid. I'd gladly die in this shithole if it means everyone I hold dear is safe.

Gion pulls out his phone again and types out a message. It's on the tip of my tongue to ask what he's doing, but I refuse to give him the satisfaction of knowing he's getting to me. When he's finished, he looks up at me with a grin, and I feel a boulder drop into my stomach.

"I wonder how long it'll take him to get here?" He shows me the text message with an address on it. The address for where we are staying.

"What?" I ask.

"Your boy, the one who makes you purr when he calls you Kitty Cat," he sneers.

"Gion, I told you, I would do whatever you want as long as you keep them out of it." He would goad Carmelo and Cameron into wanting to come here, and I knew it. I just didn't want to believe he would go against my wishes if I cooperated.

"I'm going to marry you. Why did you need to do this?"

"Carmelo has a mark over his head." He shrugs. "It's been there from the very first day he accepted to take over the Rampage."

"So what?" I throw my arms out. "He could've become an ally."

"My father has an old memory, and he remembers the time when an unpredictable Torres ran the Rampage. He sees similarities in Carmelo."

"Carmelo is nothing like his grandfather, Raphael, he barely shares his blood." I try my best to convince him so that maybe he will convince his father.

"He's his grandson and I see the rage that sits inside him." He taps his chest. "That look in his eyes when he's calculating, and the way his fists fly when the rage takes over. He's more like his grandfather than he is like his father."

I can see how he would deduce that from what little time he's gotten to know Carmelo, and I would think the same, only I know him more than surface level. I know his very insides and I know he is more like his father than he is his grandfather. It doesn't matter now though, nothing I say will change anything, so I need to figure out a way out of here. I'll have to find a way to keep Carmelo from dying and to get a message back to Cameron. He could stall Carmelo and then he could get ahold of Ember and my father.

The thought of losing any of them has my heart sinking, but I don't know how to get the hell out of this.

Chapter Twenty-Two

Cameron

I am awakened by a loud knocking on my door and groan when it feels like I barely slept.

"Cameron!" Trent's voice booms through the wood, and I scramble out of my bed in haste. Did he get ahold of Cat? "Tell me you know about his plans and why he would leave the compound in the middle of the night," he fires at me as soon as the door is opened.

"Who?" I wipe the sleep out of my eyes and Trent huffs in annoyance.

"Carmelo."

"What?" I know I sound a little slow, but I have no fucking idea what he's talking about, and now that I know it's about Carmelo, none of it can be good.

"Just what I feared. He is so much like his father, but I had hoped that gene had skipped him."

"What gene?" I ask as I throw on clothes.

"The one that says he needs to sacrifice himself for others."

My stomach turns over with fear and I can feel my

mouth going dry. I follow him out of the room, and we come face-to-face with Saxon. He's watching us as he leans against the wall. There's something in his casual stance that has the hairs on the back of my neck standing up.

"I have their location." He waves his phone in the air. "And my mother has been filled in."

"What the fuck is going on?" I yell into the corridor, my voice echoing off the walls.

"I have a tracker on Gionni DeRucci's phone." He shrugs and pushes off the wall. "And Carmelo's. He will reach their location in one hour. We should hurry."

Trent curses and heads down another corridor, probably to the office to call whatever reinforcements we will need.

"You should stay here," I tell Saxon. "This could get ugly."

He looks at me and chuckles. "Bro, you should stay here. The only reason I suggested you come was because you have a way of calming those two."

"Why are you coming?" I raise my brow at him, but he just shakes his head.

"Let's go." Trent comes back down the corridor. "I got the private jet ready at the tarmac. Thank God he didn't take that. Can you believe he flew commercial?"

"Does he even know he owns a jet?" Saxon asks him as they walk ahead of me.

"Probably not. I doubt your mother told him anything about his assets." Trent chuckles. "Good thing too, because we'd be fucked if she did."

"I feel left out right now," I mutter at their backs, and Saxon turns to look at me over his shoulder.

"I'll fill you in on the way there."

When we get to the tarmac, I see about five blacked-out SUVs and a pilot standing near the plane. Trent looks at his watch and growls.

"What is it?" I stare at him, my heart galloping wildly.

"We're looking at a six-hour flight, and Ember won't be here for at least that. We may have to do this alone." He looks at Saxon, who's deep in thought.

"How many men do we have?" I look around.

"About thirty. Not near enough." He paces. "We needed Ember for her skill set."

"We'll have to do." Saxon shrugs as he gets on the plane. "Let's go save the mafia princess and her toad."

CARMELO

The taxi drops me off at the bottom of the driveway, and I look at the large gate. There's no way of getting in without being noticed, and I can already see at least four cameras on me. They know I'm here, so I might as well hurry this along. I step up to the speaker and small screen to my left and tap on it.

"Hello? Pizza delivery."

"Who ordered all cheese and anchovy?" Gionni sneers into the screen. I can hear a few laughing in the background and keep my face void of any emotion. "You really came alone?"

"Yeah, are you letting me in? Or are you scared of one Torres man?"

I have sweat collecting at the base of my spine and my hair is saturated in it. The Californian sun differs from New York. It's more intense, and the air is drier. Here, close to the coast, the air holds a scent of salt, and I can already feel the exposed skin on my face being sucked dry of any moisture.

The gates in front of me swing open, not a single sound coming from their hinges, and the sight is eerie. I know I'm at the right house, even if I can't see it yet, and walk up the familiar cobblestones, knowing it'll weave through the palm trees all the way to the porch. The picture is ingrained in my mind. I take a deep breath and wish I could've slipped a knife into my pocket, but it's not like I could bring any weapons with me on the flight. As soon as I enter that house, I know what will happen. I just hope I can save Cat. It'll all be worth it in the end.

I get to the house and find Gionni standing on the porch with at least five men. "What's with the army?" I call out. "I'm not armed. I came to negotiate."

"Negotiate what?" He laughs.

"Everything the Torres own in exchange for Catalina Costa."

His laughter stops at that and he nods to his men to go inside, but he shifts his shirt to the side to show me he's armed. Not that it fucking matters, because I won't be fighting him. I just want to be put into the same fucking dungeon he has Cat in.

"I don't think you have the power to negotiate what your auntie owns," he taunts me, and I let the words glide over my head.

"Aunt Ember owns nothing. She was just keeping my seat warm until I came of age."

"And you're willing to turn everything over to me? And for what? A chick?" His chuckling begins to gnaw on my nerves.

"We both know she's not just some chick. I can see you care about her too. How could you not? You grew up together. You must see though, she doesn't want you like that."

"So, you want to hand me the Rampage and go off with Catalina Costa into the sunset to live happily ever after?" He rolls his eyes.

"No." I shake my head and finally let the sadness I'm feeling coat my words. "I know I won't be leaving here with her. You need to get rid of me or I will always be a threat to you and your empire, but I want to see her leave."

His eyebrows rise in surprise, and he rubs his fingers along his smooth chin. "You would switch positions with her? Knowing it's a death sentence?"

"Yes."

"No hesitation. I'm impressed." He steps inside the house and motions me to follow. "Let's get this done, Torres."

I take a deep breath and look up to the clear blue sky, the clouds like white wisps. Then I send up a prayer to my father to give me the strength he found when he decided Aunt Ember's life was worth more than his. I need every bit of the willpower he had to make that same decision. The terracotta tile in the foyer is clean and shiny, with a scent of cooking in the air.

"My cook made quite the spread," he tells me. "You must be famished after that trip."

"Not particularly," I mutter, and he laughs.

"Too nervous about coming here and facing me?"

"Yeah." Not even a little. "Something like that."

"Eat, Carmelo." He pulls out a chair in an obscenely large dining room. "I'm not a monster."

Laid out in the center of the long oak table are trays of food, bottles of wine, and twelve fucking chairs. Was he planning a dinner party?

"Twelve seats, just like the Apostles." He gives himself the sign of the cross. "I am like the Messiah for the DeRucci Family. I will act as such."

He's sick in the head. That explains all of this, and now I am more concerned for Cat. I need to see her.

"I need to know Cat is all right," I demand as I sit in the chair. "Why isn't she eating with us?"

"Cat is just fine." He waves me off. "That girl was trained for far worse."

I don't like that answer. What does he mean by 'far

worse?' And does he intend to do far worse? The smell of the food should entice my hunger because I haven't eaten in over twenty-four hours, but instead, I am on the verge of throwing up all over this table. I can admit I am scared. I don't like the unknown, and even if I knew how this was all going to go down, I would still be terrified. Was this how my father felt as he watched his little sister run free, knowing he was about to lose his life?

Was he scared? Was he brave? Can you be both? I know it's a brave decision I've made, but my whole being trembles with the thought of never seeing the people I love again and leaving before I could really make something of my life. Instead, I will always be known as the angry piece of shit who couldn't do anything right except die for someone else.

"I would rather not eat," I tell Gionni. "I want to see Cat."

"Isn't she your Kitty Cat?" He gives me a look that screams both jealousy and hatred.

"She is," I agree, because there's no point in denying what he already knows. "I found the bug, not in an original spot, but still effective."

"I didn't place the bug in your room." He shrugs, and I can feel my mind trying to comprehend his words. "Looks like we have a mutual friend in the compound."

"You're saying you didn't plant that bug?" He's a fucking liar. "I found you in my room."

"That's true, and if I'm being honest, I should've come up with something like that. No, it wasn't me." He grins wide at my surprised expression. "Looks like there's more than one mole in the compound."

Fuck, I was so sure it was him this entire time, and now

I won't be able to warn my family we have a dangerous breach.

"So, this is where you kill me and take every bit of intel you gained with that bug and take over the Rampage?" I take the glass of water in front of me and down it in one gulp. I'm suddenly parched.

"Unfortunately, the mole found it only pertinent to send me clips of your sex games with the woman I was supposed to marry, the woman who was under agreement to remain pure until that date."

What? A mole who was only sending our sex audios? This was an intentional setup for a conflict. This person would have to know Cat's terms of marriage and send off proof that they were violated. All to start a war with the DeRuccis. And for what? This person wants to take down the Rampage and I can't figure out why.

"It's fascinating watching all the emotions flicker across your face. When I was a kid, that was the first thing my father trained out of me. Never to show how you're feeling under any circumstances. Do you know how he did that?" I shake my head and his grin becomes almost manic. "By beating the shit out of me, by inflicting different tortures, both physical and psychological, until my mind turned off." He lifts his shirt and I see his skin is marred with scars. "Hot pokers, sharp knives, and sometimes poisoned darts, just to see if I would survive."

"Sounds like an asshole," I retort, and he laughs.

"I hated him for a long time. I was the one who took his abuse as my older brother, the heir, lived unscathed. I was always meant to become the monster that protects this family." He takes a sip of wine and then grins at me. "Sometimes, your Kitty Cat would be there with me, enduring some of the same pain. That's how we bonded."

I hate that he's calling her my nickname, and I know he's enjoying the reaction he gets from me every time he says it, but to hear Cat was tortured alongside him makes me fucking livid.

"I can see that pissed you off." He points into my face. "I can't tell what angers you more, that I'm calling her your pet name or that she was tortured as well."

"I think I dislike them both equally." The disgust is clear with every syllable he spits out.

He laughs at my answer before scooping a mouthful of pasta into his mouth. "I promised Cat when we were kids I would never torture our children like that, and I would kill my father if he even tried."

"You should just kill your father." I shrug, and again, he laughs.

"Makes sense coming from you, you never had a father." His words don't affect me because they're the truth. "My father is the most revered here in California. The people love him because he provides protection, and his men fear him so they never step out of line. He's cruel, and he's respected for it."

"Sounds a lot like my grandfather, which is strange since he hated him."

Again, Gionni laughs as he chews his food like a cow. Through all that torture, they couldn't teach him basic manners?

"Oh, yes, Raphael Torres, also known as the Mad Torres." He drinks some more wine. "People still talk about him to this day and how his very own daughter killed him."

"Tortured him first," I mutter, and he laughs again.

"My father very much respects Ember Torres. He thinks that if she was born a man, we would be in a lot of trouble."

They are in a lot of trouble regardless, because once she finds out I'm here, she will come for me. I say nothing because as sexist as he is, he was raised that way, and the DeRuccis only see the most obvious use for a woman. Too bad they don't know how lethal Aunt Ember is, and they really shouldn't underestimate Cat either.

"I need to see Cat."

Gionni nods and wipes his mouth with the napkin on the table. "I'm sure she would want to see you too." He drops the napkin and purses his lips. "Today is our wedding day. In five hours, to be exact." He looks at his watch. "I didn't tell my father about her impurity. He would have her killed for it, and I much rather like Catalina alive, even though she disappointed me."

Gionni stands, and I do the same, following him to the large industrial steel door I saw in the video. He turns the three locks and hauls open the heavy slab. The thing looks to be about five inches thick. I would assume no noise can penetrate it and the thought is unnerving. Why would he keep Cat down there if he plans on marrying her?

We go down the familiar stone steps and I can tell it's considerably colder down here, like there's a separate AC running to keep it this frigid. What would it be for? Keeping dead bodies fresh for longer than normal? The bottom floor is dark, and I follow him toward a room with a light streaming out under the door. Is Cat down here in this freezing temperature? I crush my teeth to hold my anger at bay, and when he opens the door, he turns on me quickly.

"You must be the stupid one in the Torres family," he

sneers, and then the butt end of his gun slams into my head.

Chapter Twenty-Three

Catalina

"Boss wants to see you downstairs," one of Gion's men says as he stands in my bedroom doorway.

I am looking at the most hideous wedding dress that's ever been made as I turn from side to side in front of a large standing mirror. Throwing down the ugly matching veil, I follow the guy from my bedroom. We head downstairs and through the kitchen, stopping at the steel door.

"Why are we going down there again?" I ask as he opens it.

"Boss' orders."

"Whatever." I roll my eyes and push past him to descend first. I'm not afraid of these men because they're controlled by the Don, and he wouldn't want anything to happen to me. The stairs are cold on my bare feet, and my body begins to tremble as we get closer to the bottom. I hate how cold he keeps this place.

I hear voices coming from the room he held me in when we first got here and head that way. The pitch of Gion's laughter sends chills down my spine. He only ever sounds like that when he's gloating over the newest toy his daddy bought him. I didn't know that was on the docket today, unless...

I run into the room and see a strung-up Carmelo, his arms tied together over his head. He looks unconscious and has a large nasty bump over his left eye.

"What the fuck did you do?" I scream as I run in, toward the man I love.

Gion grabs me around the waist and rests his chin on my shoulder, his nasty breath hitting my ear. "Someone came to save you. To offer himself up in exchange for your release. So romantic."

"Get him down right this instant!" I screech at the two men flanking Carmelo.

I know what this room is used for. The stains below his feet are the bodily fluids of victims before him, and the frigid temperatures are for the bodies that are left in here long after they expire. They didn't give Carmelo the same courtesy they gave me. I, at least, could keep my feet planted on the floor so my shoulders bore none of my weight. Carmelo's shoulders are straining under his weight and his toes only slightly brush the floor below him.

"Wake him up," Gion demands, and one man picks up a bat, driving it into Carmelo's stomach.

"Stop!" I yell just as Carmelo groans awake.

"Looks like the conditioning you endured didn't extend to the people you love, hmm, Kitty Cat?" Gion taunts into my ear. "Knowing that makes me slightly angry, considering I sat beside you during most of it, and not once did you scream like that for me."

I can't give in to him. If I tell him right now that I never loved him, he will kill Carmelo, and I will be to blame.

Carmelo's eyes open—well, one does, the other is swollen shut—and looks at me, a small smile curving over his gorgeous lips. Even like this, beaten and hung up, he still has no sense of self-preservation.

"Still mad at me?" he croaks out, and I almost rip Gion's arms from me to hit Carmelo with the bat myself.

"Even more so now," I retort, and I'm shocked when I watch his stomach flutter in laughter. "Why did you come here? You must've known this was a trap. Or are you that stupid?" Even as we stand here, him flirting with death and me in the arms of another man, we still manage to fight.

"Just that stupid for trying to come here and save you," he rebuffs, and the fucker even tries to shrug.

"We need to get to the church," Gion rasps in my ear, and my heart breaks. Carmelo came here to save me, and little did he know, I never needed saving. "Thank you, Mr. Torres!" Gion booms. "You have given me the best wedding gift." He releases me and strides forward, grabbing the bat from one of his men. Then, with a quick smirk to me over his shoulder, he slams it three times into Carmelo's stomach and ribs. "Don't kill him until I get back. I want him to see me as a married man."

He drops the bat and I school my features into nonchalance. If I show I care any more than I already have, I could tip Gion over the edge. He grabs my arm and forces me from the room, the sounds of Carmelo's anguished coughs fading behind me. I don't look back, because if I do, the walls I have carefully erected for the past ten years will crumble at my feet, and then we are all dead. At least Gion is keeping him alive until after the wedding.

When I come back here, I will be a DeRucci, and I will save Carmelo using that name.

CAMERON

Saxon and Trent left me here about an hour ago in a motel room and told me to 'hang tight.' What the fuck does that mean? I have been calling both Carmelo and Cat's phones, but they are both turned off. I want to kill them both. How did I become entangled with two people who are almost exactly the same?

Before he left, Trent was pacing this room, his phone glued to his ear. I heard something about a wedding, and I can only assume that it's Cat's. What about Carmelo? Where is he? There are too many emotions clouding my thoughts, so thinking clearly is impossible. There's so much I want to say to both of them, so much I want to do with them, and now I can't help but feel like it's all gone. I want to be optimistic and not give up hope that they are fine, that we'll all be back at the compound to rip each other's throats out, but I just can't muster the strength.

I have a terrible feeling and it has a lot to do with the fact that we have no backup. Ember is on a flight here with Emmett and Vin, but she's not landing for another hour, and all we have is Saxon. No offense to him, but he's not his mother, and right now, we not only need Ember, but an entire army. How the hell can we take on the DeRucci Mafia?

I've worn a permanent burn into the fabric of the cheap carpet from my pacing, and I am feeling useless here. I'm guessing the DeRuccis would be pretty popular, especially if the Don's heir is getting married today. As I pick up the receiver in my room, I suddenly feel like I can be helpful. Thankfully, the lady at the front desk sounds pleasant enough. I tell her I'm here with my family to celebrate a wedding, but we got separated from the group. I give her a long, drawn-out story about being from Canada and traveling here for the first time to see my cousin, Gionni DeRucci, get married.

"Gionni DeRucci is your cousin?" Her voice becomes hushed as she whispers into the phone.

"Yes, of course. His father, Don Julius, will not be happy if I miss it, and I'm sure he would appreciate it if you ordered a car to take me to the church."

"Of course!" She sounds like she's slightly out of breath. "I will contact someone to come get you."

"No!" I yell into the phone and then take a deep breath when she gasps. "It's a surprise."

"Oh." I can hear she's slightly wary of me now and I'm not sure if it's because she doesn't believe me or she's a little unnerved by my association with the crime family. "So, you just need a taxi, sir?"

"And the church address. I'm not from around here, remember?" Then I lower my voice, inserting a bit of seduction. "Actually, I need a date too."

She giggles into the phone, and I know I have her hook, line, and sinker. "Me? Go to a DeRucci wedding?"

"Why not?" I purr.

"I don't have a dress!" Fuck me and females who need to fuck up my day.

"I'm sure you look amazing. This is your one and only chance," I coerce, and hear her huff.

"Okay. I will meet you down in the lobby in twenty minutes. Finding a taxi here will be difficult."

"Thank you, Miss…?"

"Adela."

"Adela. That's pretty."

She giggles again and then hangs up. I let out a breath and fall back on the bed, the mattress springs digging into my back. What fucking cheap-ass motel are we in? And fucking why?

I meet Adela in the lobby about fifteen minutes later and force a smile when I see she's old enough to be my mother, much to her delight. She grabs my arm and smacks my ass, then leads us out of the lobby. I'm not sure how to feel about the whole thing and I'm more shocked at the fact that I didn't completely dislike it. She has a firm hand but ends the smack with a slight cupping. It feels nice.

I'm losing it. It must be the lack of sleep and the constant worry this family puts me through. Maybe I need a therapist and about a truckload of prescription drugs.

"You are handsome," she coos into my ear, and I swear she licks it.

The car pulls up and we both get into the back, Adela's hand landing firmly on my thigh.

"He's Canadian," she tells the driver. "And his family has a lot of money, right, handsome?" She looks at me.

"Yeah." I nod.

Her hand moves farther up my thigh and then she's suddenly grabbing my junk, literally sinking her claws in.

"I will not pull up to the church," the taxi guy warns, his brows coming together. "They will shoot a car they don't know."

"Sure," I squeak as Adela squeezes again.
If Carmelo isn't dead, I'm going to fucking kill him for this.

CARMELO

How did I end up here?

My arms are trussed up above my head and my body is swinging over a darkened cement floor, which is darkened with what can only be bodily fluids. I can smell the ammonia and iron plainly from here.

Voices sound from my left, but it's hard to see that side with my eye swollen shut, and my body hurts too much to force it to turn. They warned me this could happen, that fucking with these people would have me killed.

But she was worth it.

Being a Torres by blood hasn't been easy considering where it's gotten me, but I can't help that. I'm not too worried because my name also means people are coming to help me. I can rest assured I'll either be rescued or avenged. The DeRucci Family has no idea what they're in for.

My Aunt Ember needs little convincing to fight or shed blood, and I can only hope I'm alive when she rips this place apart for me. That's a sight I want to see.

Suddenly, the voices have hushed, and I don't know how long it's been this quiet. Then I hear a creepy whistle sounding from down the corridor. I try to swing my body to see better out of my one eye, but it's fucking useless. The sound grows louder as they grow closer, anxiety tightening my chest.

Are they whistling "Kissin' Cousins" by Elvis Presley? Then it dawns on me. I know exactly who the fuck that is, and I don't know whether to be elated or petrified. I keep trying to turn, but the pain becomes too much on my shoulder blades, so instead, I wait for them to find me.

Once the whistling is directly to my left, I swing slightly and come face-to-face with the source. Their face is covered in blood, both drying and fresh, and a sinister smile lines their lips.

"Just hanging out, I see."

Saxon is standing in front of me, his face half painted with a skull, and the other sprinkled with blood. He has on a black hoodie and he's twirling a large knife in his hands. He looks around the room and his gaze lands on the stool in the far corner, the one they used to get me up here, I imagine. Saxon goes to it and brings it back, his face the only thing I can focus on. He stands on the stool and cuts my hands free, making me drop to my feet. The pain is unbearable from the jarring, and I fall to my knees, my arms refilling with blood.

"Did they break anything?" he asks, and I look back up into that eerie face.

"Maybe a rib or two." I stand up and sway a bit on my feet. "I'll be fine." He notices me staring at him and he grins maniacally. "You're her replacement," I state.

"Black Slaughter in the house." His hands push toward the ceiling as he bounces on his toes.

"What?" I must've been swinging here a while because I don't understand a thing he's saying.

"Never mind." He wraps a hand around my waist and leads me out of the room. "I killed the ones who were here, but more could come at any moment. I don't know if they have surveillance or whatnot. Didn't have time to check."

"Right."

He leads me up the stairs and back out to the front of the house. It's fast, but I have just enough time to see the blood everywhere. He's left handprints and blood splatter on most of the walls. Just when we get to the front door, I look down at the floor. There's writing on it, but it's backwards from this view, and when we leave the house, I look behind me to read it.

Black Slaughter.

Chapter Twenty-Four

Catalina

The material of this hideous dress scratches against my skin and the mountain of makeup used to cover all the scrapes and bruises on my face itches as well. Then there's the heat here in Los Angeles. It screws with my hair, making it frizzy, and my skin is constantly dry. I want to be back in New York with Cameron and Carmelo.

Carmelo.

I want to ask Gion to grant me one wedding gift, one I will be forever grateful for, and I would remain loyal to him forever. I want to ask him to set Carmelo free, let him go home to his family, and we can live a long and prosperous life here. He may be willing once he hears me say I do, proving to him I keep my promises. Regardless of who I love, Gion is who I will stay with. I would do all that to ensure both of my guys are safe, even if it means I wouldn't be with them.

I stare at my reflection in the mirror and see a girl I no longer recognize. This one looks sad and weak. I became weak the moment I fell in love with not one, but two men, the moment my heart began to beat for them instead of me, and it's a weakness I will gladly accept. I've been told that a woman's emotions are a weakness because we love so intensely.

It rules our logic, and I believed it for most of my life. I didn't want to fall in love for fear I would become an emotional mess entombed inside my skin. I didn't want to be ruled by those emotions, and I wanted to always think before I act.

First, Carmelo drew out the anger, taking my strikes with ease and taunting me with more. He unearthed the mountain of pain and anger I had built up over the years and gave me an outlet to release. Then Cameron came along, and he showed me patience and unconditional love, things I never knew I could possess. Now, I just want to experience every human emotion and I don't see them as weaknesses. Because of them, I am even stronger. I want to be someone my mother would be proud of. I want to be someone who Carmelo's father would have approved of, and I want to be the person who Cameron's family accepts with open arms.

I know I can't have all of those things anymore, but I can make sure they move on and one day find it again. I can do that because I am strong. Then maybe in the next life, we can all find each other again, and we can give it another shot. Our love will transcend, it's that strong.

I press my hand over my stomach to keep the trembling at bay. I always thought we would find a way out of this, and I would never have to marry into this family of monsters. There was always a part of me that knew I wasn't ever getting out of it, that these ruthless people didn't just become an evil force overnight, and defeating them would be next to impossible. I always knew deep down, this is where I would end up, standing in front of a mirror in a God-awful dress and wishing my life were different. I was always meant to take this path.

"Miss Catalina?" I hear a woman call from the doorway of the small room I am in.

This monstrous cathedral is one of the oldest in Los

Angeles and the rooms are all scattered and tiny. The rumors of tunnels beneath the structure are real, I've been inside of them many times, and the noises this place makes are surely supernatural.

"Yes?" I turn and look at her.

"The service will be in twenty minutes." She wrings her hands, and I can feel the instant anxiety coming off of her. "Have you seen Mister DeRucci?"

"Don Julius or Gionni?" I raise a brow.

"Gionni," she hums and then looks around anxiously. "His father is looking for him and no one can find him."

It's easy to get lost in this place, and even though I feel a twinge of hope, I don't let it grow.

"He's probably in a room with a woman." I wave her off. "Trust me, he will show up."

She gives me a quick nod and scrambles from the room. I wouldn't be so lucky for Gion to be a runaway groom. No, he's too worried about pleasing his father to do anything he wants for himself, and he's just biding his time until the old man is dead. Not that I blame him. That old man took his mother from him too, and Don Julius always told Gion it was because she was too weak for the DeRucci Family. We shared that grief in common, both of our mothers brutally killed by the orders of that man, and we shared the same hatred.

We just wandered down separate paths as we grew older, him on a path to please the man he hated, and me on another to destroy him. I understand they share blood, and that's why I couldn't fault Gion for his choice, but it doesn't mean I follow along with his choices. That was never going to happen.

A throat clears behind me, and I turn to see the very monster himself. The sight of him used to instill fear, now he's nothing but an annoying old man, albeit a dangerous one.

"Yes?" I make my tone neutral, my face void of any emotion as he gives me a cursory glance.

"Have you seen my son?"

"Yes," I reply as I adjust my veil. "We came here together a few hours ago."

"And after that?"

"No." I shake my head, letting the lace crowd around my shoulders. "I have been stuffing myself into this beautiful dress."

He snorts and looks down the hallway. "Just like him to fuck this day up."

"Yes," I agree, not bothering to sugarcoat anything.

"There's a reason I chose you for him." He means stole me for his son. "He will be weak, especially for women. He can't ignore his weaknesses, and he likes flashy things. You are more the man I wanted in my sons and that's why this marriage is essential. Catalina, you will one day run this family."

His words come as a bit of a shock, knowing how he feels about women and how he treated me most of my life.

"I can't change your son, Julius." It's the truth. Gion is beyond changing. "I will be there to offer my help whenever he needs it though."

He nods again and turns to look over his shoulder. He's sitting at around sixty years old, but he looks no older than late forties. His hair is dyed regularly, but it's still full and thick. His face isn't too deeply lined, and his body is trimmed and strong.

Nothing like the average sixty-year-old man. The women still flock to him and flutter their eyelashes. They all know who he is, of course, but it's even better that he's still handsome. Speaking of, I see a woman approach him, her cheeks red and eyes wide in admiration. Is she wearing a hotel uniform?

"Mr. DeRucci?" she asks tentatively, and I watch as Julius gives her a slow appraisal. She's older but curvaceous.

"Yes?" he answers her promptly.

"I am lost." She touches her palm to her head and sighs. "I came here with a cousin to the DeRucci family. He's Canadian, and now I seem to have lost him on my way back from the bathroom." She does a full circle.

My stomach drops at the mention of a Canadian cousin, and I can feel the impending doom, like humidity, thick in the air. The DeRuccis have no family in Canada. Maybe she is mistaken, but I know she's not and so does Julius, as cunning as he is.

"Oh, really?" He looks over at me as he grabs the woman's hand. "A cousin from Canada is here. You must take me to them." He knows they tied Carmelo up in Gion's basement, and now there's someone else here at the church. If he's riled up enough, he will gun the whole place down. Religion be damned.

I watch them walk away, no change in my demeanor until Julius is out of sight, and then I gasp into my hand. Is it Cameron? Would he come here without backup, looking for Carmelo and me? If it were my father, she would've said he was American. Even Ember and Emmett could pass as cousins for the DeRucci family, but not Cameron. His blond hair would stick out like a sore thumb and those bright baby blues scream Caucasian.

How the hell am I going to save everyone? And in this ugly as fuck dress?

CARMELO

This suit fucking scratches against my skin and the stiff material is agony against my screaming ribs. Saxon ditched me here on the road outside of the church, and even though I'm wearing sunglasses, I know it'll be hard to get any closer without recognition. All I need is for one of Gionni's men to see me and this whole thing goes up in smoke. I spoke to Trent about an hour ago and he told me Aunt Ember, Uncle Vin, and Uncle Emmett had landed and were on their way here. I wonder how worried they are about Saxon, and I can't wait to tell them he's completely fine… and psychotic. Did Aunt Ember see that in him? That he was the one to take over her extracurricular activities without issue?

There's a cemetery connected to the monstrous church, and I decide to head in there. No one will be in the cemetery on a wedding day. At least I hope not, but this is a mafia wedding, you just never know. I open the gate and step inside, letting it shut softly behind me. Just as I thought, not a single person is interested in the cemetery today, and why would they be? It's a DeRucci heir's wedding, people will come for the luxury alone. It's like they're royalty here.

I find a wrought iron bench that was once white but is now peeling and rusted, and the delicate design is lost in the orange flakes. It looks the way I feel, tarnished and beyond repair. Sitting on the seat, I know the rust will stain my suit, but I'm still uncaring. I came here to save the girl I love and instead needed saving, pulling my family into the most dangerous situation they've been in yet. I don't even want to think about seeing Aunt Ember after this, because she just might finish the job Gionni started.

"Gion!" My heart jumps when I hear that voice, and I stand slowly. "Are you out here?"

"Cat?" I call out, and I hear an intake of breath.

Suddenly, there's a cloud of white taffeta and satin veering around a mausoleum. Then she's standing directly in front of me.

"How?" Her hands cover her mouth as tears fall over her cheeks.

"It's a long story and slightly strange. No, it's a lot strange. I'll tell you when we get home." I step toward her.

"No." She shakes her head. "I can't leave. They will hunt you all down and kill you. I have to marry Gion."

"You don't have to do anything—"

"Yes, I do," she cuts me off, and then her eyes widen. "Is Cam with you?"

"No, he's back home—"

"No, he's here." She stomps her foot in frustration. "Don Julius is going to find him any second."

"You saw him?" I quickly scan the surrounding area.

"No." She grabs up her skirt, turning away from me. "He came with some older woman."

"Excuse me?" I ask, confused.

"Stay here. I will find him and send him out here. This seems like the safest place right now."

"Cat!" I call out to her retreating back, and she looks back at me. "I love you."

Her face registers shock, and then it relaxes into sadness. "I love you too." Then she disappears back to wherever she came from. I want to go investigate and find her, and force her to come with me, but I know Cat and she's fiercely independent, not needing or even wanting my help.

I sit back on the bench and wait for everyone around me to do everything for me. I got us into this mess and now they have to risk their lives to get us all out of it.

CAMERON

I finally found a fucking bathroom in this hideous place they call a church. I thought my dick was going to explode after all the fucking squeezing Adela was doing to it. This building is so old that this large bathroom only has one sink and two stalls. I skip inside one quickly and relieve myself, moaning in appreciation. Then I hear the bathroom door open and the sound of fabric swishing around. Please, God, this is your fucking house. Do not let that be Adela.

"Cameron? Are you in here?"

Her voice has me shoving myself back into my pants and flying out of the stall without doing them up. "Cat?"

She's standing there in a monstrous dress, but still, she somehow makes it look ethereal and breathtaking.

"Oh, thank God," she moans and rushes forward, grabbing me in her arms. "You are the stupidest pair of idiots I have ever met."

I am enveloped by her scent, and I scoop up all of her frills to hug her close. She smells like her usual citrusy self, and I almost tear up from missing her.

"Carmelo is outside in the cemetery." She pulls away, and my mouth dries at her words.

"They killed him?"

"What?" She looks at me in shock. "No! He's literally right out there." She points at the large window that sits about six feet off the floor. "That's the cemetery."

I rush over to the window and pull myself up to stand on the radiator, holding my breath as it wiggles under my weight.

"Hurry," Cat demands. "That old lady you brought with you found Don Julius and he knows you're here."

"That old cougar bitch!" I exclaim, and she erupts into a stream of giggles.

"Honestly, you could die here. Can you hurry?" she finally gets out.

It takes a bit of effort, but I finally get the window to open, and to my luck, it's an old-style swing out without a screen. I lean out the window and over the ledge to see the drop is about eight feet, not small, but totally doable to jump out of. I do a quick scan and find him sitting on a weird-looking bench with his head in his hands.

"Hey!" I whisper-yell out of the window. "Asshole!"

He looks around and then stands to his feet, never once looking up. "Cam?" he calls out quietly.

"Look up!"

He turns finally and looks up to the window, his face breaking out into a grin. He's wearing sunglasses, but I can see his face is a mess and it pisses me off. I look down the wall, trying to see if he can scale it when I see a tombstone.

"Use that." I point to the tombstone.

"Jesus," he curses and walks over to it slowly. "Angela Delgado is gonna haunt me."

"Wait." Cat rushes up beside me. "You're making him come in here? Are you both so fucking stupid?"

"He needs to be here to see our girl get married!" I look at her. "When that priest asks who objects, we can both say we do."

"And then you'll be killed," she retorts.

"Worth it," Carmelo says as he throws himself through the window. "Your fly is low." He points at my crotch.

"I hope you're killed first."

"Same." He grins wide and I haul him in for a hug. It feels good to have us all back in the same room again.

"You guys done?" Cat stands there in that grotesque dress with her hands on her hips, yet she still looks devastatingly gorgeous.

I pull her into me and grab her chin, forcing her to look up at me. "You're so beautiful, especially when you're pissed at us." Then I lean in and crush my mouth to hers, slipping my tongue into her mouth. She pulls away all too soon with a wince on her face and that's when I notice the split on her lip.

"What the fuck?" I grab her chin firmer and force her to turn her head from side to side, noticing all the marks on her face. "I'm going to kill him when I see him."

"What's done is done." She backs away. "I knew it would happen when I hit Gion."

"Let's just leave." I look between her and Carmelo. "We're all here and now we can just fucking jump out that window."

"They'll find us and torture you two in front of me before killing us all." She looks over her shoulder at the door. "I've got to get back out there and find Gion. You guys wouldn't know where he is?"

"If I did, he'd be out there chillin' with Angela." I thumb over my shoulder and Carmelo coughs out a snicker.

"I love you, Cameron." Cat laughs and shakes her head, pressing her mouth to mine gently.

"I love you." My insides warm as I tell her what I've felt it for a long time. I was worried I wouldn't have the chance to say it, and now at least we have that.

Then she's gone in a cloud of white and her citrus scent lingering behind her. I miss her already.

"So, who's the old lady you came with?" Carmelo snickers, breaking the silence.

"She's like the Hannibal Lector of dicks. I thought she was gonna rip mine off and eat it." I tip my head back and exhale. "She's a scary bitch."

"I don't want to know." Carmelo chuckles.

"Are you okay?" I reach out and take the sunglasses off his face, his mottled skin a patchwork of blues and purples.

"I've been better. I wish I wasn't the reason we're here." He sounds defeated.

"This was always going to happen, maybe not exactly like this, but Cat was always going to end up here. Now, we have to save her."

"How?" he presses me like I have the fucking answers.

"Not by standing in here and talking about it. It stinks like three-hundred-year-old shit. Let's go."

"Wait." He grabs my sleeve. "I need my glasses. Gionni's men will recognize me."

I hand them back and watch as he carefully puts them on his face. Something about him is different. I know he's been through hell, and I wish I had the time right now to talk about it because it looks like he needs it.

"I won't let anyone touch you." I mean every word I say. "They'll have to get through me first. Sorry I wasn't there when you needed me—when you both needed me."

I can't see his eyes, but I see his chin and jaw working to keep his emotions at bay. I grab his shoulder and pull him in for a hug, tightening my hold on him when I hear him sniff.

"You can never fuck up enough to lose me," I vow to him. "We were always going to do this life shit together." He nods into my shoulder, and I release him, smoothing out his jacket. "Pull yourself together, Torres. Your dad is watching, and I bet he's hella proud of you right now."

Then I open the bathroom door and poke my head out real quick. It's quiet. I wandered off pretty far from the church and down toward the backend because there were paintings I got caught up in. Now finding my way back will be difficult.

Luckily, I find the line of paintings that held my attention the whole way here and we make it back to the nave. I peek inside and see Cat standing in front of an older gentleman while a group of men crowd around them.

They seem to be in the middle of a heated argument, so I grab Carmelo by the arm and stuff us both into a confessional. It's cramped, but at least I can keep a lookout around the curtain.

"This is fucking uncomfortable," Carmelo hisses, and I give him a look.

"Shut the fuck up and sit down. Jesus hears everything in here," I threaten him.

"Forgive me, Daddy, I have sinned." He snickers, and I turn a shocked face on him.

"It's Father!" I hiss.

"Oh, my bad."

I slap my hand over his mouth when I notice two guys walking side by side toward the confessionals.

"I thought I heard something," one of them says.

"Nah, this place is haunted. The worst place to get married."

"Catalina is going to kick the shit out of Gionni every day. She's crazy, and he's a fucking pussy," the first one says. I think I like him.

"She's so hot."

They walk away toward the front of the church, gathering with the crowd, and I watch as the older gentleman points his finger into Cat's face.

Chapter Twenty-Five

"How can no one find my son in this whole cathedral!" Julius booms, and I stand completely still, watching as the man loses control over his emotions. "There must be an explanation. What did you do, Catalina?"

"Nothing." I shrug. "I'm here, aren't I?"

"Sir, he followed two… ah… females into the sacristy." A mafioso points to a door that leads behind the altar. "We checked it, but he's not in there right now."

"Maybe there are other exits in there?" I suggest, not caring if he went in there with women. I hope he gets a dick rotting disease and I get to see the thing fall off.

"Did you check for that?" Julius turns on his son's men, the ones sworn to watch his every move. "Did you see if there were other ways to exit from inside there?"

"The place is so old, the other exits look unused and dark," one man explains.

"Sounds like the perfect spot to enjoy female company," I add with a shrug.

Julius nods and snaps his fingers at two of the men.

"You, go in there and look for him. The rest of you spread out in this church. Now!" The priest jumps from his spot at the altar and gives himself a quick sign of the cross before quickly exiting the room.

"Sir, shouldn't a few of us stay here with you and Miss Costa?"

"No." I can feel Julius' gaze burning into my skull. "My daughter-in-law has proven on several occasions that she's better than two of you soldiers."

The man nods, and I watch as they all span out and leave the nave, in search of a stupid Gion. Why would he pull this shit on our wedding day? He's begging for his father to stick a knife in his neck, and Julius would because he has no sense of familial ties, just what works and what doesn't for his organization.

I step down from the altar and sit in the front pew, the hideous dress billowing up almost like it's smothering me. I don't think I would object to it either. Julius sits beside me and sighs, sounding like he has the weight of the world on his shoulders.

"I did not find this Canadian cousin," he murmurs, and I look over my shoulder at the older lady sitting a few pews back. She notices me looking and gives me a frantic wave.

"Are you sure she has all her wits about her?" I turn back to find him smirking. "She could've very well thought she was following the whole Canadian army to this damn wedding."

He laughs and reaches out to pat the puffy material. "Yes, you're probably right. Besides, those Canadians we both know are too smart to get involved in such things."

"For sure," I mutter and roll my eyes. All of them are blasting fucking idiots.

"I just need you to bear a son and then you can kill Gion for all I care." His admission astonishes me, and I look at him in surprise. "Truly, if I could do it, I would've forced you to marry me instead."

I hold the bile steady and breathe in through my nose, the images of what he suggested flitting through my mind. He must see the disgust on my face, an emotion I couldn't hold back if I tried right now, and laughs. "I know, I could be your grandfather."

"Yeah, I knew no family outside of my father. I know I have aunts and uncles, but I have never met them." Not sure why I am bringing this up, but if he's going to sit beside me, then I need to fill the silence.

"I knew your mother well and her family." Him mentioning my mother, like he didn't have her murdered in cold blood, has me on edge. "Estrella was beautiful and aptly named because she truly looked like a bright, shining star."

"Unfortunately, I've only ever seen pictures," I grit through my teeth and see him nod in my peripheral vision.

"I know you must hate me for what happened, and I can understand that, but I also think after all this time with us, you know how we operate. Sometimes death is necessary and teaches us that loving someone too much is a weakness. They become your weakness."

I've heard this many times from him, and it's always the same well-versed saying. Loving anyone is weak and they will be used against you if necessary. I don't contradict him, but I also don't agree. I sit in silence, not wanting to speak to him anymore, and the minutes tick by without a single sight of Gion.

I'm about to tip my head back and nap when I hear a

commotion at the entrance of the Nave.

"Sir!" We both turn and see one of Julius' soldiers running in, his black hair looking wet with blood, and he has blood running down the side of his face as well. "They're here…" Then he falls to his knees, his mouth opening wide in a silent scream before dropping forward face-first into the stone floor, a knife protruding from his back.

"What is this?" Julius jumps to his feet, his voice booming throughout the church. I move to stand in front of him, my back to his front, and wait to see who it is. I have a good idea it's the Torres', but Julius also has a brother who would love to see him dead. The old cougar Cameron came with runs from the room, screaming like a banshee.

Emmett strides inside and grabs the knife, pulling it out of the soldier's back. He wipes the blood off onto his dark pants and then replaces it back into the belt around his waist. He stops at the entrance, his arms crossed over his chest and a small smirk on his mouth. In this instant, I can see where Carmelo inherited that cocky look he gets.

There's another commotion at the confessionals, and I watch in shock as Cameron and Carmelo fall out of the small box.

"Uncle Emmett!" Carmelo exclaims and rushes to Emmett's side.

Emmett doesn't spare him a look as Ember and Vin step into the room behind him, both covered in blood and Ember with a freaky-looking sugar skull painted on her face.

"Oh, look!" she exclaims as she comes inside. "I've dressed accordingly for a luxurious mafia heir wedding. Haven't I, Don?"

"Yes, Ms. Torres," he replies quietly.

"It's Greene," she corrects and walks into the center of the room, giving me a pointed look. "Cat, are you okay?"

"Yes." My voice comes out in a squeak.

I step away from Julius and he throws me a look that has traitor written all over it, but what he doesn't know is he raised this traitor to one day stab him in the back. A sudden noise from behind us has me whipping around and cursing that I have this dress on and not a single weapon. It's unnerving to be unarmed right now.

Saxon comes out of the doorway, his face half-painted with a skull and saturated in blood. He's holding a scared-looking Gion with a knife to the throat, and he has a sinister smile on his face. So much like his mother's, it's scary.

"Saxon," Carmelo calls out, humor in his voice. "You got a little something right here." He motions to his entire face.

"Killing is a messy business." Saxon shrugs, but the smile stays firmly on his face. "You need better trained guards," he says to Julius, who gives him a single nod of acknowledgement.

Then I watch in shock as my father steps out of the sacristy, sheathing his knife, and also covered in blood.

"Daddy!" I exclaim and run to him, wrapping my arms around his waist. I don't even care if this dress runs red with blood, it'll probably look better.

"Julius!" Vin calls out and steps up next to Ember. "Your team of fifty men was taken out by the handful of people you see in this room right now. We didn't leave one standing, except for your heir."

I look at Saxon and his hold on Gion, one looking amused and the other unsure. Saxon releases him with a chuckle and kicks Gion in the ass, making him fall forward into his father.

"It is a sin to commit murder in a church of God," Julius calls out, and Ember laughs, the sound sending chills down my spine. When she's like this, she's nothing like the woman I know.

"It's a sin to do just about anything that's fun in the church of God, spoilsports those Catholics, really," she huffs.

"You are a useless man." Julius turns on Gion, his face red with rage. "Since the day you were born, I knew you would be more like your mother, and completely useless. Thankfully I made your uncle a deal to take over the family when I'm gone."

I can see the moment Gion's face changes, the exact moment when he decides where his loyalties lie, and just how much he remembers of his life with his father. His father held his respect with fear, but now that he's here, all their men killed and faced with the reality of death, he's ready to detach from that fear.

"And you are a stupid old man," Gion bites back. "Thinking you earned your respect from me and her!" He points at me. "You killed our mothers! You ripped our souls out and stuffed us with ice. What did you think would happen? That we would stand by you forever? I have been counting the days until I had the power to kill you."

Julius' face drains of color and he stands there in the center of the room, staring at his son with shock.

"Why do you look so shocked?" Gion asks with a tip of his head. "You taught us to never gain weaknesses, to never form bonds with people that can be used against you. You should be proud. You succeeded."

"So, you will kill me now." Julius nods, but shockingly,

I can finally see pride in his eyes. "Do it."

"As much as I want to, I will gain just as much pleasure letting someone else do it, someone just as deserving as me." Gion turns to look at me. "Do it."

The desire to grab my father's knife and throw it between Don Julius' eyes is overwhelming, but there's someone else more deserving. Someone who lost more than Gion and me.

"Daddy." I look up at him. "This is your chance to avenge her and me. He took us both from you."

I can feel the tremble in my father's body as I back away, and he unsheathes the knife, the hatred apparent in his features. I can only imagine what this moment feels like for him. I know what my mother meant to him, I know how much he loved her, and I know he will never be with another. Julius DeRucci took that life from him, and he almost took me as well, his only surviving family.

My father steps down from the altar and stands in front of the Don. "I've prayed for this day, and right now, I can see Estrella crying in happiness." He stabs the knife into Julius' belly, the sound like a hot blade slipping through butter, and steps in closer. "She is still praying for your soul because she was pure like that, but me, as God is my witness in his very house, I condemn you to Hell."

It's the absolute worst curse you could ever give a Catholic, and especially in God's temple, condemning them to Hell. I watch as Julius' mouth opens and tears slip down his cheeks, blood running from between his lips. Then he slumps forward and into my father's arms, seemingly in a loving embrace. My father releases him, and we watch as he falls to the floor, writhing in pain. I was raised a Catholic with the DeRucci family, so I sign myself and send a quick prayer to the

Lord above for forgiveness.

"Cleanup in aisle Jesus!" Saxon calls out as Julius draws his last breath, his blood seeping into the church carpet. Then he steps over the body and sits at the front pew, crossing his legs and looking around expectantly.

Everyone's attention turns to Gion, and he swallows thickly, probably fearing the same fate as his father. It's Ember who steps forward and stands beside him as they both stare down at his dead father, an end to the reign of terror for the DeRucci Family.

"You have a few choices," she tells him. "I know we look like a sadistic bunch, but I can assure you we are fair. A wise man once told me, 'The sins of the father are to be laid upon the children.'" Her face looks sad and scary with that makeup. "But as the product of an evil father myself, I try to change that. I am giving you a chance, Gionni. Just one."

"A chance for what?" He looks at her.

"To do the right thing, to convince your uncle to change this family into something worthy of respect and to become the man your mother would've wanted." I can see the effect her words have on him as his eyes widen with realization, and he gives her a single nod. "You have the chance to start over and forget the teachings of your father. Release him and the hold he has over you."

"Welcome to the daddy issues club," Carmelo says as he sits beside Saxon.

I don't know if Gion will follow in his father's footsteps or forge his own path with his Uncle Dante, the new Don. I don't know if he realizes the threat that looms over his head if he makes the wrong decision, and only time will tell how this will all go down.

For now, I just want to go home and be with the men I love.

Chapter Twenty-Six

Carmelo

"I should've stabbed him," I grumble as we settle into the jet. "Just once for planting that bug in my fucking room."

A small throwing knife flies and sinks into the soft leather of the seat next to my head. "Do it then," Saxon taunts.

"What the fuck?" I snatch the blade out of the seat as everyone talks heatedly around us.

"I planted that bug in your room and I was the one who fed information to Gionni. I saw an opportunity to spur us all into action and I took it." His facial expression is similar to one you would find on someone reading off a recipe. "I made a plan, and I went with it."

"You could've gotten her killed." I point at Cat, who's curled up in Cameron's lap.

"All of us could've been killed." He shrugs. "But sometimes death is necessary for change. I took the chance, and you should be happy I did."

Uncle Vin puts a hand on my chest when I bare my teeth and step toward Saxon. "I will agree he should've spoken to us, and we should've been given a choice." He pushes me back toward my seat. "I also agree with him that something needed to happen, and at any point, any of us could have been killed. We don't live normal lives, our jobs aren't conventional, and we know this when we decide on it. We all understand the risks and I think we should be happy today went down the way it did." He looks at Saxon. "We are family, and if it can be avoided, we don't use each other as pawns. If it's necessary, then we discuss it as a family."

Saxon nods, and I calm down, sitting back in my seat and waiting for the plane to take off. I will never admit it, but I admire Saxon for his courage and logical way of thinking. At his age, I was fucking as many girls as I could and getting pounded in the face every other day. He has a lot to learn, but he's already way ahead of me, and that, I can appreciate.

"Thank you," I tell him. "For at least coming up with a plan when the rest of us couldn't."

Saxon looks at me, exhaustion heavy in his eyes, and nods. He saved me, he saved Cat, and he pulled us out of the clutches of the DeRucci Family. Technically, he's still growing and maturing, but once he's at our age, he will be a formidable force.

When we are finally back on US soil, Trent, Cat, Cameron, and I exit the plane. The rest are continuing on back to Whitsborough and their lives there. All of us are weary and sore, with brand-new perspectives on our lives and what it means to live it to the fullest every day.

Cameron carries a sleeping Cat as we pile into a blacked-out sedan that will bring us back to the compound. I will enter a new phase in my life as the newest leader of the Eastside Rampage and the Head Corp with Trent as my right-hand man. Cat will oversee all training and Cameron will manage the facilities. Fighting was once my outlet, and I loved the feeling of adrenaline when it hit my body, making me feel invincible, but now I have a girl who does that and also makes me feel completely loved, even if we spend most of the time at each other's throats.

Uncle Vin was right. We don't live normal lives, and if I'm being honest, I don't think I ever want to.

CAMERON

We enter the compound, and everyone is waiting for the return of their leader. I watch as each person comes forward and pledges their loyalty to Carmelo, some from his father's time, who looks misty-eyed, and everyone looks relieved that he's safe. I can feel something around us. It feels protective, and I'm sure it's his father, shining his love and pride down on his son from above. Carmelo isn't perfect, but he possesses qualities very few people have, and once he loves, he does it with his whole being.

I carry Cat to her room, bypassing Trent and Carmelo as they greet everyone, and lay her on the bed. She changed into a tracksuit of mine, but I know she's aching for a bath and proper sleep in her own bed. I know because I'm wanting the same things. I head into her bathroom and run the water, giving it time to warm up and looking under her sink for the bath salts she loves.

I smell her citrus scent and turn to the doorway to find her standing there, watching me intently. "I don't know how to explain to you what I feel, and the first time I told you was so rushed," she begins and chews down on her bottom lip. "I was raised to believe feelings are for weak women. I grew into this hardened woman who had no attachments and refused to feel a damn thing for fear I would be weaker because of it."

"I know—"

"Wait," she cuts me off. "I can't tell you the moment it happened because I fought it so hard, and no longer think I am weaker because of it. I am so much stronger. I love you so much, Cameron Williams."

"Are we having a moment?" Carmelo comes up behind her and his arms wrap around her waist, his teeth sinking into her neck. "Because I really want in on this." He punctuates the word with a thrust of his hips.

"I love you too, Catalina Costa." I smile and stand in front of her, undoing the zipper on my hoodie she's wearing. She has nothing on underneath, and I can feel myself hardening as I slowly lower it.

Nothing else is as important as the two people standing in this room with me. Nothing. I'm ready to start this life and experience every up and down with them. When they fight, I want to stand between them, and I also want to enjoy the good times. I am ready to love them unconditionally for the rest of my life.

CATALINA

I kicked them out of the bathroom, much to Carmelo's protests, and slipped into my bath, soaking the despair from my muscles. To finally be free of the DeRucci Family is hard to put into feeling. On the one hand, I am elated to be back here with the people I love and to live my days without worry, but on the other, I consider Gion and the life he has now been forced into. I know he never really held any of the same concerns for me, but that's just how he was raised, and I refuse to be so weak as to not think of others.

"Kitty Cat," I hear Carmelo call out from the bedroom. "I'm not into dick, but I'm horny enough to take advantage of my cousin here."

"We're barely related!" Cameron retorts, and I cover my mouth to hold in my laugh.

"Okay, I take it back. I think Cam is horny enough to take advantage of his cousin," Carmelo says around his laughter.

I pull myself out of the bath and wrap my body in one of my softest towels, a luxury I didn't realize I had. I will never take the simple things for granted ever again. Opening the door, I find them both scrolling on their phones, lyying side by side. Both are topless and looking freshly showered. They must've gone back to their rooms while I was soaking.

"Feeling good?" Cameron asks me as he puts his phone on the side table.

"Yes." I nod.

"Good," Carmelo rasps as he puts his phone aside. "Come here then."

Who am I to keep them waiting? I drop my towel and crawl up the bed between them, my smile growing wider the closer I get. It's like they both work in tandem as I watch the outlines of their cocks grow at the same time. I don't know how I ever thought I was going to live without them.

Carmelo is the first to grab my face and haul me up and over his body, whispering how much he loves me as he kisses down my neck. We made up for our last fight, promising to be better, and yet knowing we'll probably fail, but that's life. I'm still going to spend each day with them because that's the definition of unconditional love. Nothing will come between us.

I feel Cameron kissing his way down my back, and I moan into Carmelo's mouth when I feel his fingers swipe through my folds. I know I'm wet and ready. It's what I need after this ordeal, and I want so desperately to feel how much they love me. Carmelo is plunging his tongue into my mouth just as Cameron sinks two fingers deep inside me, and I feel myself tighten around him, craving to be closer.

"She's so fucking wet," Cameron groans, and Carmelo pulls away from our kiss, throwing me a wink.

"Let me taste."

Cameron pulls his fingers out and Carmelo sucks them into his mouth, moaning like it's a fine dessert. I will never tire of watching them do this and sharing these intimate moments with both of them.

"I don't think I have the patience for soft and sweet," Cameron warns from behind me as I feel the lubricant run down my rear hole.

"There's always next time," Carmelo taunts with a smirk as he pulls his pants down enough to free his cock.

"I'm not wearing a condom either," Cameron states, sounding petulant.

"Same." Carmelo chuckles.

"You will deal with whatever consequences then." I shrug but tremble from the want of feeling them both inside me, skin to skin.

Carmelo is the first to guide me down over his length. The slight burning of the stretch feels so good, and I fall forward to capture his mouth with mine.

"I know I prepared this hole," Cameron murmurs as he circles his finger inside my ass. "But do you think we can both fit in here?" He slips two fingers into my pussy alongside Carmelo, thrusting in time with him.

"I think you can squeeze in." Carmelo grins up at me. "Would that make us cock rubbin' cousins?"

I giggle and then gasp when I feel Cameron working his way inside my pussy too, the stretch feeling like too much. Just when I think I'm going to split apart at the seam, he bottoms out, settling in right beside Carmelo.

"You are fucking dripping, Kitty Cat." Carmelo grins up at me. "Do you like both of your men inside you? Rubbing our cocks together, skin to skin?"

I moan and nod as they both thrust inside me, their groans mingling in, and the sounds my pussy makes are just as loud. Then, as if of one mind, they both slam into me, making me scream, and I can feel something coiling tight. It's different, stronger, and something I know I won't be able to control.

"Feel that squeeze, Cam?" Carmelo husks. "Feel like we're going to get a shower."

"Think so?" Cameron hums, sounding out of breath

as he keeps thrusting inside me.

I don't know who it is, but one of them keeps bumping a certain spot inside me, and each time I can feel my pussy clench of her own accord, the feeling shooting streams of sensation up my spine. This differs from any other orgasm I felt before. I can tell what's going to happen, and I am happy I read into these things beforehand.

"I'm going to come," I warn them as my body vibrates and my pussy clamps down tight. Then the most amazing release washes over me and I scream into Carmelo's neck as I feel the gush of liquid from between my thighs.

"Fuck, yes," Cameron moans from behind me and slams in, coming with my name on his lips.

"This feels so good," Carmelo gasps as he slowly thrusts through both mine and Cameron's cum. "So fucking warm and wet."

Then he speeds up, his breathing accelerating, and just as Cameron pulls out, Carmelo shoves himself all the way in and comes. As soon as he's done, I roll off him and onto the bed with a groan, eyeing the wet spot on Carmelo's pants. Fuck, that looks so fucking hot. I reach my hand down between my legs and run my fingers through my pussy.

"I need another shower. This is a fucking mess."

They both laugh as I hop off the bed and rush to the bathroom. Sex is so much dirtier with two men and I'm so fucking lucky that I get to have this for the rest of my life.

EPILOGUE

Emmett

I sling my knife into the dead body as I wait for Em to hurry and come back with the tarp. This particular brand of rapist preferred the ladies with walkers as opposed to the ones without. Strange, but still a fucking pervert.

"Sorry!" She hurries back into the retirement home's kitchen with the blue tarp. "They have butter tarts over there on the counter," she mumbles around a mouthful of food.

"Are you fucking serious?" I head in the direction she's pointing, moaning when I see the little pastry desserts until I reach out to grab one and notice the blood on my hands. Fuck that. "I need to wear gloves when I do this shit with you."

"This is the last," she vows, sounding sad. "I'm retiring, and I'm ready to spend all my time with my family."

"You're gonna miss gutting these fuckers." I chuckle as I kick the fat cook. The piece of shit posed as a cook at a retirement home so he could rape all the nanas after hours.

"I am, but I have the perfect replacement." She looks at me, pride glowing in her eyes. "I actually think he's better."

"I think so too." Saxon is strange and oddly perfect as a stone-cold killer.

"Carmelo is also the perfect fit for the Rampage."

"Yeah, he is." I nod, feeling proud of that. "He really is."

"Let's get this fat fuck out of here and get to that party. Vin is always grumpy when I'm late."

By the time we get back to the compound, the place is fucking packed, and I groan as I try to find a place to park. "We should've taken the bike."

"Fuck that," Em huffs. "You passed that trait onto my son too."

It's so fucking cool that Saxon is just as into bikes as I am, and it feels good to have at least one person to talk to about them. I finally find a spot to park, and we head inside, still spotted with the rapist cook's blood. This is our usual though, so we're unphased as we step off the elevator and head to the dining hall. It's Trent's birthday and Catalina threw him a large party, inviting the whole family. When we enter the hall, I take a deep inhale and feel myself choke up. We are all so fucking lucky to have each other.

I notice Trent sitting with Carmelo and Cameron, his hands flying around over his head as he tells them some outlandish story, probably one of the same as he used to tell me when I was a kid. I see Ivy, Cat, and Neil sitting at a table with a row of shots between them—tequila, I bet—as Neil sips on a beer and shakes his head. Ember heads over to where Vin is sitting with Travis and Adri, all three laughing, reminding me of being in the cafeteria at Precious Blood Academy oh so many years ago.

"Unc." Saxon stands beside me, also with splatters of blood on his forearms and T-shirt. "Why are you just standing here?"

"Who did you kill?" I ignore his question and ask my own.

"Some guy who gave me the middle finger," he states with a shrug.

"Are you fucking serious?" I exclaim.

"Yeah." He grins, the look so much like Em's. "But only after I found out he had a rap sheet with rape accusations longer than this hall." I'm still staring at him, and he laughs. "It was a job." He rolls his eyes and heads to the bar.

"I don't even know if I believe him," I mutter to myself.

I know I should be happy at this moment, seeing my family together and enjoying themselves, but being in this compound always makes me nostalgic. I miss my brother, and time hasn't diminished that. So, before anyone notices, I slip back out of the hall and walk down the corridors that lead to his office, or his son's office now.

The funny thing is, after all these years, I can still sense his presence here, and I know he is watching over his son. I just hope I did things the right way. When I open the office door, I see Carmelo has kept it the same. I sit in the chair I always sat in as a teen to listen to Carm's lectures, and I can almost see him sitting there.

"I know you're watching me, probably laughing at me sitting here looking sad, and now that your big mouth can't interrupt me, you'll listen to what I have to say for once. You have an amazing son. He's everything you would've hated." I laugh. "But also everything you would've been proud of. He's brave and strong, he loves so fiercely, and most of all, he's selfless, more than any of us ever were.

"He's a Torres through and through, just as fucking crazy too. He loves to fight, and he can run his fucking mouth sometimes, and it drives me fucking nuts. Then I think, in those moments, that must've been how you felt about me. When I would argue with you about every little thing and your right eye would twitch." I chuckle into my hand. "Now I know just how badly you must've wanted to pound the living shit out of me.

"If you have been checking in, you'll know I struggle sometimes, and I feel all the things I have piled inside here"—I tap my chest—"that I never got to say to you. So, I need to say them and then I need to let you go. You have a son to look after anyway."

The tears run down my cheeks as I lean forward and put my hand on his desk. "You were an amazing big brother, and I was always trying to walk in your shadow. I would copy the way you dressed, your hair, and even that swagger you had. I thought there was no one better than you, and when you brought me to Ember, I fucking knew I would be forever in your debt.

"She's doing good, by the way. Her kids are all Torres and no Greene." I laugh. "Just as crazy as us when we were growing up. But I never really thanked you properly for giving me back the part of my soul that was missing. It also led me to the people I love with my whole being. Adri and Travis are doing well, and our kids are fucking hellions. I don't care how bad you thought I was, you never had to deal with twin children, and these are like demons who got into crack."

I sit back and rest my foot on my knee. "But having a family is an amazing experience and I think I always held on to this guilt that I got the chance to have it when you didn't. That's why I pushed him so hard, yelled at him too much, and forced him to strive for more. I just imagined what you would've been like as his father and tried to be that. I hope I did it right, Carm."

I stand up and run my hand along the shining mahogany surface. "I miss you and I'll always love you. You were my idol and still are to this very day. I'm still hoping to be you when I grow up."

I walk to the door and open it slowly, feeling the lightest I've been in so many years. "Keep an eye on your son, but don't forget to check on me too now and then."

FOR ALL BOOK UPDATES AND SOCIAL PLATFORMS, CHECK OUT MY WEBSITE

C.A. Rene lives in Toronto, Canada with her family, where most of the year varies from chilly to frigid. Most days you'll find her wrapped in her many blankets in bed while reading or writing her next dark, twisted story.

Her stories boast of inclusivity and refusal to be conformed in any small box. Writing across genres is a hobby and drinking wine is a must… Or coffee … with a splash of Baileys.

For all book updates and social platforms, check out my website

Also by C.A. Rene

The Whitsborough Chronicles
Through the Pain

Into Darkness

Finding the Light

To Redemption

The Whitsborough Progenies
Ivy's Venom

Carmelo's Malice

Saxon's Distortion

Gabriel's Deception

Desecrated Duet
Desecrated Flesh

Desecrated Essence

The Reaped Series
The Reaper Incarnate

Hunting the Reaper

Claiming the Reaper

Hail Mary Duet
Blue 42

Red Zone

Steel Dragons MC
Dragon Slayer

Dragon Strife

Dragon Scorch

Hell's March MC Duet
Hell's Viper

TBA

Fusion Core Duet
Tension

Release

Second Chance Standalones
Fighting the Tide